Secrets of Blackhand Creek

A Jake Cashen Novel

Declan James

ONE

L aughter. He said something funny. Or maybe not funny at all but she reached for him. Running a hand across his cheek. The bubbles from the hot tub rose and surrounded them. Dusk now, the LED lights underneath them changed colors, going from purple to green, then orange to blue.

"Come here," he said to her. "I told you you'd like it here."

"It's nice," she admitted as she moved through the water and straddled him.

The killer moved closer, staying in the shadows. They would never see him. Never hear him. The jets from the hot tub whirred, disrupting what should have only been the tranquil sounds of the surrounding woods. Those ridiculous colored lights seemed an affront to nature. Neither of them looked up. They were missing the real show above them, a brilliant blanket of stars unspoiled by light pollution.

"Where are you going?" the man asked her. Water sluiced off her nude body as she rose and stepped out of the hot tub. She grabbed a blue-and-white-striped towel from a rack on the deck.

"We're just missing one thing," she said. "I'll be right back." She threw her hair over her shoulder. She let the towel drop and the killer looked away.

"Don't start without me!" she teased as she went inside the cabin.

It was modern-built, but made to look rustic and old. The kind of place that charged at least five hundred a night in peak season.

A moment later, music blared from the Bluetooth speakers mounted on the deck. A lilting saxophone. Lord, he thought. If she keeps it on Kenny G, his bullets would be a mercy to all of them.

"Joey, come on!" the man yelled. "Come back."

The killer could see her through the kitchen window. She couldn't see him. She opened the fridge and pulled out a bottle of champagne. Two glasses from the cupboard. She would be a while.

Now, he thought. He could do it now. Two quick pops. She wouldn't even know what happened until she came back out to the hot tub.

He could leave it at that. Maybe that was the merciful thing. Leave her out of it. As the killer stared at the man in the tub, his blood heated.

Oblivious. Careless. Wallowing in luxury. Each breath he drew was an insult.

The killer took two steps toward him, keeping to the shadows. Would he let him see? Let him understand as he drew his last breaths? Would there be satisfaction in that?

He heard water running in the kitchen. The song changed. Celine Dion now. The woman sang along at the top of her lungs. Her voice wasn't bad. She was good, actually.

What a waste, the killer thought. She could have done a hundred different things with her life. Made even one alternate choice.

The killer took another step. He was in range now. One shot. He aimed his gun. Count to three. Let out a breath.

"Joey!" the man yelled. She couldn't hear him, though. Soon, she never would again.

"Hey?" The man saw him. Saw something, anyway. He started to rise in the tub.

Pop!

The killer got the first shot off. Flesh chipped off from the man's bicep. There was that split second when he didn't realize what happened. Adrenaline coursed through him, preventing his brain from processing the pain. But it only lasted an instant.

"What the hell, man!" he shouted, still trying to rise. But his foot slipped on the slick ledge of the hot tub. The LED lights turned purple again, masking the blood that started to fill the tub.

He doesn't realize who I am yet, the killer thought. The man looked down. He saw the blood pouring from his arm.

"Joey!" he shouted. Was it to warn her? Did he actually care if she was in danger, too?

"No," he said. "No, man. No. Whatever it is. Whatever you want. I can ..."

Pop!

The killer didn't remember making the choice to pull the trigger again to deliver that fatal shot. It caught the man in the forehead, dead center between his eyebrows. There was that nanosecond before he died. The look of shock. Then he slumped back into the hot tub and sank below the water.

It felt good. That's the thing you don't account for. The power of it. Pure dominance. It was godlike, the killing. Adrenaline coursed through the killer's veins now. God, he'd been stupid enough to think he'd have at least a fleeting moment of regret. There was none of that, though. There was only the thrill.

"Oh my God!"

He hadn't heard the slider open from the kitchen. She'd been carrying a bowl of strawberries. They tumbled to the deck.

"Jax!" she screamed. "What have you done? What did you do?"

She saw him. Though Jax had been oblivious, she seemed to know. Even in her shock, she read his face. Her eyes darted back and forth as she no doubt etched his features into her memory. When the shock wore off, she might understand.

"No!" she screamed. Then she did something nonsensical. She ran right toward him. The sliding door behind her was still open, but she went forward, passing close to him as she ran down the deck stairs and toward the dark woods.

It caught him off guard. Of all the things, *that* was the one that gave him pause. She ran streaking into the woods, her brown hair flying behind her like a banner.

"Joey!" he called after her, just like the man had done.

It was no use though. She would never stop on her own. So the killer did the only thing left to do. He raised the gun and took aim.

The first shot hit her on the back of her right thigh, just below her buttock. Even then, she took two more staggering steps forward before falling onto the embankment just above the creek bed.

He could take his time now. The ground was dry and hard. He'd been careful about that.

She whimpered at first, then let fly a stream of obscenities. Would he be merciful? He raised the gun once more.

She had a life. A future. Only she'd thrown all that away the moment she let the likes of Jaxon Waters in. He might be gone now, but there would be someone else. There would always be someone else.

She went up on her elbows, trying to crawl forward. She didn't cry. She didn't beg. She just tried to get away. But it was too late. She had seen too much. She hadn't done enough. So the killer did the only thing there was left for him to do. He squeezed the trigger. The fatal shot entered right below her shoulder blades, ripping straight through her heart.

The killer felt it in his.

In the distance, he could still hear the faint notes of Celine Dion singing about how her heart would go on. Funny that, he thought.

He looked back at the woman.

"There's nothing to fear," he whispered.

Then he holstered his weapon and disappeared.

Two

"It's crooked! Like I told you!"

The sound of Grandpa Max's voice went through Jake like a cannonball. He had to remind himself this time, he wasn't the one in the crosshairs.

"It's not crooked," his nephew Ryan protested. Jake came around the bar where he'd just hung Gemma's new neon sign.

"It's crooked!" the old man shouted. "Jake, hand me one of those rocks glasses." Jake reached under the bar, grabbed the glass the old man wanted, and filled it with water from the beverage gun.

"He doesn't know what he's talking about," Travis Wayne whispered. Ryan had recruited him along with two other members of the wrestling team to earn extra money this summer helping get the bar up and running. Gemma wanted to open for business two weeks from today. They'd make it. Just barely.

Jake stepped around the bar. "Take it easy on 'em, Gramps," he said. "It's tough to find good help." He winked at the boys.

"These kids don't wanna work," Grandpa mumbled. Jake put the rocks glass in his hand. Grandpa walked over to the coppertop and set the glass on it. Just as he predicted, the water dipped to one side in the glass.

"I told ya!" he said. "Not level. See this thing?" He picked up a long yellow box level from the main bar. He tossed it lightning quick at Ryan. Ryan got his hands up just in time to catch it before the thing would have hit him right in the jaw.

"How does he do that?" Travis asked. "He can barely see."

"He senses movement," Jake muttered. "Like a velociraptor."

"Use it," Grandpa said. "And use these heavy duty screws. Not the cheap crap from overseas. Good American-made hardware."

The front door opened and Gemma burst through. She looked young today. Younger than Jake had seen her in a while. She didn't normally dress like this, in a faded tee shirt and blue jeans. She had her hair pulled back and no makeup on. Using her forearm, she wiped the sweat from her brow.

"It's perfect!" she exclaimed. The copper top had been a surprise gift from the old man. The thing had to be over a hundred years old. Up until two months ago, it held a place of honor in Grandpa's basement. A relic from the last time the Cashen family had owned a bar. Grandpa had conscripted Ryan and his younger brother Aiden to polish it back to its former glory before installing it here. It would be one of the best seats in the house. Gemma wanted Grandpa to take up a permanent perch there with his friends from the Elk's Lodge. From there, Max could oversee the operations and add all the local color Gemma could want.

"Looking pretty good," Jake said. "The boys have been working their tails off."

"I see that. I've even got Aiden out there pulling weeds. I need to call Rick Schuler again. He might need to treat again for dandelions."

"That stuff takes over once it gets a foothold. This place was vacant for too long."

"Lucky for us." She smiled. It was then she noticed the neon sign Jake had just finished hanging.

"Is it hooked up?" she asked, clapping her hands together.

"Just waiting for you to get here," he said. "It'll shine more in the evening."

"Do it!" she said.

Jake picked up the remote from the bar top. He had the lights set on a timer. The neon sign had a button all its own. He pressed it.

Gemma slid her arm around him as she marveled at the sign. In brilliant green letters with a shamrock in the lower corner, the sign read, "Cashen's Irish Pub."

It was bigger than the one Grandpa saved from the original bar. Grander. This one cast a dazzling reflection in the mirror behind the bar.

"It's getting real," Gemma whispered. His sister's eyes misted with tears. She'd been weepy like that a lot lately. Jake knew it had to do with more than just the impending grand opening. Her eyes settled on Ryan. He and Travis had made the adjustments Grandpa told them to. The copper top was finally level. They busied themselves polishing the metal to a shine. The thing was gloriously dented from decades of bar patrons using it.

In just shy of two months, Gemma's baby boy would leave the nest, possibly for good. Ryan had gotten a partial scholarship to Putnam University, a small four-year college outside of Akron.

Close enough Gemma could visit when she needed to, but too far for Ryan to commute. He'd be living in the dorms. Jake couldn't be more proud or excited for him. But he knew Gemma would be a wreck, maybe forever.

"Thank you," she said to Jake, resting her head on his shoulder. He pulled her close. He had a feeling he'd need to do a lot of that this year.

The sign had been Jake's birthday present to her a few months ago. He'd worried the thing was too big. But now, blazing to life above the bar, she was right. It was perfect.

"Can we take off for the day?" Ryan asked. "Nate Cooper's grad party starts in a couple of hours. He's having it out at the quarry."

Gemma opened her arms. Ryan darted a look at his friends, then let his mother hug him. Briefly.

"Just be careful," she said. "Don't get in a car with anyone who's been drinking. And you call me if you need to be picked up. No questions asked, okay?"

Ryan shot his uncle a sheepish look. Jake knew kids had been drinking out at the quarry for eons. It was a rite of passage. He narrowed his eyes and transmitted a nonverbal message to his nephew he knew Ryan would understand.

Don't be stupid. Don't do anything that'll get brought to my attention. Don't expect me to bail you out if you do.

"We'll be fine, Mom," Ryan said, though he kept eye contact with Jake. He hugged Grandpa Max too and gave the old man back his level. Then the boys packed up their gear and left out the back door.

"He's a good kid, Gemma," Jake said. "Don't worry about him."

"I know," she said. "It's all just happening so fast, you know?"

Before Jake could answer, his phone rang. He checked the caller ID and braced himself.

"Hey, Darcy," he said. Darcy Noble was Worthington County's main dispatcher. She rarely called Jake's cell phone with good news.

"Hey, Jake," Darcy started. "Sorry to bug you on your day off. I know you're busy with Gemma's bar. A bunch of the guys were talking about it. Man, they are planning on filling it up opening night. I can't wait."

"What's up, Darcy?" Jake asked.

She let out a sigh." We had a 9-1-1 call out at Blackhand Creek. You know those cabins they built a few years ago? The north side? When you head down from Duckbill Road?"

"I know it."

"Okay. Dan Tuttle's out there. A bunch of sorority girls were tubing down the creek. Right at the bend just before it splits off before the waterfall? You know where old Neville Potter's shanty used to be before that thing finally caved in on itself?"

"I know the area," Jake said. It was a prime fishing spot. Jake and Ben Wayne used to cut school in the spring and spend hours out there.

"One of the girls found a body out there," Darcy continued. "Tuttle's with her. Like I said, I hate to bug you on your day off. Tell Gemma I'm sorry."

"It's okay," Jake said. "We're just about finished up here for the day anyway. Tell Tuttle to keep it together for me. I'll be out there in twenty minutes or less."

"Will do, Jake. I'll call Lieutenant Beverly and tell him you're on your way."

Jake clicked off the call. Before he could even draw a breath to explain to Gemma, she held up a hand.

"Save it," she said. "Darcy has a speaker phone voice even when she's whispering."

Jake smiled. He gave his sister a quick peck on the cheek, then headed for the parking lot.

D eputy Tuttle parked his cruiser at the top of the hill near the footbridge overlooking the creek. He had a girl sitting in the back seat, her head buried in her hands. She looked up, teary-eyed, as Jake approached.

Lord, she was young. Twenty-one but she could have passed for half that. She wore a pink bikini top and black board shorts. Tuttle had put a blanket around her shoulders.

"Hey, Jake," Tuttle said. "This is Kayla Bishop. She's the one who found the body. It's down there. Just past the clearing. She got caught on the rocks where the current shifts. If she'd have broken loose, she might have gone downstream, who knows how far."

"Kayla?" Jake said. The girl was shaking though it wasn't from the cold. She was in shock.

"She was just lying there," Kayla said. "I couldn't stop. I slammed right into her. She had something crawling out of her mouth. I can't breathe. I can't ..."

Two more cruisers pulled up. He recognized one as belonging to Lieutenant John Beverly. Birdie Wayne drove the other. She had Deputy Morse with her.

"Stay with her," Jake said to Tuttle. Jake scanned the area. He saw no footprints or broken branches or anything that would have indicated anyone besides Tuttle and Kayla Bishop had been this way. He started to make his way down to the creek bed.

The body was easy to spot. Her legs stretched across the rocks, her head and arms were still submerged.

She was naked. Long brunette hair floated around her face. Covered in mud and sludge, Jake could see her wounds clearly. A gunshot wound below the right buttock in the meat of her thigh. Another hole through the center of her back. There was no way to tell if it was an entrance or exit wound at this point, but Jake had a sense the woman might have been running away.

No tattoos. No scarring. She was thin with an athletic build. Her head was turned. She lay on her left cheek. She was young. Maybe not much older than poor Kayla Bishop. Twenty-five, Jake guessed. He didn't know her. He knew of no missing persons in the area.

Up the hill, roughly fifty or sixty yards, sat one of the modern cabins Darcy mentioned. The closest cabin was large with a custom fieldstone chimney. Expertly designed landscaping. Behind the cabin were the hilly forests of Blackhand Hills.

Neville Potter's family had sold off this acreage a decade ago. Since then, four modern-built log cabins had been put in along the creek with ten acres in between. They'd been rented out to tourists looking for a "rustic" getaway. It was exactly the kind of thing Gemma wanted to do with part of Grandpa Max's property on the other side of the gorge.

Jake couldn't see anything up at the cabin from this distance.

"Jake?" Birdie stood at the top of the hill.

Jake made his way up to her. He told her briefly what he'd found. "Do you know who owns that cabin?" Jake asked.

"I think Edgar Lattimore still owns it. He makes a fortune renting it out to rich people looking to rough it without really roughing it, you know?"

"I need to know who's renting it," Jake said. He met Lieutenant Beverly just a few yards from Tuttle's cruiser where Kayla Bishop kept crying.

"What do you need?" Beverly asked.

"More deputies," Jake said. "I want the bank of that creek secured at least fifty yards each way from the body. Nobody goes near it. I'm calling Mark Ramirez and getting BCI and the ME out here. Bird—Deputy Wayne, head up the hill with me. I want to see if there's anyone staying in that cabin. Odds are that's where she came from. I don't recognize her as a local."

"Nobody's been reported missing in the last twenty-four hours," Beverly said, confirming what Jake thought.

"All right," Jake said. "I'll see what I can find out. Have Tuttle try to get a hold of Ed Lattimore. We think he still owns this property?"

"I'm pretty sure," Beverly said. "I'll have one of the deputies get on tracking him down."

Jake motioned to Birdie. The two of them started up the hill toward the cabin. As they approached, Jake saw a white Range Rover parked in the driveway. Ohio plates. No rental stickers on it anywhere.

"Do you have a guess how long she was down there?" Birdie asked.

"Not long," Jake said. "I'm guessing no more than twenty-four hours. Ramirez will have a better guess."

Jake went to the front door and knocked.

"They're charging six fifty a night," Birdie said. She had something pulled up on her phone. Jake looked. It was a rental listing from some app. Birdie scrolled through the interior pictures. It looked gorgeous. High-end fixtures and wood flooring throughout.

"Hello!" Jake called out. "This is Detective Jake Cashen, Worthington County Sheriffs. Anybody home?"

No answer. He peered through the side window. He could see into the great room. There was a robe draped over the couch, but no other signs of life.

"I'll try around back," Birdie said. "Listing shows a hot tub and screen door leading into the kitchen."

She pocketed her phone and disappeared around the corner. Jake walked over to the Range Rover and looked inside. There was nothing unusual, just two half-drained bottles of vitamin water in the center console cup holders. A wadded-up receipt on the passenger side floor. Blankets folded in the back seat.

"Anything?" he called to Birdie. She didn't answer at first. His phone beeped. An incoming text from Mark Ramirez with the Richmond office of the Ohio Bureau of Criminal Investigations.

> I thought it was your day off, Cashen.

He smiled as he read the text.

> Sorry. I'm gonna need the full team. Here's the address.

Jake sent Ramirez a pin to his location.

"I'll be out within the hour," Ramirez texted back. "Do me a favor and quit taking days off, Cashen. Seems like bodies tend to show up when you do."

Jake couldn't argue the point. He sent a thumbs up emoji to Ramirez.

"Jake!" Birdie called out. "You better get back here!"

Jake's blood heated at the tone of her voice. His hand went to the heel of his weapon. Jake sprinted up the driveway and went around the side of the cabin.

Birdie stood in a ready stance, her gun drawn as she stared at the hot tub on the back deck.

Jake followed her line of sight. Then he felt the blood drain from his face.

THREE

Birdie Wayne wasn't squeamish. An Army combat veteran, she'd done two tours in the Middle East. One in Afghanistan, one in Iraq when the fighting was intense. When Jake rounded the corner and found her with her gun drawn, every nerve ending in Jake's body went into high alert. He took one step forward, as Birdie bent at the waist, covering her mouth with her arm. Jake got to her side. The hot tub built into the center of the elaborate wood decking had turned into something out of a horror movie.

The second victim floated face down in a brownish, soupy mixture. The jets were still going full blast, churning gore.

"Gunshot wound to the right arm," Birdie said, recovering enough to stand upright.

"No one answered the front door," Jake said. His instincts kicked in. The back slider was slightly open. He went to it, gun drawn.

"Police!" he shouted. "Anyone inside? Make yourself known!"

Birdie was right behind him. Together, they entered the cabin and cleared it. There were only three rooms. The large kitchen and great room, then the luxury master suite down the hall. The place was designed for couples. Rich honeymooners. The bedroom contained a king-sized circular bed draped in a canopy of pink chiffon. The bathroom had a tub built for two in a giant wet room. Four shower heads aimed toward the center with a marble bench along one tiled wall. Jake spotted red silk women's underwear in a wad near the tub. Two sets of toothbrushes were propped up next to the sink, toothpaste still on them.

"It's just the two of them," Birdie called. She'd made her way back to the kitchen. She stood in front of a stainless steel fridge.

"Lattimore Luxury Suites," she said, reading from a magnet on the front of the fridge.

"Edgar Lattimore," Jake said. "You think he owns all this property back here?"

"Old man Potter made a fortune when he sold his acreage off," she said. "Or his kids did."

Jake pulled out his phone and punched in Beverly's number. His lieutenant answered immediately.

"Beverly," Jake said. "We have a second victim up at the cabin. Gunshot wounds as well."

"Oh man," Beverly said. "Oh geez, Jake. What do you need?"

"I need a couple of deputies to break away to help me secure it up here. I need to call Ramirez and have BCI send a second unit."

"Got it. Tuttle's got things under control here. I'm sending Morse and Stuckey. I'll come with them. Ramirez's van just pulled up down here. I'll tell him about the situation. What else?"

"I need a warrant for the house," Jake said. "When in doubt, write it out. The vehicle too. White Range Rover. Can you take the plate down for me?"

"Go ahead," Beverly answered.

Jake and Birdie were back outside in the driveway. Jake rattled off the plate number for Beverly.

"You said Ramirez just pulled up?"

"Yeah," Beverly said.

"Do me a favor and send him straight up here. We need to extend the crime scene to the whole property."

"Sheriff Landry will divert all units we can spare," Beverly said. "Christ, Jake. There are two other cabins on Potter's old land."

Jake's stomach churned. He found himself praying for whoever might be in those other cabins. Lord, he thought. Please don't let this go beyond what we see here.

"Send two units," Jake said. "One to each of the other cabins."

"Jake," Beverly said, his tone filled with distress.

"I know," Jake said. "I know. Let's not get ahead of ourselves. We don't know anything until we know something."

"Ramirez will be up there in five minutes," Beverly said. "I'll give Sherriff Landry the quick rundown, but she's gonna want to be briefed by you as soon as possible."

"Copy that," Jake said. He clicked off with Beverly.

"I've never seen anything like that," Birdie said. She stood at the top of the driveway. From here, they could almost pretend the hot tub horror wasn't there. Almost.

A few minutes later, BCI's crime scene van pulled up and parked alongside the white Range Rover. Agent Mark Ramirez got out along with two of his agents.

"What do we got, Jake?" Ramirez asked. He shook Jake's hand.

"We gotta stop meeting like this," Jake said.

"Hey, Erica," Ramirez said. He shook her hand, too. "You okay?" He shot a look at Jake that seemed to read, "She okay?"

"It's gross," Birdie said. "And I don't get grossed out that easily, but it's awful back there."

Ramirez wrinkled his nose. He gestured to his two agents. They gave him nods and disappeared behind the house. "What can you tell me?" Ramirez asked.

"Nobody else inside," Jake said. "No signs of a struggle. The back slider was open about two inches. Like they got caught off guard. Didn't see any blood when we cleared the house, but you'll tell me if I'm wrong on that. No sign of forced entry."

"Perpetrator surprised them," Ramirez said. He and Jake walked around to the back of the house. Ramirez's techs stood on the hot tub deck. One looked like he was about to be sick.

Ramirez peered over the railing and looked down into the hot tub.

"Jeezus!" he said. "You weren't kidding."

"I've got a call into the ME," Jake said. "He's on his way."

"He better hurry. Another hour and things in there are gonna get a whole lot worse."

"How can they get worse?" Birdie asked. Then she put up a hand. "Never mind. Don't answer. I don't think I want to know."

"You ever seen anything like that?" Jake asked.

"Once," Ramirez answered. "Victim was in a backyard pool. But that wasn't as bad. The water was cold. This? This is …"

"Yeah," Jake said. "Human crockpot."

"Ugh," Birdie said. She stepped further away.

She took out her cell phone and made a call.

"Victim at the creek," Ramirez asked. "Was she local, do you know?"

"Not that I know of. This place is a rental. Looks like it caters to honeymooners and other couples looking not to get found if they don't want to."

"It's a lucky thing your other victim wound up in the creek," Ramirez said. "If she'd been up here in the Jacuzzi with loverboy … if that's what he is … it might have been days before anyone knew anything. Then we'd have had …"

Jake put a hand up. Like Birdie, he decided he'd rather not know the gory details.

"Jake." Birdie came back. "We've got incoming."

"What do you mean?"

"Just talked to Deputy Chaplin. Ed Lattimore is her uncle. Lattimore is already on his way up here. Somebody tipped him off there were emergency vehicles up here on the property."

"Good," Jake said. "Make sure Tuttle heads him off at the pass. I don't want anyone else coming up here."

As he said it, Beverly pulled up along with another marked cruiser. They were the extra deputies Jake asked for.

"Okay," he said. "We'll keep it clear up here for you."

"I'm gonna need those warrants sooner rather than later, Jake," Ramirez said.

"You'll have 'em."

"ME's ten minutes out," Beverly said. He exchanged quick pleasantries with Ramirez while Jake gave the deputies their marching orders. A third cruiser pulled up behind them.

"Anything else these guys need," Jake said to Beverly. "If and when Ed Lattimore shows up, I want to talk to him. In the meantime, Bird ... er ... Deputy Wayne and I want to make sure this thing hasn't gone any further than this property. Lattimore's got two others?"

"Yeah," Beverly said. "If you follow the road where it curves around. According to his website, this is Unit 1, Rustic Pines. Unit 2 is about a half-mile west of us. Unit 3's a half-mile past that."

"I need to clear them," Jake said. "Make sure we're not dealing with any more victims." Deputy Jordy Holtz got out of the second cruiser.

"They're all clear, Detective," Holtz said. "We've just come from that way on our way in. There's nobody in either one but the cleaning crews. Their weekend renters left two days ago. They're getting them ready for new guests for tomorrow morning."

"Good," Jake said, relief flooding him. "Any of the cleaning crews see or hear anything?"

"No, sir," Deputy Holtz said. He was new. Young. Green. God, Jake thought. The kid barely looked older than his nephew Ryan.

"The girl I talked to said they haven't been down to this unit all summer. She said these are long-term renters. We didn't say anything about why we were asking."

"Good," Jake said. "Good man. Let's keep a lid on this as long as we can. I don't need the local news out here."

Jake's cell phone rang. Dan Tuttle's ID popped up.

"Whatcha got, Tuttle?" Jake asked.

"Jake, Ed Lattimore showed up at my barricades. He's mad as hell and demanding to be let on to his property. I thought it was gonna come to blows for a second. I've got him cooling his jets in the back of my car, but he's demanding to talk to whoever's in charge."

"I'll bet he is," Jake said under his breath.

"Got it," he said to Tuttle. "Tuttle, just keep him on ice for a few minutes. I'm on my way back down. I've got just as many questions for him as he's probably got for me."

"Will do," Tuttle answered.

In the background, Jake could hear a man's voice swearing a stream of obscenities. Ed Lattimore, no doubt. Jake pocketed his phone. He turned to Ramirez.

"I'll have those warrants ASAP."

The ME's van pulled up just as he said it.

"Good enough," Ramirez said as he started to walk toward the van. "We've got a bunch to keep us busy until you get 'em."

"Come on," Jake said to Birdie. "Let's see if Ed Lattimore can help us ID our victims."

Birdie grabbed her campaign hat off the hood of Jake's car and climbed into the passenger seat of his cruiser.

Four

"Sir, you can't go down there." Deputy Tuttle had his hands flat on the chest of the man in front of him. An older gentleman, maybe seventy years old. Snow-white hair combed back from his tanned face. He wore a pink golf shirt and seersucker pants with a white belt. He still had golf cleats on.

"You can't tell me what I can and can't do on my own property, son," the man said. "Now, I suggest you get out of my way before I call your boss."

"Today, I'm his boss," Jake said. He pulled a card out of his wallet and handed it to the man.

"Detective Cashen," Deputy Tuttle said. "This man says he's Edgar Lattimore. He's the property owner. He tried to drive through our barricade."

Lattimore glanced at Jake's card, then handed it back to him.

"I don't care who you are. But you need to care who I am. I got a half a dozen phone calls telling me you all were driving emergency vehicles all over my property. Disturbing the peace of my tenants.

This is a secluded area. Private property. Somebody should have called me before you descended on this place like a plague of locusts. Do you have a warrant?"

"Mr. Lattimore," Jake said. "We need to have a conversation but this isn't really the place to do it. How about you follow me back to the sheriff's department? I'd rather talk in my office than out here in the open. We can make you more comfortable there, too."

"You trying to drive me off my own property?"

"Not at all. But we have a serious situation and I need to apprise you of it. But not here. So why don't you just get back in your vehicle and follow me down the hill?"

"Do I need to speak to my lawyer?"

"I've told you. You're not under arrest. But you are about to drive right into the middle of my crime scene. I'm not gonna let you do that."

Lattimore's tanned face went a little paler.

"Crime scene? What's going on? I demand you tell me exactly what you're doing down there."

"I intend to. But not here. Just do as I asked, okay? We'll continue this conversation in my office."

Another vehicle came up the road and pulled in behind Lattimore's black Lincoln. Jake's heart sank. It was a Channel Nine news van.

"Jake," Birdie started.

Lattimore's entire demeanor changed. Panic came into his face.

"They can't be here. Hey, there! You can't be here!"

"Deputy Tuttle," Jake said. "Do you think you could handle that?"

"Yes, sir!" Tuttle held on to his hat as he sprinted toward the driver's side door of the news van.

"I don't want a camera in my face. I don't want them filming here."

"It's a public road," Jake said. "But as far as them filming you, just get in your car and follow me down like I've asked you to three times now. I'll meet you in my office in thirty minutes. I've got something else to do that takes priority."

Finally, Lattimore saw the wisdom of Jake's demand. He nodded quickly and made a bee line for his own car.

"You want me to hang back and help Tuttle?" Birdie asked.

"Not a bad plan," Jake answered. "I want to talk to Landry about conscripting you to partner with me on this for the duration. I need to get your overtime approved."

Birdie kept her face unreadable, but he saw the spark in her eye.

Lattimore kicked up gravel with his back tires as he turned and started back down the road. Jake got behind the wheel and went after him. The man floored his accelerator and took the turn onto County Road Seven at a recklessly high speed. Jake had half a mind to pull him over again, but he slowed, catching Jake's eye in the rearview mirror.

As they got back to downtown Stanley, Jake almost expected Lattimore to peel off in the other direction. But he pulled into the public lot in front of the sheriff's department. Jake gave him a friendly wave and held up one finger, indicating he'd be there as soon as he could.

T en minutes later, Jake had his warrants.

"I appreciate this, Judge," Jake said. Judge Finneas Cardwell had thrown his arms through his robe but kept it open, revealing his Pink Floyd concert tee shirt and red gym shorts underneath. He'd just come in from a run at the indoor track at the Y two blocks over.

Judge Cardwell handed Jake his paperwork and perched himself on the end of his desk.

"Sounds like you've got a real mess out there."

"Word's traveling, huh?" It wasn't surprising, but Jake really hoped to be able to keep a lid on the details of this as long as possible.

"It is," Judge Cardwell said. "But you can't really expect anything less in Blackhand Hills, Jake. Were these locals?"

"I can't say anything about that yet. Even if I knew for sure. I've got Ed Lattimore cooling his heels back in my office."

"Aw, hell," Cardwell said. "Ed's gotta be fit to be tied. He's gonna see nothing but vanishing dollar signs. That's his property out there."

"That's the gist. Yes."

"Well, you tell Ed I expect him to cooperate fully. If he gives you any trouble, you let me know."

"Will do. And thanks for this." Jake held up the warrants. "BCI needs to get in there."

In the half hour since Jake left the scene, Ramirez had texted him three times, asking for a status report.

"Then I won't hold you up here," Judge Cardwell said. "And I'll keep a good thought for a speedy resolution. Just hurry up and catch the son of a bitch who did this. My granddaughter was one of the girls in that sorority that was out tubing in the creek."

That answered how Judge Cardwell heard the details so quickly. "She doing all right?"

"I don't think she saw the body. But her mother says she's pretty shook up."

"Well, I'll keep a good thought for her and your family, Judge."

Jake thanked him again and made his way down the hall. His phone blew up again with texts from Ramirez and Sheriff Landry. He forwarded copies of the warrants to Ramirez and made his way across the parking lot to his office where Ed Lattimore was hopefully still waiting.

FIVE

Darcy made Ed Lattimore reasonably comfortable in the interview room. She got him his brand of sparkling water and a bagel. Jake walked in with a pen and pad of paper and sat in front of Lattimore.

"You gonna tell me what the hell's going on now?" Lattimore asked as he unscrewed the cap to his water. "I've been sitting on my ass here for almost an hour!"

"Mr. Lattimore, two bodies were found on your rental property this afternoon. None of what we're about to discuss is for public dissemination yet."

"You think I want people knowing any of this?" Lattimore started to sweat. His hands trembled as he put his water bottle down.

"No," Jake said. "I don't imagine you do. Though we're not going to be able to keep a lid on it for long."

"What happened? Was it an accident? Do you know?"

"No," Jake said. "This wasn't an accident. Things are still very early in my investigation, but the two individuals appear to have been shot to death. This was foul play."

"Oh God. Oh hell. This is terrible. Oh. Oh."

"Mr. Lattimore, I need to know who you had staying in the Rustic Pines."

Lattimore's eyes seemed to cloud over. Jake's words hadn't fully sunk in for him. Finally, the man got a hold of himself.

"Married couple," he said. "The husband contacted me late this spring. It's a long-term rental. Guy wrote me a check for thirty-two thousand dollars to cover June, July, and August."

"Names," Jake said, sliding the pad of paper in front of him.

"Waters," Lattimore said. "Jax Waters."

"Jack?" Jake asked.

"Jax," Lattimore repeated. "J-A-X-O-N. I had him spell it for me three times. Jaxon Waters. I only talked to him once on the phone when he inquired about the initial booking. Most of my interactions after that were with the wife. She introduced herself as Joey. Joey Waters."

"What do you know about them?"

"They filled out a rental app. I would normally do a credit check for a long-term rental like that, but the man's check cleared. My renters don't normally pay upfront for the whole season like that. I do a deposit then have them pay the first of the month after that. But this guy ... he just wrote me a check for the whole burger, you know?"

"Do you have a rental agreement?"

"Of course. If you'll give me a sec ..."

Lattimore took out his cell phone. He squinted at the screen, then slipped on a pair of readers he kept in his shirt pocket.

"We do everything online now," he said. "Paperless with one of those legal document signers. Makes it easier, I guess. Though I sure do miss the days of carbon copies, you know? Or maybe you don't. You look pretty young. Here it is."

Lattimore turned his phone over to Jake. He'd pulled up a PDF of a rental contract. As Lattimore described, the tenants' names were Jaxon and Joey Waters.

"Do you know why they needed a three-month rental? Was it a honeymoon?"

"Not a honeymoon. And I didn't ask too many questions about their why. I never do. But the guy said his business was mobile. That all he'd need was a laptop and an internet connection and he'd be working through the summer. A real know-it-all. Said he runs a real estate investment firm. Was asking me all kinds of questions about the region. I think he was scouting, though that's just me speculating."

"He signed this lease as an individual," Jake said. "Not as an agent of any business."

"That's right. But he kept telling me crap I should do to improve the resale value of my property out there. Stupid stuff that showed me he didn't know what the heck he was talking about. But like I said, I only really communicated with him in the beginning while we were working out the terms of the lease. After that, it was the wife I dealt with. Real sweetheart. Pretty. Brunette. You ask me, Waters was out of his league with her. But he had money, so maybe that was the attraction, I don't know."

"Did you see them together? See them interact?"

"No. The wife came into the office a couple of times early in the summer. She was interested in the different attractions we have out here in Blackhand Hills. Wanted to know where she could rent kayaks, that sort of thing. And she bought one of our gourmet baskets my secretary puts together. She does it for couples' weekends. You know, champagne, glasses, strawberries. She sticks in gift certificates to the spa out on Norvell Road. They do couple's massages. I always thought that sounded like a horrible idea, but the guests seem to love it. I don't know if they used the gift cards or not."

"How did she seem to you, Mrs. Waters?"

"Well, I told ya. She was a sweetie. Just pleasant. Smiling. Please and thank yous. Saying how much she loved the cabin. Appreciated the decor, the attention to detail. Well, that really put her in Verna's good graces, cuz she picked out a lot of the decor."

"Verna. She's your secretary?"

"Yes."

"When's the last time you had any communication with Mr. or Mrs. Waters?"

"Are they dead? Are they the ones who are dead?"

"That's what I'm trying to figure out," Jake said.

Lattimore shook his head. "I couldn't tell ya. Well, Joey, the missus. She came in three days ago to buy that basket. I haven't talked to her since then. I mean, there'd be no reason to. I don't go out there on a daily basis or anything. The people who rent from me? They want to be left alone. That's the draw out there. Rustic weekend getaway. Well, as rustic as you can get with plumbing, electricity, high-speed internet. Plus, those cabins are all high end."

"For eleven grand a month, I would think so," Jake said.

Lattimore buried his face in his hands. "This is gonna ruin me. Don't think I don't know that. You're saying they were shot to death? You're sure?"

Jake pursed his lips and nodded. Even Lattimore seemed to realize it was a ridiculous question, but the man was clearly trying to process the tragic news.

"What about an emergency contact?" Jake asked, scrolling through the rental agreement on Lattimore's phone. The space on the form where the Waters would have filled that out was blank.

Lattimore shrugged. "If they didn't write that down, then I don't know. It wouldn't have occurred to me to force the issue."

"Can you send me a copy of this agreement?" Jake asked.

"Go ahead," Lattimore answered. Jake pulled up the send option and texted himself a copy of the rental agreement. A half a second later, his cell phone buzzed with the incoming text.

"Do they know?" Lattimore asked. "I mean, do I have to tell them? Do I have some legal obligation?"

"Tell who?"

"I've got renters coming into Units 2 and 3 today. Are you extending your crime scene to include my entire property?"

"Not at the moment," Jake said. "The scene's being processed by agents of the Ohio Bureau of Criminal Investigations as we speak. And the medical examiner is out there. Mr. Lattimore, it's going to be a long while before we'll be able to turn the cabin back to you. I'm sorry about that. As far as your other tenants, there's no way they're not going to catch wind of what's happened out there."

"God. The coroner. I mean, of course, the coroner. It's just ... there's gonna be body bags. Right?"

"At some point, yes."

"Those reporters. Vultures. They're gonna plaster pictures of body bags being rolled out of there. It's gonna ruin me. I'm sorry. I know that sounds callous. I care about what happened to the Waters. If that's them. But ..."

"It's a lot to take in. It's okay for you to feel how you need to feel."

"Are we done? I mean, can I go? I have to figure out what to tell my other renters. They might already be out there. Your deputy ..."

"You do what you need to do. I may have more questions, but for now, you've been very helpful."

Lattimore rose and shook Jake's hand. Gone was the confident, arrogant man who'd rushed to the scene from the golf course. He seemed befuddled, bewildered, and maybe a little broken. It was going to be a long, dry summer for Lattimore rentals.

Jake showed Lattimore out the door. He knew Sheriff Landry would be waiting for him in her office as soon as he was through.

Six

She was alone in her office when Jake got there, pacing in front of her desk like she always did when she was agitated. Meg Landry had a hard time sitting still when her brain was spinning.

"Jake," she said, breathless when he walked in. "Tell me some good news."

Jake shut the door. "Not sure what constitutes good under the circumstances, Sheriff. Warrants are signed so the leash is off for BCI. The ME showed up just as I was leaving."

"Who are these people, the victims?"

"We're gonna have to wait for positive IDs, but it looks like they were long-term renters from Delaware, Ohio."

Meg's shoulders dropped, but she scowled again just as quickly.

"Not local. You know, I don't know if that's good news or bad news. Long-term renters. So rich, right? Those cabins are among the most expensive lodging we have out there."

"I talked to the landlord, Ed Lattimore. He said they paid upfront for three months. Real estate investors. Married couple."

"I know Ramirez has to do his thing. But what did it look like to you? You know I trust your eyes."

"Meg, I gotta be honest. I don't know. Just a cursory glance and it didn't look like a robbery or burglary. The back door was wide open. No forced entry. Both victims were buck naked and looked like they were in the middle of a romantic evening. Guy was found in the hot tub. Woman was found at the creek bed. My guess is she tried to run so she was probably shot second."

"The hot tub?" Meg wrinkled her nose.

"Yeah. I've seen a lot. But that one's got to rank up there in the top five grossest things I've ever seen."

Meg covered her mouth in disgust, then sank into her desk chair.

"Birdie ... er ... Erica was even having a tough time with it if that gives you any indication."

"What about the other rentals? Do you think there's a chance whoever did this was targeting them?"

"The two other cabins in Lattimore's property were vacant. Cleaning crews were out there getting ready for the next renters. So far, it doesn't look like anyone else was targeted, but it's early. Way early."

"Okay. Okay. Ugh. Okay. What do you need?"

"Probably everything," he said. "Beverly's out there now keeping the scenes secure."

"Scenes?"

"The creek bed where we found the woman. The cabin where we found the man. I already had to run off one news van. Judge

Cardwell already knew all about it. One of his granddaughters was with the sorority group who found the female victim."

"This is already getting out of hand. I'm going to need to get out in front of it. You can expect the county commissioners breathing down my neck any second."

"No doubt. I just don't know enough for you. BCI just got clearance to go in."

"How long will it take them?"

"Ramirez has two units out there. ME's already out there. Ramirez will work efficiently but he won't be rushed."

"Right. Good."

"You asked me what I need. I need a partner. I want Deputy Wayne running things down with me. And I'd like to make it official."

"We've been over this. I can't get budget approval for another detective right now. I'm sorry. You know I'm fighting for it. But right now, I'm hamstrung."

"Fine. Well, not fine. But then pull me off this temporary detective sergeant crap. I never wanted it in the first place."

"Nobody wants it," Landry said. "You know I offered it to Majewski and he turned it down. With Jeff Hammer's demotion to the property room, there's just nobody left to fill the void. I know you hate it. I hate it for you. But it would be worse if I filled that position with just any warm body. You'd hate that worse. I'll take as much as I can off your plate, but for right now, we don't have the budget or manpower to do everything we want."

"Everything. I need you to take everything off my plate while I'm working this case. I'm telling you it doesn't look like a robbery. I'm telling you it doesn't look like anyone else has been targeted. But that could change with one phone call from Ramirez. Or one more sorority girl further down the creek. I just don't know yet."

"Okay. I get it. You know I get it. Just do the best you can. I'll do the same. And we'll pray this was just some disgruntled ex and it goes no further than that."

"We can hope. But again, if the county commissioners get worried about their precious tourist season, maybe remind them that it's pretty damn hard for me to solve a double murder when they won't approve the resources I need and their inaction is forcing me to pull focus on crap I shouldn't be. If they want it cheap, it won't be good. If they want it good, it won't be cheap or fast."

Landry looked introspective. She paused for a moment.

"What?" Jake said. "You want to say something? I know that face."

"Jake," she said. "You're not going to like this. And I need you to know this isn't because I disagree with you. I *do* agree with you. Deputy Wayne is an outstanding cop. She's going to make a great detective someday if that's her ambition. But ..."

"There are no buts," he said.

"There are. I'm just saying it hasn't gone unnoticed that you have a particular affection for her."

Jake felt his ears turn hot. "Affection? What? This has nothing to do with that. Yeah. I've known Birdie since she was a toddler. But that ..."

"Jake, you don't help your case every time you call her Birdie!"

Jake let out a hard sigh. "You know what I mean. For chrissake, name me another deputy out there with her skill set or natural instincts."

"I just told you I think she's a phenomenal cop. Her resume speaks for itself. I'm just wondering ... and others might wonder ... if maybe you shouldn't be the one pushing so hard for her promotion. Everyone knows how close you were to Erica's brother. It's only natural for you to want to look out for her since his passing."

"His murder," Jake spat. "Since his murder."

"Be that as it may," Landry said. "All I'm saying is, you'd do yourself and Deputy Wayne a lot of good if you kept this process at arm's length. Let me do my job. Don't ruffle feathers you don't need to ruffle. And have a little faith in my administrative capabilities. As good a detective as you are, I'm a good sheriff. For both our sakes, I'd like to be able to keep my job. We're four months from an election that is by no means a lock for me."

Jake hated when she brought that up. He hated even thinking about the prospect of losing her behind that desk. But he also wasn't naïve about politics. As much as he hated admitting it in the heat of the moment, he knew she was right.

Something about his posture changed enough for Landry to take notice of his thoughts. She smiled.

"Okay," she said. "So I have my marching orders. I'll try to hold off the media as long as I can. I'll try shuffling some things around to take as much off your plate as I can. For now, Deputy Wayne can be your right-hand woman on this. As for the future, let's just deal with one day at a time. Hell, one hour at a time."

"Yeah," Jake said. "And I do appreciate it. And your insights."

After a light knock on Landry's door, Birdie poked her head in.

"Sorry," she said. "Darcy told me where I could find you, Jake. I've got a few things I didn't think could wait."

"Go," Landry said. "Both of you. Catch me a murderer, will you? Hopefully before the six o'clock news."

Jake took his leave. He and Birdie walked back down to his office. On the way, he filled her in on his conversation with Ed Lattimore. Birdie sat down at Jake's desk and fired up his laptop. Within a few seconds, she had a website pulled up.

"Well, Lattimore's story tracks with what came up when I ran the plates on the Range Rover," she said. "It's a company car registered to a House Money Holdings. I googled it and came up with this."

Birdie turned the laptop toward Jake. "I found a website for House Money Holdings Real Estate Investments," she said. "That's a pretty nebulous description. There's no mention of any specific projects or anything. But take a look at the about page."

She clicked on the menu bar. The next screen showed two professional headshots. Jaxon Waters was listed as company president. Josefina Waters was listed as vice president.

"That's them, isn't it?" Birdie asked.

Jake squinted at the photos. Jaxon Waters was good-looking enough, with a thick, square head. He had a look about him that reminded Jake of a bodybuilder who partook in too many steroids. But it was damn hard to match the photo on the screen with what he saw floating in that hot tub. But the woman. Pretty. Dark-haired, with a dimple in her cheek. It absolutely looked like the woman found on the creek bed. They'd need positive IDs through dental records if no next of kin could be found, but Jake would bet his next paycheck they'd found their victims.

"This is good work," Jake said.

"It's a start," Birdie agreed. "But I just can't shake the feeling that whoever did this might still be lurking out there in those woods."

A shadow fell across Birdie's face. He knew she was thinking of her brother. Ben had been murdered in the woods not unlike the way Joey Waters had been. It sent a shiver of dread through Jake as well.

Not again, he thought. Please, not again.

A call from Mark Ramirez mercifully brought Jake out of his own head.

"Hey, Jake," Ramirez said. "We've still got a lot to do out here, but I've got some preliminary findings you're gonna want to know about right quick."

Birdie heard Mark's voice even though he wasn't on speaker. She flipped Jake's laptop shut and grabbed his keys.

"We'll be out in fifteen minutes," Jake answered.

SEVEN

Agent Mark Ramirez stood at the edge of the creek. Flood lights and crime scene tape marked the spot. The full moon's reflection wavered in the water. Jake and Birdie stepped carefully, avoiding the taped-off areas. Ramirez turned and walked up to meet them.

"Thanks for working so fast," Jake said. "We think we've got an ID on the victims, but we're still trying to figure out next of kin."

"Josefina DeSilva," Ramirez said. He held a small tablet. Pulling up the first of his crime scene photos, he tilted the screen so Jake could see. "We found her purse on the kitchen counter," he said. "Credit cards, a hundred and eighty bucks in cash, all crisp twenties like she'd just gone to the ATM. And she had a rock on her finger. I'm no expert but it looked to be a two or three carat square diamond. I mean, it could have been a fake."

"I doubt it," Jake said. "Rental property owner said the guy paid 32K upfront to rent the cabin for the whole summer."

"DeSilva," Birdie said. "Not Waters?"

"Maiden name probably," Jake said. "If they were recently married, she might not have had time to change it, if she was even inclined to."

"Well," Ramirez said. "Anyway, I think you can safely rule out robbery as a motive."

"What can you tell me about her?" Jake asked.

"ME's still doing the post mortems. But he's telling me she was out here maybe twelve to eighteen hours before your sorority girl found her. Two gunshot wounds. One just below the right buttock. Second one through the upper back. Exit wound right between her breasts."

Ramirez swiped to another crime scene photo. The woman's body had been flipped over onto the stretcher, already in her unzipped body bag. Had there been any doubt, the straight-on image of her face in death matched the headshot Jake and Birdie found on the House Money Holdings website.

"She was running away," Birdie said.

"Most likely," Ramirez said. We found one bloody footprint in the leaves up there. Nothing coming out from the cabin. The ground's been pretty dry. If your killer shot her up at the cabin, I would have expected to see a trail of blood all the way down here. So your killer was a good shot."

"Wouldn't have to be that good," Birdie said. "Shooter would have had a clear shot from an elevated position. If he's up there and the creek's down here. Plus, she couldn't have been moving too fast with that leg shot."

"Good point," Ramirez agreed. "Anyway ... we'll know more about her specific injuries after your ME's done. But I don't think she would have suffered long. Girl was probably dead when she hit the ground."

"Small mercy," Jake said.

"There's no outward sign of any other trauma to the body," Ramirez said. "Again, I defer to Dr. Stone, but this doesn't read like rape to me. Her clothes were in the bedroom in a hamper, underwear on the floor but intact. Didn't look torn off. I mean, your killer could have held her at gunpoint or something, but she took her clothes off on her own."

"Anything else down here of note?" Jake asked. It was the cabin he really wanted to go through.

"That's about it. Let's head up."

Jake followed Ramirez back up the hill. Birdie stayed transfixed for a moment, staring at the indentation in the mud where Joey DeSilva's body had lain. An odd expression came over her face. For a moment, it seemed as if she were looking at something beyond the creek in front of her. Then she recovered, turned, and followed the two men up the hill.

"No sign of forced entry," Ramirez said as they approached the deck at the back of the cabin.

The hot tub was silent now. Part of Jake didn't want to go up those steps. He wasn't particularly squeamish, but the condition of Jaxon Waters's body was gonna stick with him in his nightmares for a while.

"We had to drain the tub before we pulled him out," Ramirez said. "Water temp was a steady 104. Plus, with the jets going. Man ... this was one for the highlight reel, if you know what I mean. Your property owner's gonna be digging out chunks for a while."

"I'll tell him to just tear the whole thing out," Jake said, wrinkling his nose.

"Yeah. Anyway ... two gunshot wounds on your guy, too. One through the arm, the other right between the eyes. Exit wound out the back. We found a pretty much intact bullet in the bottom of the hot tub. Probably the one that hit his arm. Looks to me about a .38 caliber."

"They were caught off guard," Birdie said. She hung back. "Shooter could have been standing on that little hill beside the cabin. It would have put them almost level with the deck."

"With tree cover," Jake agreed. Two giant arborvitaes shielded the deck and hot tub from the driveway. They'd likely been strategically planted for that very purpose when Lattimore's developers built the property.

"That'd be my guess," Ramirez said.

"He scoped it out," Jake said. He walked to the hill with the arborvitaes. Birdie was right. This would have been a perfect little sniper's nest. There were no windows on this side of the cabin. Anyone sitting on the deck, especially after dark, would be hard-pressed to see someone standing here.

"Any casings found anywhere?" Jake asked.

"Not so far," Ramirez answered. "We've done some digging out here and down near the creek bed. We found some other things below the ground. A civil-war-era belt buckle, old buttons, a few coins. Nothing new. Like I said, no visible footprints from the house."

Jake walked up and down the small hill at the side of the house, looking toward the hot tub.

"It's like he was assassinated more than murdered," he said.

"That's what I'm thinking too," Birdie said. "Waters might not have even known what hit him."

"I've got no footprints leading up to the cabin from there," Ramirez said. "Doesn't mean your killer didn't make his presence known. But with the way the body was found, I'd say yeah. Poor bastard was caught by surprise. Naked too. Which is why this doesn't read like a sexually motivated crime to me. Your victims were probably naked for each other, you know?"

Jake walked up to the back slider door. In his mind's eye, he could see it as he and Birdie first came upon it. Strawberries on the ground. The opened bottle of Moet was on the counter just inside. Shattered champagne flutes out on the deck.

"She came up on him," Jake said. "Sees her husband as he's shot or right after he was shot. She drops the glasses, the strawberries. She makes a run for it."

"If he was here," Birdie said, coming out from behind the trees, "she would have had to have run right past him to get to the wooded trail down to the creek. Why would she run toward the shooter?"

"Unless she didn't see him," Ramirez said.

"Body was found at two p.m.," Jake said. "You're saying Doc Stone thinks she was down there twelve to eighteen hours? Either way, that puts the critical window in the dark of night, or dusk at best."

"No robbery or burglary," Birdie said. "So the killer wants them dead because of who they are? Or is it somebody who wants someone like them dead no matter what?"

"Nothing going on at any of the other cabins on the property?" Ramirez asked.

"No," Jake answered. "They were empty."

"I've only got one set of tire tracks coming in," Ramirez said. "They're consistent with your victim's Range Rover. Like I said, the ground's pretty dry. So I can't conclusively rule out any other vehicles in the vicinity. But nothing obvious is showing up."

"Where did you come from?" Jake whispered, looking back at the pines on the hill. His mind played a dozen different scenarios. Did the killer hike in on foot? Park a vehicle further down the road?

"We need to know a hell of a lot more about these victims," Birdie said, as if she'd tapped into Jake's thought process. "Find out if they were seen with anyone else this week."

"Or were they seen at all?" Jake answered. "Lattimore said the woman's the one who came off as more extroverted. She was down at his office chatting up his secretary. That champagne and those strawberries were part of a guest gift basket she bought at the office."

"I can go talk to her," Birdie said. "That'd be Verna Howell. She's been working for Ed Lattimore for eons. My mom played bunco with her before she and my dad moved to Florida. I knew her son Kent back in the day. She had him call me before he enlisted in the navy. I think she wanted me to try and talk him out of it."

"Good," Jake said. "Yeah. Whatever you can find out. Ramirez, what about phones?"

"Got 'em," he said. "Both of them had the newest iPhones. Both locked. We found them on the charging docks in the kitchen. I'm sending them to ONIC if you're okay with that."

"ONIC?" Jake asked.

"Ohio Narcotics Intelligence Center," Ramirez said. "They're fairly new. The governor and AG put this together. They're an intelligence tool that assists drug task forces throughout the state. Mostly drug-related cases and organized crime. But they will occasionally assist in crimes like this. I've been working with them a lot lately. They've got the resources to get through the phone forensics a hell of a lot faster than I can. I figured the sooner the better for you on this one."

"Good. That's great. I think we're gonna need all the help we can get."

"It'll still take a couple of days to get a full analysis back. But these guys are extremely good at what they do."

"Was there anything else?" Birdie asked. "You said Ed Lattimore said Waters told him he could run his business anywhere he had an internet connection. Was there a laptop?"

"No laptop," Ramirez said. "But there was something else. Something you're not going to like, Jake. At all."

Ramirez gestured for Jake and Birdie to follow him into the master bedroom. There a small safe sat on the ground. It had been sawed open already. Beside it, lined up in small evidence bags, Jake counted ten additional cell phones and a large bag of currency.

"Burners," Jake said, his stomach churning.

"Looks like," Ramirez said. "This is the other reason we need ONIC involved. Like I said, this is way too much for me to handle on my end as far as the phones. There's also a little over 30K in a backpack in the closet."

"Drugs?" Birdie said, staring at all the phones and cash.

Jake could already hear the alarm in Meg Landry's voice when he broke it to her. If Jaxon and Josefina Waters were running something illicit through the Rustic Pines cabin in the heart of Blackhand Hills, murder might have been the best thing that happened to them.

"Sorry, Jake," Ramirez said. "I know this thing got ten times more complicated for you. You know I'll give you a call as soon as I have anything that'll help."

Jake thanked him. That full moon filled the floor-to-ceiling window in the master suite overlooking the woods. Two clear evidence bags sat on the nightstand beside the round bed. Jake walked over to it. Waters's ID lay face up inside one of the bags.

"Who the hell are you?" Jake whispered as he stared at Jaxon Water's driver's license. "And what the hell did you bring to my town?"

EIGHT

Eight a.m. the next morning, Darcy stood outside Jake's office holding out a steaming cup of coffee for him. It was the first sign of trouble.

He took it from her, dubious. She kept a smile on her face.

"What did I do?" Jake asked. "Or more to the point, what did you do?"

"I'm just looking out for you," she said. "You're up to your elbows in crap. I just wish there were something more I could do."

The coffee was good. Strong. Hot. But in the three years since Jake came to the Worthington County Sheriff's Department from the FBI, Darcy had never once brought him coffee. Nor was he shortsighted enough to ask.

"Thanks for this," he said. "But it's no good."

"It's not? I used those Jamaican beans everybody likes. I ground them fresh just this morning."

"Not the coffee. The coffee's great. But you. Whatever you're buttering me up for. It's no good. Just come out with it."

"Roll call," she said. "Sheriff wants you to handle it again this morning."

Jake grumbled. So much for Meg trying to take more off his plate.

"I'm waiting for a call from the ME. And I'm trying to run down next of kin for two out-of-town murder victims. Those poor people out at the cabin have been missing for their relatives for going on two days now. That's my priority. I'm heading down to Delaware, where we think these victims were living. I've got an appointment with a detective down there. I need to get on the road. Tell Majewski to handle roll call. He should be doing Hammer's job now anyway."

"He won't. Anyways, he can't. He took PTO for a colonoscopy or something today."

"A colono ... I've got a double homicide on my hands."

Jake realized having a colonoscopy sounded like a vacation compared to the day he knew he was about to have.

"Roll call can wait," he said. "I'm on my way over to see the sheriff before I light out for Delaware."

He gulped the rest of the coffee. She followed him, her heels clacking down the hallway. When he got to Landry's office door, he realized the real reason for Darcy's attempt at subterfuge.

"The timing couldn't be worse, you know that," Rob Arden's voice boomed. Meg's door was open a few inches. Jake could see his Uncle Rob planting his palms on Meg's desk. She sat in her chair, her fingers steepled beneath her chin. From the looks of it, Uncle Rob had been yammering at her for a while.

Snorting, Jake handed Darcy back her mug.

"Don't go in there," Darcy whispered. "I wouldn't ..."

He ignored her. He gave a cursory knock and let himself into Landry's office.

"Jake," Landry said, sitting up straighter in her chair. "I was just informing your uncle that we're doing everything we can to clear these cabin murders as quickly as possible. All hands on deck."

Rob didn't turn to look at Jake. He kept his gaze straight on Meg.

"You're worried about the tourists?" Jake said. "So am I. I'm trying to make sure they're not in danger of getting shot to death."

Rob pushed himself off Meg's desk.

"I need you to get out in front of this or I will, Meg. There should have been a press conference last night. All sorts of wild rumors are starting to spread. You wouldn't believe the kinds of calls my office is getting. Every crackpot in town is crawling out of the woodwork. That ridiculous true crime group on social media has a couple of viral posts. They're saying those people were dismembered and there are body parts all over Blackhand Hills. Like some sort of grisly Easter egg hunt."

"That's ridiculous," Jake said. "I don't know where people are getting their information. It's not coming from us."

"That's the problem!" Rob shouted. "The longer your office stays silent, the worse the rumor-mongering gets. It's not just about the tourist industry. That's bad enough. But next week, we're hosting the statewide county commissioners' convention. I've already got a few members staying in town. They're spooked. This is a terrible look."

"Rob, we all understand the urgency of this matter," Meg said. "I'll say it again. We are doing everything humanly possible to clear this case quickly."

Jake bit the inside of his cheek. He felt his fists curl. Meg saw it and gave him a stern look. He knew she didn't want him to antagonize Rob Arden. He also knew just sharing the same air with the man usually did that. He held a ridiculous grudge against Jake and his sister for simply existing. They were a constant reminder that his sister, Jake's mother, had sullied herself with a man the all-powerful Arden family considered beneath her.

"Are we safe out there?" Rob asked. "That's the question everyone is asking. This just couldn't have happened at a worse time."

"We'll try to plan our murders during the off season next time," Jake muttered.

"Jake," Meg said.

"You think this is a joke?" Arden said. "Tourism is what keeps this county going. We don't have the mills like we used to. You people are bitching about pay raises during negotiations. Manpower increases. If we don't have a tourist industry, there won't be any raises. In fact, you can expect more layoffs and it's out of my hands. So yes. I suggest you solve this thing quickly. And I expect a press conference within the hour. If you can't turn down the temperature out there, I'll do it for you."

"If you do anything to impede my investigation, I'm going to ..."

"What?" Rob said, red-faced. He turned and took a step forward, getting into Jake's personal space.

Jake's vision clouded. The hatred in Rob Arden's eyes seemed to have weight.

"Jake!" Meg shouted. She was out of her chair. She came around her desk and got between Rob and Jake.

"No," she said. "You know what? I'm tired of this. Whatever beef the two of you have with each other, work it out and keep it out of my office. You both seem to forget that we're all on the same team. This is our county. We all want what's best for it. And nobody wants to let this murder investigation languish or scare people away."

Meg's intervention did nothing to lower the temperature in the room. Jake saw the muscles in Rob's neck contract. He, too, had his fists clenched.

Hit me, Jake thought. Just take a swing. One swing.

"Fine," Meg said. "Kill each other and be done with it!"

She did something Jake wasn't expecting. She moved out from between the two men then stormed out of her own office, slamming the door shut behind her.

It caught Rob off guard just as much as Jake. He finally took a step back. For a moment, Jake realized his uncle was actually scared of him.

"You love this," Rob said.

Jake's eyes went wide. "Love what?"

"This is some kind of power trip for you. You think you're the smart one. The great savior of Worthington County. You've got Landry snowed. But not me. Never me. Don't forget that."

"What the hell are you talking about? You think I like people getting murdered in my county? Because it inconveniences you?"

"Look at you," Rob said. "If she hadn't checked you, you would have done it. You still want to do it."

Rob stepped forward again. His eyes flashed with hatred. He could smell the onions Uncle Rob probably had with his omelet this morning.

"You want to wrap your hands around my neck and strangle the life out of me? Hit me. Draw blood for the sport of it. Just like your old man. That's how he got his jollies, too."

Jake's blood seemed to thicken in his veins ... to bubble and boil over. Yes, he thought. It would feel good to just knock the smirk off Rob Arden's face once and for all. There was something else though. Something he could never get away from no matter how wrong Rob was.

Rob Arden's eyes were just like his mother's. Deep set and ocean blue. They were the same eyes Gemma had. As much as Jake hated it, he could see Sonya Arden clearly in her brother's face. Blood. Family. And he knew Uncle Rob saw the same thing staring back at him.

"You don't know what you think you know," Jake said, letting his fists uncurl.

"I could say the same thing to you," Rob said.

"You didn't know him," Jake said. "And you don't know me."

"Oh, I knew him. And I warned her. The thing is, she knew it too. But by the time she was willing to do anything about it, it was too late. Because *you* were here."

Jake took a step back. "Me? You're blaming me for what happened? Jesus. I was a little kid. I was seven years old when she died."

"I'm blaming you for who you are now," Rob said. "You're not who Meg Landry thinks you are. You're not like my sister. You're like him. I can see it. The same swagger. The same temper. And someday, you're going to end up just like him. And once again, it'll be me having to clean up the mess. You should do us all a favor and disappear. Leave town like you did before."

"Well lucky for you, I belong here. And I'm going to do my job. Despite your interference and your bullshit, I'm going to figure out who killed those people out there and try to make sure nobody else gets killed. If you care at all about that, you can stay out of my damn way."

"You reek of it," Rob said through gritted teeth.

"What are you talking about?"

"Violence," he said. "You're a devil. Just like your father was. Everything you Cashens touch turns to shit. You think I didn't have this same conversation with him? You think he didn't say the exact same things you did? Make the same promises? That he'd do the right thing. That he'd take care of her. That he wasn't the person I knew he was. He was a liar. Just like you are. And he ruined her. Then he gutted her. Shot her in the face so they had to identify her by her fingerprints. My mother wanted to see her one last time and I was the one who had to hold her back. My father too. So I'm the one who went in to that stinking morgue to get my sister back. And it's in you. You know it. Don't you dare stand there and try to tell me you're different. You're the same. You're a poison. You and your sister both."

The rage flooded back in. His fingers twitched. It would be so easy. One punch and his nose would explode. It soothed Jake to think about the pain he could cause.

But it was that tiny flicker of satisfaction lighting Rob Arden's eyes … his mother's eyes … that pulled him back from the brink.

"Get out," Jake said. His voice sounded foreign to him. Cold. Distant. Dangerous.

He took a step back, grabbed the doorknob, and held the door open.

That smug smile never left Rob Arden's face as he brushed past Jake and made his way down the hall.

Jake felt thunder inside of his head. He took a breath, letting it roll through him. He didn't know how long he stood there holding that doorknob. But it was Birdie's voice that brought him back out of his own head.

"Jake?" she said. "Are you okay?"

"No," Jake said. His voice still sounded like a stranger's. It was enough to fill Birdie's face with alarm.

He found a weak smile for her. "But I will be," he said.

NINE

"Jake?" Birdie had to practically sprint to catch up to Jake. He needed air. He needed to punch something.

"Jake!" she said. For a moment, Jake hadn't even realized where he'd gone. His need to put distance between himself and Rob Arden was his only motivation. He stood at the door to the service lot. He pushed through it with enough force to bounce the thing against the brick wall outside.

"Are you okay?" Birdie persisted.

It was then the blood seemed to circulate again. Jake's right hand burned. He looked down. He'd gripped his car keys so tightly, the metal had gouged the flesh of his palm. Birdie saw it before he could hide it. She acted quickly, taking the keys from him.

"Come on," she said. "I'm going with you over to Delaware. That's where you're headed, right? Background on the victims? I'm driving."

"You don't have to ..."

She put a hand up. Her face went hard in the way he'd learned meant there was no point arguing with her. Jake let out a grumble, but followed her to the car.

To her credit, Birdie didn't say anything for the first twenty minutes out of Stanley on their way to Delaware north of Columbus.

She blared the radio instead. Nineties alt rock. After the last strains of Soundgarden's biggest hit, she stabbed the power switch and turned to him, taking her eyes off the road for a brief second.

"That got pretty ugly back there. You wanna talk about it?"

"Not even a little," Jake said.

"I figured you'd say that. Still, Arden shouldn't have said those things."

Jake rubbed his eyes. "How much did you hear?"

"Uh. Thin walls, Jake. You drew an audience. Pretty sure everybody on the floor heard. So you may not wanna talk about it, but they all will."

"Great. It's nobody else's business."

Birdie nodded. "Sure. Like that will matter."

"Rob Arden's an asshole."

"You won't get an argument from me on that."

Jake looked at her. She kept her eyes straight ahead but he knew there was more she wanted to say. More that he wished she wouldn't.

"Good," he said, hoping she'd let that be the end of it.

"The thing is though," she started. Jake sighed. "Is it true what he said? Was he really the one who found your mom?"

"No. That was Gemma's special honor," Jake said, his voice going flat.

"God. Right. Yes. I knew that. I'm sorry. Only ... the rest of what your Uncle Rob said. About his parents. That had to be rough."

"Why are we talking about this?"

"Look, I get this is none of my business. At least, I know that's what you're about to tell me. Only ... and don't get me wrong. We're in agreement. Rob is a jerk. That he holds what your father did against you and Gemma? That's just sick and cruel. It's just ... I know what it's like to have to go do what he did. At the morgue. With my brother. The anger of that, it sticks with you. It's just sad to me that's all Rob Arden seems able to hold on to."

"And that's not my problem, Birdie. For him to throw that crap in my face ..."

"I'm on your side, Jake. I am. I'm just saying. There was a lot of collateral damage when your mom and dad died. It's just sad for everyone all the way around. I just want you to know that I know that. And if you ever wanna talk ..."

"I don't," he snapped. He regretted his temper, but for now, he couldn't get past it. Birdie capitulated. She turned on her blinker and took the exit into downtown Delaware. She'd put Jaxon Waters's home address from his driver's license into the GPS. The navigation screen indicated they were just ten minutes out. Birdie stayed mercifully silent for those ten minutes, letting Jake cool down again and try to forget how badly he wanted to rip his uncle's face off.

An unmarked patrol car sat parked in the driveway of their target address. It was a manufactured home off a country road in the middle of nowhere. Jake spotted a newer development further back. Beyond that, there was nothing out here but corn fields.

Birdie parked, pulled out the keys, and handed them to Jake. "If you're good, I'll let you drive back." She smiled.

A woman got out of the driver's seat of the unmarked sedan. Middle-aged with a round face, Jake recognized her from the photo ID that popped up in the emails they'd exchanged. Detective Angela Graff of the Delaware County Sheriff's Department.

"Hi, there," Detective Graff said. She shook Birdie's hand and came around to Jake.

"Thanks for meeting us," he said.

"Oh, no problem," Graff said. She smiled, displaying buck teeth and big gums. But her handshake was firm and she walked with purpose, wasting no time on her way up to the front door.

"Got your warrants this morning," Graff said. "We're clear for the house and the House Money office. It's not far from here. Only two miles down the same road. I got the keys from the landlord already."

"That's great," Birdie said. "Do you know anything about Mr. and Mrs. Waters?"

Detective Graff shook her head. "Neither of them has ever crossed my radar. I pulled the deed for this place. They bought it for cash two years ago. Put the house on it right afterward. He's also got his name on a vacant lot in that new subdivision going in over there. Whispering Pines, I think they're calling it. Which is funny. Not a single pine tree around here anywhere. Anyway, that's gonna be a gated community with a man-made, hundred-acre lake when they're all done. From what we're hearing, it's a pretty strict HOA as well. All the new owners have to be approved. I've got a call into the president. I'll see if I can get my hands on Waters's application."

"I really appreciate that," Jake said.

"Oh, that's easy," Graff said. "But I have a feeling it's the only real insight we're gonna get into these folks. I did some asking around out here. Nobody knows them. There are only a couple of people moved in over there in the new sub. Waters and his wife haven't made their faces known. The lot they're supposed to build on? They've got a next-door neighbor. He says he's never met him. I mean, it's pretty remote out here, but your people are ghosts, Cashen."

Birdie held the set of keys found in Jaxon Waters's rental cabin. She tried the first few on the ring, then finally got lucky.

"Ta da," she said, when the lock turned. Part of Jake was disappointed. It would have felt good to kick something down today. The thought must have crossed his face. Birdie gave him her own look, rolling her eyes.

"Hello!" Detective Graff shouted, though they all knew it was futile. "This is Detective Graff. Delaware County Sheriff's. Anybody home?"

A moment later, the three of them walked into the front room. The place was spartan. Still had a new carpet smell. Jake could see a few footprints in the plush gray pile, but the place didn't look lived in.

Birdie went back out the front door and started walking toward the road. Jake went through the living room and into the kitchen. Graff followed him and started opening cupboards.

"Nothing here," she said. The cupboards were mostly bare. Just a few cans of soup, some unopened bags of potato chips. Jake opened the fridge. It was completely empty.

Graff walked down the hallway. He heard her pull back a shower curtain.

"There's some shampoo bottles," she called out. "Toothbrushes in the holders."

Jake spotted some mail on the kitchen counter. The postmarks were dated two months ago. Junk mostly. What looked like a magazine subscription renewal. A few coupons to the department store. No utility bills, but that wasn't surprising. Most people paid online now.

Jake went down the hall to join Detective Graff.

"She's got some styling products," she said. "Curling iron. Blow dryer. Diffuser. He's got an electric shaver."

Jake went to the bedroom at the end of the hall. A king-sized bed sat in the center of the room with one tall dresser in the corner. The bed was made. The dresser had casual clothes in it. Tee shirts. Jeans. Sweatshirts.

Graff went to the closet. Two men's business suits hung on one rack. The other held four black dresses.

"Designer," Graff said, reading the labels. "It's weird though. This place doesn't look like anywhere they spent a lot of time. More like someplace they just crashed at from time to time."

"The rental property owner where they were found says they were paid up there for three months. Maybe that's how they lived for the most part," Jake said.

Jake heard the front door open. Birdie came down the hall and joined them.

She held a stack of mail in her hand. "Just junk in the mailbox," she said. "Postmarks start three months ago. They might have put a stop order with the letter carrier. This is all spammy advertising."

"No television anywhere," Graff observed. "I'd say your victims haven't stepped foot in here for several months. I'm sorry there's nothing valuable here."

"Well, knowing how they lived might help me figure out why they died," Jake said. "So I wouldn't call it a complete dead end."

"You wanna head out to their office space?" Graff said. "Like I told you, it's just down the road. It'll take us about three minutes to get there."

"You wanna finish cataloging stuff here?" Jake asked Birdie.

"You bet," she said.

Jake followed Angela Graff out to her vehicle. He climbed into the passenger side. Graff had a lead foot peeling out of Waters's gravel driveway. Jake held on to the dashboard to keep himself upright.

Just as she said, Waters's office was right down the same road as his house. Graff pulled into a small strip mall across from a gas station and a chiropractor's office.

"This is it," she said, pulling into a parking spot right in front of a nondescript white door. On one side was a seamstress shop, on the other, a used video game store.

Graff and Jake got out of the car. She stepped forward and slid the landlord's key into the lock. She opened the door and let Jake go in ahead of her.

If Waters's house seemed sparse, his office space was basically barren. There was one cheap desk against the wall with two chairs in front of it. No phones. No computers.

"Why would somebody spend a grand a month renting this dump and not even use it?" Graff asked.

Jake felt his spine tingle. Why indeed? He went to the desk and opened a few of the drawers. They were empty save for stray paperclips.

"Did the landlord have anything useful to say?" Jake asked Graff.

She shook her head. "Sounds a whole lot like what your cabin owner said. Waters paid upfront a year's worth of rent after the first of the year. I talked to the lady who runs the seamstress shop next door. She's there practically every day. All hours of the day and night because she can't get good help to meet the demand. Lost art, you know?"

"Sure," Jake said. He ran a finger across the top of the lone desk. It came away coated with dust.

"Anyway," Graff continued. "Ina, that's the seamstress's name. Ina Godfrey. I've known her for years. She used to own a bridal shop years ago in this very space. She said she's never met the Waters couple. Said as far as she knows, they've never even crossed the threshold here. Which kind of suits her fine. Makes things quiet and her customers use the parking spaces out there."

"It's a front for something," Jake said.

"Can't be good," Graff said.

"No," Jake said, walking to the one window overlooking the parking lot. "It can't be good."

"I wish I had more I could tell you," Graff said. "Nobody in Delaware has reported these two missing. Nobody seems to know them at all."

"It's gonna be hard notifying next of kin I can't find."

"They're not from Delaware," Graff said. "I can tell you that much. No record of a Jaxon Waters or Josefina DeSilva being born here. I checked with the township, they're not registered to vote here either."

"I really appreciate you running all that down for me."

"Oh, it's my pleasure. Anything we can do to help."

Jake walked to the back of the office. There was a small bathroom. He opened the door. The smell of sulfur hit his nose.

"They're on a well out here," Graff explained.

Jake noticed mice droppings in the corner near the toilet.

"Landlord ought to set some traps," Jake said, closing the bathroom door.

As he made his way back to the front of the office, he saw Birdie pull up. She had her cell phone against her ear.

"Thanks again, Graff," Jake said as he waited for her to go out the front door before locking it behind them.

"Jake," Birdie said. "We've got to get back. That was Deputy Bundy. We've got a lead. Maybe. He said a woman showed up at the cabin about an hour ago. She was looking for Joey Waters. He didn't tell her anything. He got her to agree to come down to the sheriff's department. But she's spooked. He's afraid she's going to bolt. I told him do whatever he could to keep her there until we can get back."

Jake turned to Angela Graff and shook her hand. "Thanks, if there's ..."

"I got it." She smiled. "You better skedaddle if you want to get clear of Columbus traffic before rush hour. You're my first call if anything interesting turns up here."

Birdie kept the car running. She slid into the passenger side. Jake gave Detective Graff a final wave, then drove south as fast as he dared.

TEN

She was pretty. No. Not just pretty. Fancy. Deputy Bundy had set her up in the interview room. Birdie would observe while Jake talked to her. Bundy stood outside the door. The kid looked lovesick, staring at the woman's chest. A withering look from Birdie and Bundy had the decency to look embarrassed.

"She drove up in that," Bundy whispered to Jake. From the window, he pointed to a silver BMW parked crooked in the visitor's lot.

"On it," Birdie said. Jake didn't even have to ask. She'd run the plates while Jake talked to the woman.

"She won't say much," Bundy said. "Just that she and Joey Waters are friends and she came down to hang out with them today. She's spooked though."

"You're sure she didn't get close enough to the cabin to get suspicious?" Jake asked.

"No. No way. We've got it blocked off at the road. You can't even see the cabin from there."

"Good," Jake said. He grabbed a notepad and pen from his pocket and walked into the interview room.

"Sorry to keep you waiting so long," he said. "It's real good of you to come down here."

"I don't know why I'm here," she said. "Have I done something wrong?"

"Not at all. I know you had a brief conversation with Deputy Bundy, so if I'm asking repeat questions, sorry about that. I'll do my best not to waste any more of your time. You told him your name was Samantha Banco?"

"Blanco," she said. "With an L."

She tapped her manicured fingernails on the tabletop. Long and red with little crystals stuck on them. Her red skirt and high heels matched the color perfectly. She came in wearing a black leather jacket, but had thrown that over the chair next to her. She had a black silk tank top underneath and her chest strained the straps. Jake would not stare the way Bundy had. But he surmised the fingernails weren't the only thing fake about Samantha Blanco.

"Is Joey in trouble?" she asked.

"Can you tell me how you know her?"

"We're friends. Well, more than friends. I work for her and for Jax."

"What's the name of the company?"

"House Money. It's a uh … um … real estate investment firm."

"And what do you do for them?"

"I told all this to that other cop. I'm a secretary."

"You work in the office?"

"Yes," she said, irritated. "That's generally what secretaries do."

"You like that term? I didn't think it was used much anymore. Secretary."

Samantha shrugged. She had jet-black hair long enough to touch the table when she leaned forward. She kept throwing it back over her shoulders but it wouldn't stay there.

"Office administrator," she said. Samantha pulled a card out of her purse and put it on the table in front of Jake. It bore the House Money logo he'd seen on the door outside the office in Delaware. All very official looking. Only he already knew she was lying. She had no way of knowing he'd just come from her so-called office.

"How long have you worked for House Money?"

"I don't know. Three years maybe. Listen, I'm not an idiot. I know something bad is going on. I know there's a reason your deputy wouldn't let me go to the cabin today. Is Joey okay? I've been trying to get a hold of her and she's not answering. If she's in some kind of trouble, I can ..."

"Ms. Blanco, why were you looking for Joey and Jax today?"

"What do you mean? I told you. I work for them."

"Right. But I understand that most of their business they conduct behind a laptop. So why did you need to see them in person?"

She sat back. "I just ... I got worried. I've called a few times and got no answer. I had some paperwork Joey needed to sign that couldn't wait. I was in the area, so I thought I'd just stop by and see her."

"In the area. But you live in Delaware? Near the House Money office?"

"No. I live just outside of Cleveland."

Jake frowned. "Cleveland. That's like, what, two hours from Delaware? Do you commute?"

"It's like you said. A lot of what we do we can do from a computer. So I'm mostly working from home."

"Except for these documents you need Joey to sign."

"Right."

"The ones that couldn't have been done over the internet."

"Right. She was supposed to do it last week at the office but it must have slipped her mind. They're time sensitive." Her story grew less convincing the more she talked.

"When was the last time you saw Joey or Jax Waters at the office?"

"I don't know. Last week some time."

"Uh huh. Ms. Blanco, can you excuse me for a few minutes? Can I bring you back something? Water? A soft drink?"

"I'd like a Dr. Pepper Zero if you've got one."

He raised a brow. "That's pretty specific. I'll see what I can do."

She draped one arm over the chair and wiggled her nails at Jake in a condescending wave. He shut the door behind him. Birdie was just coming down the hall from the other direction holding a piece of paper in her hands.

"Well," Jake said. "She pretty much hasn't told me one true thing since she sat down."

"I'm not surprised," Birdie said. She handed Jake the paper.

"Well." He sighed as he read the woman's rap sheet. "I guess she told the truth about her name."

"She's been popped half a dozen times on solicitation charges," Birdie said. "And she gets around. Columbus, Vegas, D.C. She's got two outstanding warrants in Atlanta."

Jake felt as if he'd swallowed a two-ton boulder. He crumpled the rap sheet in his fist.

"Dammit, I was really hoping it wasn't gonna be something like this."

"Come on," Birdie said. "We both knew it was going to be something like this."

"Yeah," he said.

"Does she realize what's going on?"

"She knows something's up. It's curiosity keeping her in that room right now."

"Well, she's telling the truth about one thing. The plates on that Beamer out there are registered to House Money Holdings."

"Thanks. I think I'm done being nice with this one."

"Let me know if you think she'll respond to a woman better."

Jake walked over to the vending machine. He slipped a dollar in and punched in the number for a Diet Coke. The can fell to the bottom.

"Dr. Pepper Zero," he muttered. Birdie looked confused.

"Don't ask," he said as he walked back into the interview room.

Samantha wrinkled her nose at the Diet Coke but said nothing.

"Okay, Ms. Blanco, here's the deal. You're not stupid. You know the drill. I know you're not being forthright with me. Now, I really don't care about whatever trouble you're in in Atlanta or wherever else. What I do care about is what you're really doing in my county. So how about you drop the act and tell me the truth?"

She didn't seem scared. Samantha stared at a point on the wall and took a breath. Jake knew he was right. She knew exactly how this game was played.

"What was it?" he asked. "Your weekly drop? Is that it? You meet Joey and Jax at the cabin? You get your cut. You get your next client?"

"I was just concerned," she said. "Joey wasn't returning my calls. She always returns my calls. That's it."

"Do you want to know why she wasn't returning your calls or have you already pieced that together?"

"Where is she?" Samantha finally met Jake's eyes again. "Look. Whatever she's telling you. I'm not part of it. I'm clean."

She put her arms straight out on the table. Clean, he thought. No track marks. She didn't have that glassy-eyed look or nervousness that came from withdrawal.

"If Joey's in trouble, she deserves to have her lawyer here. That's why I agreed to come to the station with that cute deputy."

Samantha pulled another business card out of her purse. In doing so, Jake caught a glimpse of something else poking out of a side compartment. Samantha Blanco was carrying a large wad of cash.

"Here," she said, slapping the card in front of Jake. It was an attorney's name in Columbus.

"Joey gets a phone call, doesn't she? Don't I?"

"You're not under arrest. And Joey's not in trouble, Samantha, she's dead."

It took a moment for his words to sink into Samantha Blanco's brain. When they did, a tremor went through her. That cool demeanor went right out the window. She started shaking as much as any junkie he'd ever interviewed, only he knew it was from shock, not withdrawal.

"What are you telling me?"

"I'm telling you Joey Waters was found dead about fifty yards from that cabin you were trying to visit today. She was shot in the back. And I'm trying to figure out why."

Samantha furiously shook her head. "No. No way. I need to get out of here. I can't be here. You tricked me. You're trying to trick me."

"I'm trying to find out what happened to your friend. Don't you want to help me with that?"

"No. Not Joey. Nobody would ever touch Joey. You don't understand."

"So make me. Though I've got a pretty good idea what was going on at that cabin already. Jax was turning you both out."

"I don't have to tell you that. I know I don't have to tell you anything."

"No, you don't. But I also don't have to let you go."

"You can't arrest me. I haven't broken any laws."

"Not yet. But I'm guessing you're supposed to be somewhere else at some point, aren't you? What happens if you don't show up? What happens if word gets out that you've been in here talking to me all afternoon?"

Tears burst from Samantha Blanco's eyes. "She's dead? She's really dead? Was she ... did they ... um ... hurt her?"

"What? You mean other than putting a bullet in her back?"

"No. Oh God. No. I mean. Jax was supposed to protect her. She wasn't just out there on some street corner. It's not like that."

"What's it like? Who makes the arrangements? How do you know where your next client is?"

Samantha fiddled with the tab on the Diet Coke can. She gave up after a moment, her hands were shaking so badly.

"Joey tells me. Sometimes Jax. I get a text. They tell me where. They tell me when. Then at the end of the week, I meet Joey and it's like you said. I make the drop."

"Only this time, you couldn't get a hold of either one of them."

"No. That's never happened before. I knew something was wrong. Oh God. Jax is going to lose his mind. You don't understand. He's really in love with her."

"Samantha, Jax Waters is dead too. They were both shot to death out at that cabin."

She covered her mouth with her hand.

"I told you. Right now I don't care what other trouble you're in. I care about finding who killed those two. If you can help me, now's the time to do it. Do you understand?"

"I don't know," she said. "I swear to God I don't know. I just ... I do what I'm told. Go where I'm told. I don't have anything to do with the bigger business. Jax takes care of us. If I don't like a situation, I don't have to be part of it. I work when I want to. He understands. He treats me right. And he treats Joey like a queen."

"Okay. How long have you worked for Jax?"

"I told you, three years. Through Joey. She found me online. She helped me out of a bad situation. And it's good. The money's good. Sometimes three grand a night. And Jax has always taken care of us. If he's gone ... then who ..."

"Us," Jake said. "I need names, Samantha. Who else is working with you in this region? Who are the other girls?"

"I don't know them all. I swear. Most of us don't even use real names. We use handles. Fake names. Sometimes no names at all."

"Write down the ones you remember," Jake said, sliding the paper and pen to her. "When was the last time you actually spoke to Jax or Joey Waters?"

"Three days ago. Joey gave me the name of my next date. It was this guy in Dayton. He was real nice. I spent the weekend with him."

"His name," Jake said.

"No way. I don't have to give you that. And it was in Dayton. Like a hundred miles from here. That's got nothing to do with whatever happened at that cabin."

"Samantha, you've been working for Jax Waters for two years. You're out there driving a Beamer registered to Jax's shell company. You've got these phony business cards. I know the office in Delaware is a front. I just came from there. So what that tells me is Jax and Joey trusted you. You know a lot more about their business than you're telling me. So I need to know who Jax is associated with. Who might have had a beef with him serious enough to put a bullet in his head and in Joey's back."

"I don't know. I swear. I don't know. I did what I was told and Jax made sure I was taken care of. That's it."

"And you gotta understand why that's pretty hard for me to believe, Samantha. There has to be something. Somebody trying to move in on his territory, maybe. Somebody he told you to stay away from. Anything that ..."

"Marcus," she said. Her voice was so quiet, Jake almost didn't catch it.

"What?"

"Marcus Ekon. When I started working for Jax, Marcus was the muscle. He went with me a few times on my first dates. You know. Just to make sure I felt safe. I don't know what happened between them, but Marcus hates Jax. Joey told me he threatened Jax. He got arrested a while back, Marcus. I don't know what all it was about. I stayed out of the drama. But all of a sudden, Marcus wasn't around anymore. I asked once where he was and Jax got pretty pissed. Told me he never wanted to hear his name again. When I tried to ask Joey, she just shook her head, you know. Like telling me, don't even ask."

"Where can I find this guy?"

"I don't know."

"Is that even his real name?"

"As far as I know."

She wrote it on the pad and handed it back to Jake.

"What went down with Marcus?" Jake asked.

"I don't know why Jax got pissed at him."

"But I bet you can guess."

"It was bullshit, okay? Marcus got arrested. I don't know the details. Jax always told us if any of us ever got in trouble, he'd get us a lawyer. But for some reason, he hung Marcus out to dry. I don't know what Marcus did to piss him off. Or if it was the other way around or what. I swear I don't. But the last time I saw Marcus, he threatened Jax. It got pretty heated. They got physical. Which is a joke. Marcus could have killed Jax with his bare hands. But he told Jax he'd make him pay for what he did."

"What did Jax do?"

"I tried to stay out of it. It was none of my business. But I think maybe Jax made Marcus take the heat that was supposed to have been for Jax. Sold him out. Marcus threatened to shoot Jax."

"You heard this?"

"I saw him point his finger at Jax, you know, like a gun. He told him he was a dead man."

"When was this?"

"It was a while ago. It's been close to a year since anyone's seen Marcus. And things have turned to shit since then. We don't feel safe like we used to. We've tried to tell Jax. He made a lot of promises that he'd take care of things. But it's been bad."

"How bad?"

"Guys just starting to take advantage. Not with me. But I've heard some rumors."

"What kind of rumors?"

"Just that maybe we should watch our backs more. Nothing specific. I really don't know. You need to talk to Marcus. He was way more involved in the back-end stuff. I just do what I'm paid to do. That's all."

"You got an address? A contact number for Marcus?"

She shook her head. "That's all I know, I swear. I'm sorry. I just ... I can't believe this. You can think whatever you want to about me, but Joey and Jax were my friends. They took care of me. Who's going to do that now?"

She became inconsolable after that, sobbing into a tissue Jake handed her.

"Is there somebody else I can call for you?" he asked her.

Samantha blew her nose. "No. Don't you get it? Joey is the one you could have called for me."

He knew he'd gotten about all he could from Samantha Blanco. "I need you to stay available, do you understand? I can't keep you here today, but I may have more questions. So you're gonna write down a number for me that you're going to answer. Otherwise I'm gonna have a conversation with your probation officer you don't want me to have. Do we understand each other?"

"Yes," she sniffled.

"Good. Now I'm going to send in another one of my deputies and they'll help you with whatever you need."

Jake got up. Birdie was back in the observation room. Sheriff Landry had joined her. From the look on her face, Birdie had brought the sheriff up to speed.

He closed the door so no one else could hear their conversation.

"Shit," Meg said, summing up the day. "You're telling me our victims got themselves unalived because of a prostitution ring they were running out of Ed Lattimore's luxury cabin?"

"It looks that way," Jake answered.

Meg looked at the ceiling. Then she picked up a pen sitting on the table in front of them and threw it at the wall, hard enough to break it.

Eleven

The next morning, Jake met Dr. Ethan Stone in his office across town. Stone had finished his autopsies of both Jaxson and Josefina Waters. Though Jake didn't expect any surprises, Stone often picked up little details Jake might not have thought of. He was also one of the best gunshot wound experts Jake knew. A Vietnam combat veteran, his battlefield experience coupled with nearly fifty years as a coroner made him one of southern Ohio's best assets in criminal investigations.

"Got any leads yet?" Stone asked.

Jake filled him in on what they'd learned about Jaxon Waters's true business purpose in Blackhand Hills.

Stone whistled. "Man. That's gotta be making Meg Landry pretty twitchy. Not to mention your dear old Uncle Rob. He's gonna blow a gasket when he finds out somebody's been using his precious tourist haven for a brothel."

"He doesn't know yet. Nobody does." Jake knew he wouldn't have to warn Stone not to spread the information.

"Well," he said. "I'll tell ya. Your shooter knew what he or she was doing. The kill shots were dead on. Textbook. Your male victim got it right in between the eyes. There's a superficial wound to the right bicep. No way to tell whether that was the first or second shot. Logic dictates it was the first. A warning shot. You don't really see someone giving a coup de grâce in the arm. My money's on your killer wanting to get the victim's attention."

"That'll do it," Jake said.

"We're gonna have to use dental records for a positive ID. Guy's face was pretty much boiled off. It didn't fare very well when we dried him out. Not even his own mother would recognize him now. This one made me lose my appetite for two days."

Jake knew that was saying something. He was also glad Stone didn't feel the need to pull up the autopsy photos on his laptop. He'd already forwarded them to Jake in a zip file attachment.

"We're having trouble finding any next of kin for him," Jake said. "He's a nowhere man. Business in Delaware is a front. Now we know for what. His legal residence doesn't look like anyone's lived there for more than a crash pad since he bought it. I may have to resort to genealogy to find a relative for this guy. Nobody's reported him missing other than one of his other girls."

"Any luck on next of kin for the female victim? Not that it's gonna be pleasant, but she'll be identifiable."

"Not yet. We're not even sure they were using their real names. Probably not. Is there anything remarkable from her post mortem?"

"Just like I'm telling you. Shooter knew what he or she was doing. Superficial wound to the right glute muscle. Didn't hit anything important. But it would have slowed her down enough for the killer to get off the second shot. That one entered just the left of the right shoulder blade. Severed her subclavian artery before exiting between her breasts. She was a mess inside. She died quick, but not instantly."

"Ramirez said they found a three-hundred-foot blood trail through the woods until she hit the creek."

"I wouldn't doubt it. She lost her entire blood volume in that creek, Jake. Like I said, it would have been fast. A few minutes for her to bleed out. But not instant like the male victim. You have to wonder if that was intentional, you know? Well, I'll leave that for you to figure out."

"She wasn't the power," Jake said. "From what my witness indicated, Joey Waters was Jax's top girl, but she still worked for him."

"Well, the poor kid never stood a chance. If she'd been shot like that in a trauma room, they wouldn't have been able to save her. That artery was ripped to shreds. Completely severed. Nothing left of it. It's one of the main ones that carries blood away from the heart and throughout the body. If you asked me where to aim for the quickest way to exsanguinate somebody, that's where I'd tell you."

Stone pointed slightly left of the center on his own chest.

".38 caliber hollow point. Teflon coated. They called 'em cop killers back in the '80s because they could penetrate a ballistic vest. There was a huge push to get them banned in Congress."

"Well, in their line of work, I imagine they had no shortage of enemies," Jake said. "I just have to figure out who was bold enough to carry this one out."

"Any theories?"

"Not good ones. Not yet. I just don't know enough about these people."

"I hope to God they were just passing through. That they really were tourists, you know?"

"Me too."

"I wish I could give you more to go on with the pathology. Though it's not the thing I could testify to in court, from what I've seen, there's no doubt in my mind this was a cold-blooded intentional hit. The wounds are too precise. The type of bullets, too. Somebody wanted these specific people dead and I'd bet money this wasn't some crime of passion. Your victims were stalked, hunted, and terminated."

"Understood," Jake said. "And I appreciate how quickly you were able to make your report."

Stone waved him off. "Nah. What else do I gotta do? Right?"

"Glad to hear you say that. I've heard too many rumors lately that you're thinking about retiring."

Stone's face was unreadable. That he didn't immediately answer gave Jake a sick feeling the rumors might be true.

"Relax," Stone finally said. "When I'm ready to go, I'll let you know. Now that we've finally got somebody good investigating homicides around here, why would I want to miss out on all the fun?"

"Fun?" Jake smiled. "This is fun for you? I'd hate to see what you consider a downer, then."

"Okay. I'll admit. I could do without you sending me boiled dead guys like this last one. But that girl? She's somebody's daughter or sister. She was well nourished. Good teeth. Impeccable manicure. She took care of herself. No sign of any drug use. Before some psychopath shot a hole in her, she was as healthy as they come. I want to know who did that to her as much as you do. So keep me posted."

Jake reached across the desk and shook Stone's hand. "You've got my word on that."

They said their goodbyes and Jake let himself out. Stone's words kept echoing in his mind as he made the short trip back to his office.

She was somebody's daughter. Or sister. And she died alone and scared, running for her life as her heart spilled blood throughout her body. Every instinct in him told him she knew what had happened to Jax Waters before she made it to that creek. She knew what was about to happen to her and there was nobody out there to help her. The best he could do was try to find her people now and give her back to them. As he pulled into the lot, he saw Mark Ramirez's vehicle already there. He hadn't gotten a call or text from him, so it had to be important for Ramirez to make the trip out here this early in the day.

Ramirez was waiting for him in his office. Birdie had already made it in.

"Hey, Mark," he said. "Erica." He gave himself a mental pat on the back for not calling her Birdie in front of Ramirez. Birdie raised a brow, seemingly surprised he'd remembered too.

"I was just telling your partner here," he said. "ONIC got into those iPhones found at the scene."

"Fantastic. I just came from the ME. No surprises there so I hope you've got something good."

"Maybe," Ramirez said. "Though it won't be good for someone. I gave Erica the flash drive with what we've got. The gist was Jaxon Waters's iPhone didn't yield too much. He was guarded. Smart enough not to use it for anything illicit. Josefina didn't use her phone much either. Neither one of them had any apps on their phones beyond the factory settings. But she mostly used hers to call one person."

Ramirez picked up a stapled stack of papers from the table in front of him and handed it to Jake. He would thumb through the meat of the report later. But Ramirez had taken a screenshot of a series of texts they'd found on Joey's phone. They were dated three days before the murder.

Dr. Stone's words rose to the surface of Jake's mind again. She was somebody's daughter.

The last text she'd sent from the phone was to her dad. She'd told him she loved him followed by three heart emojis.

"I love you too, mija," he texted back. "Be careful. Be safe. I'll see you in a few days."

His text had been delivered, but never read.

"Raymond DeSilva," Birdie said. "We've got a good address and obviously his phone number. I checked some records online already once I could connect Joey to Raymond. He's from Westeridge down in Montgomery County. Josefina DeSilva was born there. Went to high school there. She was a star athlete. And she was his only child. Mother died when Joey would have been eleven years old. I found all this from the mom's obituary. It was just the two of them, Jake. Raymond and Josefina."

Jake clutched the photocopy of Raymond DeSilva's text to his daughter. The only person he had left. Within the hour, Jake would have to make the phone call that would shatter this man's world forever.

TWELVE

Four hours later, Jake and Birdie stood outside the entrance to the county morgue again. A silver Suburban pulled up. Two men got out. One walked with his head down, his dark hair disheveled as the other man held his arms around him. Jake stepped forward. As the dark-haired man lifted his eyes, Jake knew no identification would truly be necessary. He looked like his daughter. The same thick lashes and hooded eyes. Jake had only seen Joey's headshot on that bogus company website, but her father had a similarly shaped down-turned mouth.

"Mr. DeSilva?" Jake said. "I'm Detective Cashen. This is Deputy Wayne."

DeSilva didn't seem to know what to do. As if the common practice of shaking hands had eluded him. He was working on merely putting one foot in front of the other. Jake understood. He wished he could tell this man anything other than what he would have to today.

"Good afternoon," his companion said. He was tall. Six foot two at least. Blond hair, a well-kept beard. Jake noticed a tattoo on his forearm. A young girl's face with angel wings. There was a date beneath it Jake couldn't make out.

"My name is Dale Halsey," he said, extending his hand to shake. Jake took it. "I hope you don't mind my accompanying Ray today."

"Of course not," Jake said. "Let's get you both inside."

"Is she here?" Ray asked. "Is she ..."

"This way," Birdie said. She stepped to Ray DeSilva's other side. He let her take his arm and lead him the rest of the way up the sidewalk.

Dr. Stone was waiting for them in the small observation room next to the mortuary. It was a simple process, but devastating. Stone's assistant would bring a stretcher up to the window. When DeSilva was ready, he would peel back the black body bag just enough so DeSilva could see her face. That was usually all it took. Jake let Birdie gently explain everything to Ray. He took Halsey aside and spoke to him in a hushed whisper.

"Do you know the family well?"

"I do," Halsey said. "Our daughters grew up together. Joey was like a daughter to me too for a time when the girls were little."

"I can't," DeSilva said, breaking away from Birdie. "I can't do this."

Dr. Stone had just wheeled the stretcher into the room on the other side of the glass.

"Dale, I just can't."

Dale left Jake's side and went to his friend. Ray DeSilva collapsed against Halsey.

"We'll do it together, okay? We'll do this for Joey. So you can put her to rest. So she can be with her mother."

DeSilva sobbed, but nodded. Birdie handed him a tissue. The man wiped his face.

"Whenever you're ready," Dr. Stone said behind the glass.

"You can take all the time you need," Jake said.

"No," DeSilva said. "Now. Do it now."

He turned to the glass. Dr. Stone nodded to his lab assistant. The young man carefully peeled back the plastic and let Ray DeSilva see his daughter's face.

Of course, it was her. Jake hated that he didn't have some other way to make this less painful for her father.

"It's her," DeSilva said. Then he whispered endearments to Joey in Spanish.

Stone came through the door. He made eye contact with Jake. "You can use my office to talk."

Jake thanked him. The group of them took Dr. Stone up on his offer. But Ray DeSilva couldn't answer a single question. He buried his face in his hands and quietly cried.

"Mr. DeSilva," Jake said. "I am very sorry for your loss. I'm going to do everything I can to find out what happened to her."

"I need a minute," he said. "Just a few minutes."

"I'll get you some water," Birdie said. She excused herself. Halsey sat beside DeSilva and rubbed his friend's shoulder. There was a haunted look in Halsey's eyes.

"Can you leave me alone?" DeSilva said to Jake. "Just for a little while?"

"Of course," Jake said. "I'll be right outside."

Birdie was already in the hallway holding a water bottle. Jake put up a finger, cautioning her to wait a minute before going back in. A few seconds later, Halsey came out alone.

"He'll be okay," Halsey said. "He asked me to come out here and talk to you."

"I appreciate that," Jake said.

"I wish I could say we were surprised. Ray's been expecting a call like this about Joey for years, unfortunately. He knew the kinds of things she'd gotten involved in. He knew she wasn't safe."

"Do you know when he spoke to her last?" Jake asked.

Halsey shook his head no. "I don't. I'm sorry. I didn't think he'd heard from her in years. When she left home, he tried to file a missing person's report but she was over eighteen and made it pretty clear she wanted to be on her own. Joey took it really hard when her mom died. It was cancer. Came on quick. Maybe four months from the time she was first diagnosed. Joey was in middle school. She blamed Ray for it for a bit. Unjustified. But kids, you know?"

"Sure," Jake said. "I can't imagine how hard this is for him. It's good he's got a friend like you."

Halsey's face changed. "If I'm being honest, Ray would never have wanted to reconnect with me the way we did."

"What do you mean?"

Halsey lifted his arm, showing Jake the tattoo he'd noticed earlier.

"This is my angel. My Lena. I lost her six years ago. Accidental drug overdose. Fentanyl. She was just at a party I told her not to go to. She wasn't some junkie. She was just … unlucky."

"I'm so sorry," Jake said. It was a story he'd heard far too many times.

"Lena got mixed up with the wrong people. People she thought were her friends. The same thing happened to Joey. To a lot of girls from our hometown."

"Westeridge," Birdie said. "Joey was from Westeridge?"

"We all are," Halsey said. "Yes. When Lena died, I didn't think I'd survive. I almost didn't. But then I started talking to other people who've been through this nightmare. Then it grew into something bigger."

Halsey reached into his back pocket and pulled out a business card. He handed it to Jake. Jake read it.

Lean On Us Family Support Group

"For Lena. It started out as an online forum," Halsey said. "Other parents of kids who died from fentanyl overdoses or who'd been ... trafficked from the region. That's how Ray and I reconnected. A few years ago, when things with Joey got bad, Ray started coming to some of the support group meetings I held out of the Lutheran Church in Westeridge."

"It's good that he has something like that," Jake said. "Especially now."

"He knew," Halsey said. "Like I told you, he always expected he was gonna get a phone call from someone like you. But you can never really prepare, you know?"

Stone's office door opened. Ray DeSilva came back out.

"I'm sorry," he said.

"You don't have anything to apologize for," Jake said. "I hate that I have to ask you these questions now. But I ..."

"You have to find who did this," DeSilva said. "Who shot up my little girl like that?"

There was a row of chairs in the hallway. Jake led DeSilva to one of them and sat down next to him. Birdie guided Dale Halsey around the corner where she knew there was a breakroom.

"Mr. DeSilva, we know you spoke to your daughter a few days ago. We saw your texts with her on her phone."

"She stopped answering me," he said. "The last phone call we had, she told me she was making some changes in her life. That she was happy for the first time. I begged her to let me come see her. We were finally making arrangements to do that. We were going to meet in Stanley for lunch. It was all arranged. Then she changed things. She told me she wanted to bring that scumbag with her. Jaxon. I knew he was going to get her into trouble. I knew he was no good. I told her I didn't want to see him. I wish I hadn't done that. Maybe if I'd just let her bring him. Maybe I could have still done something to bring her back to me."

"Had you ever met Jaxon Waters?"

"Not officially, no. Once when he came to get her at the house, we had words. This was years ago. After that, Josefina knew not to bring him around me. He was trash. A user. A poser. She didn't think I knew what he was. But I saw. Joey was posting on that MOCA app. I know what that's about. He was turning her out. Making her do things Joey wouldn't have done otherwise. She always went for guys like that. The bad ones. Since we lost her mama, I just couldn't get through to her."

"MOCA," Jake repeated. He knew of the app. It stood for Men of a Certain Age. Though it was touted as a dating app, it was mostly used to solicit prostitutes and sugar daddy types.

DeSilva began to cry again, becoming nearly hysterical. Jake waited with him. When he composed himself a little, Jake pressed on.

"Joey never talked about being scared of anyone in particular?"

"No. I don't know. Not that she mentioned. Anytime I started asking too many questions, or tried to get firm with her or lecture her, she'd hang up. Then I wouldn't hear from her in weeks or months. Or she'd block my number or get a new one. Then, after a while, she'd reach out again. I thought we were getting to a good place again. I hoped so anyway. I'm sorry. I don't have anything I can tell you. Joey shut me out. She knew I didn't approve of what she was doing."

"I understand. It's okay. You've had a lot to process today. Maybe in time, if something else occurs to you, you can call me. And I'll keep in touch too, okay? I'm going to do the very best I can for Joey now. I'm going to try and find out who did this to her."

DeSilva nodded. He took Jake's hand and squeezed it.

Birdie and Halsey came back out. Dr. Stone was right behind them.

"How do I do this?" DeSilva asked. "How do I take care of Joey now? The arrangements?"

Stone stepped forward. "You just come with me. I'm going to let you talk to my girl, Sandra. She'll help you."

Halsey wrapped his arms around his friend. Jake was grateful DeSilva had him today. Jake mouthed a thank you to Dr. Stone. Then he and Birdie made their way back to the parking lot.

"That poor man," Birdie said. "It's a good thing he's got Dale Halsey with him. He told me he's running a support group for parents of girls like Joey. He lost his own daughter to fentanyl a few years ago."

"He told me. The two of them were trauma bonded. I don't think DeSilva would have done as well as he did without the support today."

"He's all alone, Jake. His wife's gone. No other kids. No family. It was just the two of them."

They stepped out into the bright sun. It blinded him for a moment so he didn't see who was standing in front of his car right away. Birdie did. She grabbed his arm.

"Detective Cashen!" Bethany Roman, investigative reporter for the local news, shoved a microphone in his face.

"Can you comment on the rumor that the bodies found out at Blackhand Creek were connected to a prostitution ring?"

"No comment," Jake said, feeling his temper flare.

"It's been days since those bodies were found and there hasn't been so much as a peep from the sheriff's department. The people of this county need to know."

"The people of this county?" Jake said. "We are in the process of notifying the victims' next of kin. Until that's done, the people of this county will have to just wait out of respect for the families."

"Jake, let's go," Birdie said, pulling on his arm.

Jake had a history with Bethany Roman. One he wasn't proud of. A whopping mistake of a one-night stand before he understood she was a reporter. She still held a grudge against him for it, and Jake knew it was partially deserved.

"All information regarding this investigation will be released through the sheriff's media liaison," Birdie said. "You showing up here is bad taste at best and unethical journalism at worst."

Bethany dropped her microphone and glared at Birdie.

"You can't keep a lid on this, Jake. Every day that goes by where you refuse to comment, things will get worse."

"Is that a threat?" he asked.

"I'm trying to do you a favor. Letting you get out in front of this. I would think your boss would appreciate it."

"My boss would appreciate you going through her office the way you're supposed to," Jake said. He pushed past Bethany to get to the driver's side door. As he did, Ray DeSilva and Dale Halsey came out. Bethany straightened and started to walk toward them.

Birdie stepped in front of her.

"Lady," she said. "You better turn around, get in your car, and drive away. You go near those men and I'll make you eat your microphone."

"Birdie," Jake said.

Bethany whipped her head around and stared at Jake upon hearing the nickname he used. Something came over her face. Fresh anger, maybe. Jake didn't feel like sticking around to find out.

"I'm not joking," Birdie said. She advanced on Bethany. "Get in your little car and drive on out of here."

Bethany looked back at her. She opened her mouth to say something, but made the wiser choice to stay silent. She turned on her heel and stormed off, just as Birdie demanded. They waited for DeSilva and Halsey to get into Halsey's truck and drive away. Jake wanted to be sure Bethany Roman didn't follow them. When she drove off in the opposite direction, Jake got behind the wheel.

"She's right about one thing," Birdie said. "Landry's got to get out in front of this thing. The rumors are getting worse than reality."

Reality was bad enough, Jake thought. He slammed the car into gear and headed back to the office.

Thirteen

S aturday morning, Sheriff Landry held her first official press conference on what were now being called the Blackhand Creek Murders. She left more questions than answers to the gathered press. Rob Arden stayed in the shadows, but kept Jake in his sights as Meg took questions. Jake chose not to speak at all. But when Arden started to make a beeline toward Meg at the presser's conclusion, he stepped in front of him.

"She doesn't report to you," Jake said.

"She most certainly does."

"She's got nothing more to tell you than what you heard out there. This is my investigation, and you don't get some inside scoop. There isn't one. You'll know things when it's permissible to know them."

"You need to be aware," Arden said. "The county commissioners' convention starts Monday. If you ..."

"That's not my concern. But I'll make sure to steer clear of anywhere you might choose to dine out. Other than that, I've got nothing more to say."

Arden looked as if he wanted to lay into Jake again, but thought the wiser of it. There were too many eyeballs on them. One pair belonged to Meg. She stood in the doorway leading out of the press room. She gestured to Jake.

Arden let a slow, smug smile creep across his face. "Mommy's calling you," he said. "Better hop to."

Jake turned his back on Arden and followed Meg out of the press room.

"Don't start," he told her.

"Oh, I don't plan to. I'm tired of mediating your battles with him. And I'm tired of him in general."

"That makes two of us."

"Go home," she said. "It's your day off. Enjoy it while you can. If something happens, everybody knows how to get a hold of you."

"What about you?" he asked.

Meg smiled. "I have an invitation I plan on keeping. Your sister insisted on it."

"You're coming to that?"

Gemma planned a soft opening of Cashen's Irish Pub that evening. Just close friends and other people important to her. She wanted to work out the bar and kitchen kinks when the stakes were still low.

"Then I guess I'll see you there," Jake said.

Jake looked back toward the press room. Uncle Rob was busy glad-handing reporters. Jake meant what he said. He had no intention of being anywhere Rob might be this weekend. That meant that the pub was the safest place in town. Arden wouldn't be caught dead in Gemma's bar. And Gemma would likely kill him if he tried to cross her threshold. For the first time all day, Jake was starting to look forward to the evening.

She was a nervous wreck. Jake watched his sister clean off the same countertop at least ten times as food orders came out of the kitchen and the tap started to flow.

He sat at a table in the corner, right next to Grandpa Max's. The old man was happy. Laughing. Holding court with a couple of his cronies from the lodge. It was good to see. Jake realized his sister might be some kind of genius with all of this. He couldn't remember the last time Grandpa Max looked this relaxed.

"She might just make it," Virgil Adamski said. When Gemma asked Jake to invite a few friends, Jake thought immediately of Virgil, Chuck Thompson, and Bill Nutter. The trio were all retired cops and usually took up a back booth at Papa's Diner in town. They'd nicknamed themselves the Wise Men, to the amusement of everyone who knew them well.

"Wings are good," Nutter said, reaching to grab another one from a basket at the center of their table.

"She looks like she's about to have a stroke though," Thompson said. "She always that uptight?"

"Sometimes," Jake said. "She's got a lot invested in this place. Money and stress. She's hoping it'll bring in what she needs to help pay for Ryan's college fund."

"Where's he going?" Virgil asked.

"Putnam," Jake answered. "He got a partial wrestling scholarship. Tuition's paid for, but he's gotta live on campus. It's still going to cost a good chunk of change."

"Living away from home's the best thing for him," Chuck said. "Get out of Blackhand Hills for a while like you did. He can always come back."

"Who needs a refill?" Their pretty brunette waitress sat in the space in the booth beside Jake. She'd taken good care of them all night, never leaving an empty glass or plate for very long.

"Count me in," Chuck said, downing the last of his draft beer and sliding the mug across the table. The waitress caught it with a quick hand.

"How about you, baby brother?" She'd been calling Jake that all night after she heard Gemma say it once. It should have bothered Jake, but somehow, she came off sweet, even though she was teasing.

"I'll take another," Jake said. "Thanks, Nora."

She shot him a wink, gathered the rest of the empties, and headed back to the bar. Jake caught Virgil tilting his head as he watched Nora's backside.

"She's into you," Bill said.

"She's being nice," Jake said. "She's trying to keep the owner's brother happy."

"Jake," Chuck said. "That girl has come back to this table like ten times. It's not even her section. You haven't noticed that Carly Beverly's been taking care of your grandpa's table next to us all night? Not Nora?"

He hadn't. But now that Chuck said it, Carly came around the bar and took refill orders for Max and his buddies. Nora was already on the other side of the restaurant, talking to tables near the pool room.

"She's cute, Jake," Bill said. "You should ask her out."

"Thanks. I don't need a matchmaker. Certainly not from the likes of you three."

"You could do worse than following our advice." Virgil laughed.

A few minutes later, Nora came back with their new beers. When she smiled at Jake this time, he felt a flush of heat. She *was* pretty. Seemed sweet. But what he'd told the wise asses was true. Matchmaking was the last thing he needed.

Just then, Meg and Phil Landry came into the bar. It was strange seeing Meg like this. Out of her natural habitat at the sheriff's office. She wore a pair of blue jeans and a Foo Fighters concert tee shirt. It made her look ten years younger. She waved to Jake across the bar then she and Phil took seats at a high top around the corner.

"I should go say hi," Jake said.

"She's got a tough one coming up in a few months," Chuck said. "I never thought I'd say it, but Zender might give her a real run for her money at the polls."

"I don't even want to think about it," Jake said.

"Nobody does. But people are getting antsy, Jake. I was talking to Fred Beaumont. You know he owns the campground out in Navan Township. People are canceling their rentals. He's freaking out."

"I was out at the quarry with my grandkids the day before yesterday," Bill said. "It was pretty empty. I've never seen it that dead this late in July."

"They'll come around," Jake said, sipping his beer and wondering if he should have ordered something stronger.

"Maybe," Bill said. "But this season's toast. If they don't show up to the vacation spots, they're not going to spend their money in town and at all the restaurants. Gemma might be picking the worst time to launch this little venture of hers. No matter how good the wings are."

"It's temporary," Jake said. "I'm going to find out who killed those people. Things will get back to normal."

"People like to come back to the same spot every year," Virgil said. "The fear is that if they take Blackhand Hills off their list this year, they'll do it next year too. And the rumor is those people were running drugs and whores out of Ed Lattimore's properties. I mean, we'd expect it out in the rough parts of Cleveland. But if Blackhand Hills itself gets that reputation, we're screwed."

"What do you want me to do?" Jake asked, his tone sharper than he wanted it to be. He took a breath to recenter himself. "I'm sorry. But you're starting to sound like my Uncle Rob."

"We don't mean to be," Bill said. "We're just worried about what happens in November at the polls if the PR part of this isn't managed right."

"Since when has that been something any of us can control?" Jake said. "You all know this job. I work the case. Follow my leads. The rest of it? It's none of my business."

"You got any new ones?" Chuck asked. "Leads?"

Jake looked around. Only Grandpa Max's table was close enough to hear anything he might say. And everyone at it wore hearing aids anyway.

"Nothing solid," he said. "There's a muscle guy Jaxon Waters might have had a beef with. He's got an odd enough name. It shouldn't take me long to track him down. When I do, hopefully I'll have more answers."

"Well," Virgil said. "I know we don't have to tell ya. You need something. We're here."

Virgil's voice dropped as Travis Wayne came to their table with a bus cart. Gemma had Ryan and a few of his friends, including Trav, bussing and washing dishes. They were doing a good job of it too.

"Thanks, Trav," Jake said.

"No problem, Coach."

"I hope my sister's paying you kids well."

"We're getting a cut of the tips tonight," Travis said. "And she said ten bucks an hour on top of that."

Bill whistled. "Not a bad gig."

"Better than diggin' ditches." Travis smiled, repeating one of Grandpa Max's favorite clichés.

"Where's your aunt tonight?" Jake asked. Birdie was the one invitee he hadn't seen show up yet.

"She's out with some new guy," Travis said.

"New guy?" Jake said, surprised. Birdie hadn't mentioned a thing about going on a date.

"Yeah. She met him at some fitness class she takes."

"How long's this been going on?" Jake asked. It was almost as if he could feel Travis's dad whispering in his ear. Birdie was Ben

Wayne's little sister. He heard himself asking the questions he knew Ben would.

"I don't know," Travis said. "She said they might show up here. But he's not from Stanley or anything. I forget what she said. You see her more than I do. Ask her if you're worried."

"I'm not worried." Jake smiled. Travis moved off to Grandpa Max's table. The poor kid's ears turned red when the old man said something embarrassing. The men at the table got a good laugh before Travis disappeared into the kitchen again.

"He's a good kid," Virgil said. "Seems to be handling things since his dad died."

"He is," Jake said.

"That's partly thanks to you," Virgil said. "It's good he's got you looking out for him."

Though he appreciated the compliment, it made him a little uncomfortable. Tonight was a time to look toward the future, not the past. But it was hard not to think Ben should be here too tonight.

He wasn't the only one. He knew his parents would have been proud of Gemma for starting her own business like this.

Ghosts, Jake thought. He would always be surrounded by them it seemed.

He ordered another drink. Enough to make him settle into the conversation and laughter surrounding him. Not enough to forget everything that weighed on his mind.

The Wise Men were right. Even Uncle Rob was right. Whatever happened out at Blackhand Creek had allowed a dark cloud to settle over his town. One he wasn't sure what it would take to clear.

Later, he said his goodbyes to the men at his table. He knew they would stay long into the night without him. But Jake needed to be alone. At least for now. He paid their tab, said a quick goodbye to his sister, and headed back to his cabin at the edge of Grandpa Max's property in the woods.

Ben would have loved tonight. He hoped Birdie was being safe. He knew Ben would have hung out with him tonight and would have said the very same thing. Jake tossed his keys on the table and emptied his pockets. He had his credit card receipt from the night with Cashen's Irish Pub in bold letters across the top which made him proud.

.

He noticed something scribbled on the back of the receipt in blue pen. He turned it over. "Give me a call sometime. Nora." She'd written her phone number on it.

Jake smiled. He and Ben would have talked about that, too. Jake crumpled the receipt again. He was going to toss it in the trash. But he stopped himself. Instead, he smoothed it out and stuck it on the fridge with a magnet.

FOURTEEN

Marcus Ekon was easy to find. He was in the system, having been recently paroled on a weapons charge. His last known address was a duplex in Dayton. He'd registered with his parole officer that he worked at a bar in a seedy part of town. That's where Jake found him, just after his shift ended the following Monday. The bartender pointed to a service door that led to a back alley. Ekon leaned against a brick wall, having a cigarette with another dishwasher and a busboy. The moment they saw Jake, they seemed to know what he was there for.

"Ekon?" Jake asked. Ekon lit another cigarette and stayed against the wall, casually bracing one foot against it in a flamingo posture.

"Who's asking?" Ekon said.

Jake took out his badge.

"Detective Jake Cashen. I'm from Worthington County. Blackhand Hills."

"You lost?"

"You got a few minutes to talk to me?"

"Do I have a choice?"

"I think your parole officer would appreciate knowing you cooperated when I came to find you."

Ekon snuffed out his cigarette, then tossed it into the dumpster across from him.

"You've got five minutes. My ride's about to get here."

"I'm here about Jaxon Waters. I think you know him."

Ekon straightened, pushing himself off the wall.

"In that case, we're done talking. Cuz I've got nothing to say about him."

"I get that. Things didn't end so great between the two of you. I understand he fired you."

"Fired me? Nah. Nah, man. I don't get fired. And I told you, we're done talking unless you got some kind of a warrant."

"No warrant. But your name came up in my investigation in Blackhand Hills. Look, I know who Waters is. What he's involved in. My intel is that you were doing security work for Waters. Keeping his girls safe. Helping him get paid. Some of the girls are saying things have been rough since you left."

Ekon's face went hard. He was tough to read. He looked the part Waters would have needed him to play. Huge. Six foot six. Muscle bound and covered in tattoos. Skin so dark he nearly blended into the shadows.

"Samantha Blanco," Jake said.

"She in trouble?" Ekon asked.

"She's out of a job," Jake said.

"She'll land on her feet. She's a smart girl."

"Look, I don't want to waste your time. If …"

"I've got nothing to do with whatever Jaxon Waters got mixed up in. Nothing. I haven't seen him in almost a year. The last time I did, I told him he better keep my name out of his mouth. Now you're here telling me he didn't listen."

"Waters didn't give me your name. Samantha did. Here's the deal, Ekon. Jaxon Waters got himself shot to death in my neck of the woods. I'm trying to find out who did it. So far, the only name that's come up as having a beef with him is yours. I know you threatened him. You told him you'd shoot him. So maybe now you can understand why you and I needed to have a conversation."

Ekon took a step toward Jake. There was an overturned milk crate on the ground next to him. Ekon put his foot up on it and rested his arm on his thigh.

"Is he dead?"

"Yeah," Jake said. "He's dead."

"Good. Now, like I told you. I haven't seen Jax's sorry ass in a long time. But if somebody finally put a bullet in him, I'd say they did the world a favor."

"Maybe. He was running girls in my town. I need to know how he operated. Who he dealt with. What I'm learning about him, Waters's business had a lot of moving parts. These girls? They were high end. I need to know what circles he was moving in. Because every instinct I've got is telling me he wasn't smart enough to handle what he was handling."

"I don't care," Ekon said. "It's got nothing to do with me."

"What about Joey?" Jake said. Ekon froze.

"What about her?"

"You knew her too? Went with her on the job? Kept her safe? She was the smart one, wasn't she? Top girl?"

"If you know all of that, what do you need me for?"

"Because she's dead too, Marcus. She got shot in the back right along with her old man."

A shudder went through Ekon. He pulled his foot off the milk crate and scraped a hand across his face.

"You're bullshitting me."

Jake pulled out his phone. He pulled up a picture of Joey on the slab in Dr. Stone's mortuary. It was just her face, drained of all blood. Waxen lips. Vacant eyes. He turned the screen so Ekon could see it.

Ekon stared at it, then looked away.

"Christ."

He took two steps forward and pounded the side of his fist against the dumpster.

"I told him. That son of a bitch. I told him."

"Told him what? Who was Waters tangling with?"

"I don't know."

"Come on, Marcus, of course you do."

"It's been a long time, man!"

"But you know Waters's business. You were inside it. You know the girls. You know where they went."

"I don't know shit."

"You knew Joey," Jake said. "And she mattered to you. She was a good kid. Smart. Pretty. She had a dad who loved her. Who was worried about her. She's his only kid, Marcus. It was just the two of them. Her mom died."

"I know all that," Ekon said. "You think you're telling me something I don't know? Joey's the one who brought me in way back when. Talked me into it. I knew Waters was trouble. That he was gonna get her killed. I told her. I warned her. Or when the time came, he was gonna hang her out to dry like he did me. Cuz that's the one thing Jaxon Waters was good at. Self-preservation."

"Until he wasn't," Jake said. He pocketed his phone.

"Marcus," he said. "Samantha Blanco said the same thing. She was worried something was gonna happen. That things weren't as tight. Stuff was falling through the cracks ever since you left. She was scared."

"I didn't leave," Ekon said through a clenched jaw.

"No. You didn't. Jaxon forced you out. Hung you out. Is that it?"

"Nine months," Ekon whispered. "I did nine months for that motherfu—"

"You get where I'm coming from right now? I got two dead bodies shot up in the morgue. The only name that popped up as threatening to shoot Jaxon Waters is you."

"You think I killed him?"

"You tell me."

Ekon put his leg back up on the crate and pulled up his left pant leg. The green light of his tether blinked.

"I'm wearing my alibi, asshole. You got any other dumb questions?"

"I've got plenty. I don't know what went down. You're standing here telling me you knew this was gonna happen. Why? Who's Waters in bed with? If he screwed you over, you know he did it to somebody else. And I wouldn't care. Because you're right. Waters probably had this coming and the world's better off without him. Only Joey Waters got caught up in this too. Samantha Blanco's scared for her life. She knows you were the best chance she had at protection and Waters put you on ice. With Waters out, how many of his girls are exposed now? You know how this works. There's a power vacuum. You know they're not all gonna land safely. There will be more body bags. Unless you do the right thing. The thing you were better at than anybody else, Marcus."

"What do you want from me?"

"Names. Jaxon's associates."

"I don't know any of that. That wasn't my job. My job was to get the girls where they needed to go, then get them back home. And I kept the money safe too. I wasn't part of the business end beyond that. I never wanted to be."

"The less you knew the better, huh? Is that how it worked? How you thought you'd keep yourself out of prison?"

Ekon walked away from Jake. The man was still shaken from seeing the photo of Joey Waters's dead body.

"You can still try to protect them," Jake said. "Tell me who else was working for Jaxon in my area besides Joey and Samantha Blanco."

"You think that would help? Names don't mean anything. Samantha's a name I gave her."

"Tell me anyway."

"I told you. I'm not in that life. I'm not in that world."

"Where did Jax find the girls? Who recruited them?"

"That was Joey."

"Joey?" The answer shocked Jake a little. It wasn't the picture Raymond DeSilva had of his daughter. But none of this was.

"Joey found Sam outside of Columbus. On MOCA. She used that a lot."

"You said you took the girls where they needed to go. Which girls? Names, Ekon. Street names if that's all you have. I can work from there."

"I won't be what Jax was. I'm not a snitch."

"And I don't care what these girls have done. I'm not looking to bust them. I'm looking to keep them from getting a bullet in their back like Joey. She was the smart one. Top girl. If she's not safe, what chance do you think the rest of them have?"

"Sam never shoulda mentioned my name."

"Maybe not. But she did."

"You gotta swear to me you're not looking to jam anybody else up for making a living."

"That's not my goal. I'm trying to solve a double homicide."

Ekon started to pace. He swore under his breath.

"I don't wanna come back here telling you somebody else got shot, Marcus. If you're not with them and Jax and Joey are gone, they're all sitting ducks."

"Morgan," he said, turning back toward Jake. "Talk to Morgan Prater. She was Jax's best girl after Joey. His top earner."

"Where can I find her?"

"Hell if I know now. She could be anywhere. She kept threatening to walk after Jax married Joey. Morgan had a thing for him, too.

She thought he loved her. Can you believe that? How those girls could fall for that crap. But she stuck around because she knew she had it good even with Joey around. But Morgan's the one who'd know something if there's something to know. She used to work at the Kitty Club about an hour from here. A dancer. And she made a killing off MOCA. She went by the handle of Pearl. If she's smart, she'd just stick with the online stuff. It's safer. But Jax was in her head too much. Maybe now."

"You have a phone number for Morgan? When's the last time you talked to her?"

"Not since I got out. But she came to see me once. She was the only one. She felt bad about how things went down. I told her to get away from Jax. She said she'd try. But the last I heard she was still working for him anyway."

"A number. An address. I know you know where she was living, Marcus."

Marcus pulled his own phone out of his back pocket. "You tell her. If you find her. You tell her this is because of Joey. You tell her I'm not looking to screw her over."

Jake took out a small pad of paper from his jacket pocket and handed it to Ekon. Ekon wrote a phone number and an address. Jake knew the odds of either still being good were long. But at least it was a place to start.

"If you talk to her," Ekon said, "see if you can talk some sense into her. Morgan's got people looking for her. Good people, I think."

"She was a runaway?"

"Probably. I don't know. I just know she wasn't like me or Jax. She had people who cared about her. I don't know what happened to her. Why she thought Joey's offer was worth taking. But Morgan's different. She could have a better life if she wanted it. I tried to tell her that. I tried to get her to go back home. Maybe you'll have better luck."

"I can tell her you're worried about her."

"Maybe if she sees. You know. Like you showed me. What happened to Joey. Maybe it'll scare her enough to go on back home. Start over. Like I did."

"I can try," Jake said. "I'm guessing it'll matter to Morgan that you're still out here giving a shit about her."

Ekon shrugged. "Yeah. Maybe."

Jake thanked Marcus Ekon. The man's concern for Morgan Prater seemed palpable. Jake just hoped the story he'd spun about Morgan and the other girls being in danger wasn't actually true. He'd only needed Ekon to buy it so he could get whatever information he had. As Jake left Marcus Ekon alone in that alley, he had a sick feeling he'd just jinxed the rest of the girls who had the misfortune of crossing paths with Jaxon Waters.

FIFTEEN

"It's eight points." Jake walked into his office to find the sheriff and Birdie already there. He checked his smartwatch. It was only a quarter to eight.

"Eight points of what?" Jake asked, sipping from the Styrofoam coffee mug he'd snagged from Papa's Diner. Tessa made him eat a plate of eggs and hash browns while he checked in with the Wise Men at what they were now calling their bimonthly staff meeting.

"The polls," Birdie said. A copy of the *Daily Beacon* sat on the table in the corner near Jake's office coffee pot. The thing was two-thirds empty, making him wonder just how long Birdie had been here this morning.

"Zender's leading Sheriff Landry by eight points in the latest polling."

Jake made a shooing gesture with his hand. "Who cares about that crap? The election's over three months from now. Plus, those things aren't reliable. How many times have you gotten a robocall on one of those things that you didn't hang up on, block, or yell at just for your own satisfaction?"

Birdie and Landry looked at each other. Birdie shrugged. Her expression seemed to say, "I'll bite."

"You routinely yell at robots, Jake?"

He was about to tell her of course. But the bemused looks on both Landry and Birdie's faces made him bite back his retort.

"Anyway," he said. "Don't sweat it. Just put it out of your mind. I hate politics. You know that's why I want nothing to do with that sergeant's test."

"Fine," Landry said. "So give me something else to think about. How did your trip to Dayton go?"

Jake filled them in on the gist of his interview with Marcus Ekon.

Landry sat at Gary Majewski's desk. Majewski was off this week at a crime scene and fingerprint conference. Birdie sat at the table. She folded the *Beacon* and tossed it in the trash.

"You're sure you can clear him?" Landry asked. "Your other witness said he's on record threatening to kill Jaxon Waters with a gun."

"I think that was maybe an exaggeration. Besides, he's tethered. I checked with his parole officer. Ekon hasn't left the Dayton area since his parole three months ago. From everything I was able to check, he's kept his nose clean since then. Shows up for work on time. Reports when he's supposed to. He also seemed genuinely concerned about the well-being of Jax's girls."

"Chivalrous of him," Birdie muttered.

"In an odd way, yes," Jake said. "If it were just Waters I was asking him about, I don't think I would have gotten anywhere. But when I showed him Joey DeSilva's picture, he folded. He's worried about another girl in Waters's stable."

Landry scrunched her face.

"Sorry," Jake said. "Poor choice of words. Morgan Prater." Jake took out his notebook where he'd written Prater's last known address according to Ekon.

"He says she's active on MOCA. Or was before he quit working for Waters."

Birdie picked up the paper.

"I can see what's what with this."

"It'll be hard to track her through the app. But Ekon said she was working at a strip club not far from Dayton. Kitty Kat or something. Maybe somebody there has more current intel on her whereabouts."

"I know this place," Birdie said. "It's only an hour away."

Now it was Jake and Landry's turn to exchange a look of surprise.

Birdie rolled her eyes. "It's not what you think. About a year ago, I went to a bachelorette party there. A high school friend was getting married and they had a ladies' night. They have male strippers there too. Anyway, I got to talking to one of the bouncers. He gave me his phone number."

"This story's getting worse and worse, Bir ... Erica," Jake said.

"Relax," she said, slapping him lightly on the arm with his own notepad. "The guy moonlights there. He's a med student at OSU. Let me reach out."

"Good," Landry said. "That's good work. Get on it as fast as you can."

"I'll make a call right now," Birdie said. She pulled out her phone and excused herself to use it away from Jake. She closed the door behind her.

"How's that working out?" Landry asked.

"What do you mean?"

"Deputy Wayne. She's good at this. How's that working out? Your partnership?"

"Like you said, she's good at this. I don't have to babysit her. She keeps up. Hell, sometimes she's a step ahead of me. Like just now."

"You know how badly I wish I could give her an outright promotion."

Jake tried not to grumble. They'd had this conversation multiple times before.

"And I wish you'd reconsider your reticence about the sergeant's test. The situation as it is is untenable. We both know it. Stuff is getting missed."

"What stuff?"

"Administrative stuff. The stuff I can't always cover. I don't just sit in my office twiddling my thumbs and lamenting newspaper polls. And as much as the Waters' murders is on the front burner and needs to be, other bad stuff is happening in Blackhand Hills that needs our attention."

"Again, I ask, what stuff? Is there something you're not telling me?"

"I tell you everything," she said. "Mostly. And maybe that's the problem. It's certainly what Ed Zender thinks."

Landry had a hard edge to her tone.

"Who gives a rat's ass what Ed Zender thinks?" Jake said. "Since when do his actions dictate how you run this department?"

She rubbed her temples. "Zender isn't the problem. I mean, he's the face of the problem. But it's more than that. I'm getting pulled in seven directions here. The county commissioner problem isn't going to go away. Word was going to leak about what was going on out at that cabin. I know you have your issues with Bethany Roman, but she's asking all the right questions. As unlucky as it is for us, the woman is actually good at her job."

Jake felt his spine stiffen. He didn't want to talk about Bethany Roman and certainly not to Landry. His poor judgment where she was concerned was a point of embarrassment for him. He couldn't help feeling like tangling with her had let Sheriff Landry down.

"What do you want me to do?" he finally said, his voice barely above a whisper.

"I don't know. No. That's not true. I want you to help me help you. Take the damn test. Let me put you in a position of command that will protect you no matter what happens to me in November. Hell, it'll help me protect more than just you. Do you want to wait around and see what somebody like Ed Zender will do to the command structure around here? It's not just you I'm worried about. If you ever want somebody like Erica Wayne slotted into a position she's worthy of, help me do something about it while I still have a say."

"Do you have a say now?" Jake asked. "We've been fighting this battle with the commissioners over more than just Birdie. Deputy Wayne!"

"Jake ..."

"Meg, I don't want it. And I'm not just trying to be difficult. This. This is what I'm good at." He pointed to the evidence files he had spread out on the table behind him.

"I'm a detective," he said. "Let me just be one."

She smiled. "You're only a detective because I strong-armed you into it. Because that's what I'm good at. Putting the right people in the right jobs and letting them do them. If I'd listened to you three years ago, you'd still be out there writing traffic tickets."

Jake made a noise low in his throat. There wasn't a single thing she said he could rightfully argue. Only, he knew himself better than she did. He would be terrible at command. Worse, he'd be miserable.

"I don't have time for this," he said. "And neither do you. The best thing I can do to help you is solve this case. You've made your argument. So tell me who else you'd like solving the murders around here? Majewski's the only one you've got eligible for a lateral move. You want him on this?"

Landry held her hands up in surrender. Before she could say anything else, Jake got a text. He'd laid his phone on the table between them. It was angled so she could read the incoming text on his lock screen.

Jake grabbed the phone. The text read:

> Hey, Jake. I hope you don't mind. I got your number from Bill Nutter. I know it's short notice, but there's a local band I like playing at a bar just out of town. The Brass Bell. Come with me. No pressure. This is Nora, by the way.

As much as he hated Meg having read it, the text effectively changed the subject of her ambitions for him. Bill Nutter? It looked like somebody was playing matchmaker, despite Jake's warning him not to.

"Nora Corley?" she asked. "Jake, she's lovely. Phil works with her brother out at the power company. I've met her quite a few times. Are you dating?"

"No," Jake said abruptly. "I just met her at Gemma's the other night. She waited on my table."

"I saw that. I also saw how much attention she paid to you. I approve."

"You approve?"

"Yes. You should take her up on her offer."

"I don't ..."

"Go! For God's sake. You've been wound up so tight. Ugh. And I know that's like the pot calling the kettle black here. But go. See the girl. Do the thing. It'll be good for you to take a night off with all this. Besides, I'll enjoy you telling me all about it tomorrow morning. Give me something to look forward to."

"You sound just like my sister."

"I like your sister. She's got a good head on her shoulders. And she likes Nora Corley too. She's a good judge of character."

"You haven't met any of her exes."

Meg waived a dismissive hand. "You don't like Nora?"

Jake looked back at the text. He wouldn't admit it to Meg, he barely wanted to admit it to himself. But the thing gave him just the slightest flutter of a thrill.

"She's nice!" Meg said. "Go out with her. That's an order."

Jake laughed. "It doesn't work that way, Sheriff."

"The hell it doesn't. Go. You want to anyway. I saw that little flicker in your eyes when you picked up your phone."

"There was no flicker. You're seeing things."

"Whatever," Landry said, rising. "Just go. I expect a full report in the morning. I'll sweeten the pot. If you go out with Nora Corley tonight, I'll handle roll call the rest of the week."

She was halfway out the door. "You were handling it anyway!" he shouted back.

"Full report!" Landry's voice echoed as she moved farther down the hall. It carried enough to draw the attention of the occupants of the adjoining offices. Jake got a couple of curious stares around the corner.

"Busybody," he muttered.

He went back to his desk. For a moment, his finger lingered over his phone screen. Then finally, he let out a deep sigh and texted back:

Sounds good. I'll meet you there at seven.

Sixteen

J ake hadn't stepped foot inside the Brass Bell since he was
eighteen years old. Spring break during his senior year in high
school, he and Ben Wayne procured lousy fake IDs and tried
their luck one county over in Marvell. They'd managed to
order two beers before getting ratted out and tossed out by one of
the bouncers who ended up being the older brother of one of their
classmates.

The place still looked the same. Dark. Green leather booths, wood
paneling, and brass lamps giving out just enough light to make
everyone look good.

"Jake!" Nora found him right away, hopping down from a
barstool.

God. She looked good. She wore her dark hair down, cascading
over her shoulders. A black tee shirt over cutoff jeans and red
cowgirl boots. If he felt a little awkward, she made up for it,
grabbing Jake by both hands and kissing his cheek. It was forward,
but somehow put him at ease. Maybe Meg was right. Maybe Nora
Corley could be good for him. A welcome diversion.

"I got us a table already," she said. "Best seat in the house. Over there in the corner. The band starts in ten minutes. Have you heard them before?"

"No," Jake said. "I don't get out much."

"That's what Gemma says."

"Did you tell her I was meeting you tonight?"

"Oh, heck no," Nora said. "Figured I'd see if I still liked you by the end of the night."

Her wide smile told him she was teasing. She had an easy way about her. Banter came more naturally to her than it did to him. As they made their way over to the table, Nora waved or said hello to at least six other tables.

Jake took the seat against the wall. A habit he'd never be able to break. It gave him a mostly unobstructed view of the bar's entrance.

Nora scooted in beside him, rather than taking the bench across from him.

She smelled good. Her shampoo or her hairspray. Clean. Not too floral.

"I'm glad you texted me," he said.

"Would you have called me if I hadn't?" she asked, her eyes twinkling. Would he have? The reality was, he probably wouldn't have. When he worked a homicide, he got so wrapped up in it, he barely remembered to eat three square meals, let alone worry about his social life. His non-existent social life.

"I wanted to," he answered. It was the truest thing he could say. Nora's smile brightened.

"You're all right, Jake," she said.

"You sure?"

"Oh, I'm sure. I know guys like you."

"We just met. What are guys like me?"

She just kept smiling. "Do you like the food here?"

"I haven't been here since I was in high school." He opted not to tell her about the fake ID incident. "So why don't you order us whatever you think is good."

"Oh, that's the fried pickles. Hands down."

Nora raised a hand and caught the attention of one of the waitresses. She came over and took their order.

"One order of fried pickles," Jake said.

"You want a burger?" Nora asked.

"Sure. Medium. Cheddar, lettuce and tomato."

"Two of those," Nora said. "Thanks, Val. And I'll have a Seabreeze. How about you?"

"I'll stick with water and whatever you have on draft."

"Give me ten," Val the waitress said. "I'll get your food out before the band starts up. It's going to get rowdy in here after that."

He didn't mean to, but Jake stiffened. Nora caught it.

"Oh. I'm sorry. Is that okay? Maybe you don't like crowds. They've got the patio open out back. If it gets too nutty in here, we can move out there."

"It'll be fine," Jake said. "And thanks for inviting me. I've been told I could use a night out."

"Yeah? I kinda sensed that about you."

"Comes with the territory."

"I guess it would. I can't imagine doing what you do for a living. Are you ... are you on call tonight?"

Val came back with their drink orders. Nora immediately started mixing hers with the cocktail straw. Jake took a sip of his beer.

"No. Not officially. That doesn't mean hell can't break loose and somebody will come looking for me. But things are quiet in Worthington County for the moment."

Nora raised her glass and clinked it against Jake's. "Here's hoping it stays that way. And I'm glad you took me up on my invitation. I have to be honest, I didn't think you would. In fact, nobody thought I could get you out here tonight."

"Nobody? What, was there a pool?"

"Just us girls at CIPs. Gemma excluded, of course."

"Sips?" he repeated.

Nora raised a finger to punctuate her words. "Cashen's Irish Pub. CIPs."

"Sips," he said. "Who came up with that?"

"Not sure. It's catchy though, isn't it?"

"Isn't it really KIPs though?"

Nora shook her head. "So you're one of those guys."

Jake raised a brow. "Those guys? So what's your definition?"

"Literal," she said. "Thinks he's logical."

"Is that a bad thing?"

Nora just took another sip of her drink and shot him that

mysterious smile. Her eyes swam as she looked at him. It made him wonder how strong they'd made her drink.

Jake leaned back against the booth, draping one arm across it. He angled himself so he could see Nora better.

"Not sure how I feel about being the subject of all the bar gossip."

"It's Blackhand Hills. Everybody's the subject of gossip at one point or another."

They sat in easy silence for a few moments, each of them sipping their drinks. Val came back with the plate of fried pickles and they lived up to Nora's hype. The things were damn delicious. Jake almost wished he'd just ordered two baskets and skipped the burger.

"I told ya," Nora said. She held one of the fried spears above her mouth and lowered it past her lips. The gesture stirred something in Jake. She really was pretty. And so far easy to talk to.

The conversations in the bar dimmed a bit as the band took the stage. Jake recognized the drummer as Denny Voigt, one of the volunteer firemen. Denny saw Jake as well, and raised a drumstick in salute.

The bass player hit a few deep notes, checking his amp.

"So," Jake said. "How'd you get mixed up with my sister?"

"Gemma sold my brother a house last year. She knew I worked at the End Zone when the Weingards owned it. When she bought the building, she gave me a call to see if I was interested in coming back under new management. I wasn't going to. But your sister's tough to say no to. The hours she offered me are perfect. I'm studying to be a respiratory therapist. She's letting me work around my class schedule. The Weingards never let me do that."

"That's great. I hope it all works out."

"Me too. I've worked for a lot of assholes in the bar and restaurant business. In fact, most of them are. Gemma's different. And she's the kind of person where it seems like she deserves a win. You know?"

"Yeah. She does."

"She said you were a skeptic when she bought the bar."

Jake stopped mid-drink. "She said that? What else has my sister told you about me?"

Nora put her index finger to her lips. "Nope. No way, buddy. You're gonna need to ply me with more than one drink to get me to spill all my secrets."

Before he could respond, the band started playing. They launched into a sped-up version of a southern rock song. The thing was louder than Jake liked, but he had to admit, they were good. The lead singer sounded a lot like a young Ronnie Van Zant.

"Be right back!" Nora sprang up. "Want anything else from the bar?"

"I'm good," Jake said. Nora grabbed her purse and made her way to the women's bathroom. He decided he liked watching her walk. She tossed her hair over her shoulder in a way that made Jake think she knew he was watching, and probably didn't mind.

Damn, he thought. She was very pretty. And so far, he was having a decent time.

He turned his attention to the band. The singer hit a screeching high note and held it there with impressive control. It got a raucous cheer from the audience.

"Jake? Are you serious right now? Jake Cashen?"

Jake looked up. A red-faced, burly guy with thinning blond hair weaved his way toward Jake's table. He looked familiar, but Jake couldn't place him.

"I'll be goddamned," the man said. He had two companions with him. An even bigger guy wearing a black shirt with the sleeves cut off and a smaller man in a red golf shirt and denim cargo shorts.

Jake rose. The burly guy offered his hand to shake.

"Jake Cashen. I heard you moved back this way. Never thought I'd see you all the way out here. What're you doing in Marvell?"

"Watching the band," Jake said. He hoped by letting the guy talk for a minute it would jog his memory. No luck. He was drawing a complete blank.

"This is Jake," he said to his companions. "State Champ from Stanley. Beat Dexter Oaks. Match of the Century. Remember I told you about him?"

The smaller of the two men seemed to recall what his friend was talking about and extended a hand to shake Jake's.

So a former wrestler, Jake thought. That narrowed things down, but not by much. High school was twenty years ago and this guy looked like he'd lived hard with every single one of them.

When Jake reached over to shake his hand, the guy tried to give Jake a bear hug. Jake tensed.

The guy stepped back. His eyes were glazed over and he swayed a bit on his feet.

"Hey, buddy," Jake said. "You look like you need to sit down."

"You don't even remember me, do you?"

"You know, I'm afraid I don't. But you do look familiar."

"Kyle Russell," he said, over enunciating the syllables. Jake nodded as if the name meant something. He wasn't sure whether he should wish it did or not.

"From Laurel Point. You were in my weight class in eighth grade. I moved up to 189 by the time I was in high school. Sure would have liked a rematch from that Grassley tournament. You remember that though."

Jesus, Jake thought. The guy was referencing some match from when they were fourteen years old. No. Jake had no memory of it.

"I told 'em. If I had ten more seconds on the clock, I'd have gotten that reversal."

"I'm sure you would have," Jake said.

"Look at you now," Russell said. "Man. You're a lot littler than I remembered."

"Who are you calling little, Kyle?" Nora reappeared. She slipped an arm around Kyle Russell's waist, then reached up and messed up what was left of his hair.

"You with Jake?" Russell asked her.

"Tonight I am," Nora said.

"Well, let's make a party of it!"

Before Jake could think of a plausible protest, Kyle Russell and his two friends pulled up chairs and joined Jake and Nora at their table. Nora gave him a sheepish grin and shrugged. Jake finished the rest of his beer. He could safely have one more, he figured. Nora nursed her Seabreeze. Russell ordered a pitcher for the table. The band kicked into high gear and drowned out the possibility of meaningful conversation. For the moment, Jake decided that was a blessing.

"We heard you moved to Chicago," Russell shouted, undeterred by the noise.

Jake nodded.

"Big damn deal, that was," Russell said. "This guy." He pointed at Jake with his thumb. "You shoulda seen him in his prime. Had the best headlock. But that's garbage wrestling if you ask me. You couldn't get away with that crap if you were on the mat today."

"Sure thing," Jake said, hoping the guy would just sputter himself out and go away.

Jake leaned in to whisper to Nora. "You maybe wanna check out that back patio?"

"One sec," she said. "This is my favorite song they do."

The lead guitarist started the first few notes of "Sweet Child o' Mine." The crowd erupted in cheers and catcalls. Nora put her fingers to her lips and let out an ear-splitting whistle.

"I watched your last match against Dexter Oaks," Russell said. Lord, this guy just wasn't gonna give it up. "Can't believe you stuck him."

"Thanks."

"You know what happened to that guy?" Russell asked.

"What?" Jake asked. Russell's voice was partially drowned out by the band.

"I said, do you know what happened to Dexter Oaks?"

"Yeah, I don't know," Jake answered. "But maybe we can talk about it later. I'm here with Nora trying to enjoy the music."

This elicited a huge smile from Nora. She slid closer to Jake and grabbed his arm, draping it around her.

There was something different about her. She sucked her bottom lip and sang along off-key to the band. She'd only had the one Seabreeze, but the way she leaned against him, she didn't seem all the way sober.

"You okay?" he asked her.

"I'm fiiiine!" she said. "Except for this asshole. Hey, Kyle, why don't you shut your yap for five seconds so we can hear!"

Kyle laughed for a second. But Jake saw the glint of anger cross his eyes.

"Come on," Jake said to Nora. "I'd really like to check out that patio like you suggested. Let's get some air."

"That's a great idea!" she said. She spun out from underneath Jake's arm and pulled him along with her out of the booth.

As she started to walk toward the exit sign, she swayed sideways. Jake grabbed her just before she would have knocked into Val carrying a tray of drinks.

"Thissss way," Nora said. Jake caught Val's eye as they moved past her. She shot Nora a look of disdain. Jake could have sworn it was a "here she goes again" kind of expression.

What in the ever-loving hell was going on with this girl?

Nora danced her way out to the patio. She knocked hips with a few people along the way. Most of them didn't seem to appreciate it one bit.

"Nora," Jake said. "Maybe let's get you some water?"

She ignored him. Instead, she kept right on dancing even though there was no dance floor out here. Just a bunch of tables and they were all beginning to stare.

Jake spotted an empty one and tried to lead Nora to it. She plunked down into a seat and rested her chin on her hands. She had that unfocused expression on her face of someone who was either plastered or high.

"Buy me a drink!" she shouted. He wanted to tell her he thought she'd had enough. Only she'd only just ordered the Seabreeze while he was here. Had she downed something in the bathroom? Or had she taken something?

"Good idea!" Jake's spine stiffened as he recognized Kyle Russell's voice. The idiot had refused to take the hint and followed them out to the patio.

"You're not so tough!" Nora shouted. "Big man. That's Kyle Russell. Always gotta one-up everybody. You know what? Jake could kick your ass today just like he did when you were fourteen, Kyle."

"We're good. It's all good," Jake said. "We're all just having a nice night out."

"Bullshit!" Kyle said. "Look at him. I grew up since junior high, Cashen."

Kyle stepped into Jake's personal space. He was right about growing. Whatever he was in junior high, the guy was six feet tall and maybe two-twenty.

"You could do it, couldn't you?" Nora asked.

"Do what?" Jake said.

"Still kick Kyle's ass. Somebody ought to. Cuz he's rude. And full of it."

"You think you could take me? The hell you could."

"Yeah. I'm not interested in trying, Kyle. Junior high was a long time ago. Who cares? We're all grown-ups now."

"A hundred bucks says you could lay him out in thirty seconds," Nora said.

Her words were met with a chorus of laughter from Kyle and his two friends.

"I'm not ..." Jake started.

"You're on, Cashen!" Kyle said, his face splitting into a gleeful smile.

Christ, Jake thought. This was not happening.

"Do it. Do it!" Nora started to chant. She pounded her fist on the table.

"Let's see the hundred first," Kyle said.

"I'm not taking that bet!" Jake shouted. "I'm here to watch the band. Nora, I don't know if ..."

"Bawk, bawk, bawk!" This from Kyle Russell. The idiot had removed his jacket and took a ready stance, his fists near his face.

"I'm not gonna fight you, Kyle. Nora's just joking. It was funny. How about I buy the next round of drinks and we all just enjoy the rest of our night?"

Jake ran through all the scenarios he could think of for how to get the hell out of here without leaving Nora on her own to get home. Finally, he just came out with it.

"Come on," he said, sliding an arm under Nora. He grabbed her around the waist. "Let me get you home safe." She was like liquid in his arms as he tried to get her to her feet. How in the hell had she gotten so zotted?

She came with him more or less willingly, grabbing her purse off the table as they made their way out to the parking lot.

"I'm sorry, Jake," she said. "Val gave me a generous pour."

"I can see that. No harm done. Let's just get you home."

He got her to his truck and propped her up against the passenger side as he fumbled for his keys.

"You scared?" The booming voice of Kyle Russell filled the air.

"What? Go inside, man. Now!"

"He's not scared!" Nora shouted. "He's gonna have you squealing like a pig, Kyle. Give you what you deserve. Go for it, Jake!"

"Let's just get in the truck."

He started to move toward her. Kyle stepped in front of her. He was fast. Jake would later give him that. He landed a sucker punch straight across Jake's lip. He felt it instantly swell and tasted blood in his mouth.

Kyle took a step back and put his fists up again.

"I know your moves now, Cashen," he said. "Show me what you got."

"Fight!" Nora shouted. "You're going down, Russell."

Kyle Russell got one punch in. He would not get a second.

He was bigger. Maybe even stronger. But Jake's instincts kicked in. He knew size never mattered once you got them on the ground.

Jake shot forward and hit him with a blast double, grabbing his tree trunk legs. Within a second, he put Russell on his ass. Jake moved up on the now stunned Kyle Russell and put him in the headlock the creep had been so impressed with. Jake squeezed and lifted his head. Russell's face turned purple from the pressure.

From there, it was quickly over. Nora's cheers drew a crowd.

Kyle spit and sputtered, but there was no way he was going to get Jake off him. Within a few seconds, he realized it.

"You done?" Jake hissed in his face. He drove Kyle's cheek into the asphalt.

"Yeah," Kyle spit out. "Let me up."

"Nora," Jake said. "Get in the car. I'm going to drive you home."

This time, she did what he asked. She slid into the passenger seat and shut the door.

"You got this?" Jake looked up at Kyle's two friends. The shorter one had the sense to look embarrassed. He gave Jake a nod.

"We'll get him home," he said. "Kyle, it's over. Quit being a dumbass."

Jake gave Kyle a last shove to make sure he got the message. Then he let him up and left him to his friends. "Sorry about that garbage headlock," Jake said.

Sweat poured down Jake's back. He had blood on his shirt. He grabbed his keys from the hood of the car and slowly climbed behind the wheel.

"Nora," he said. "Where do you live?"

"You gonna spend the night? I'd like it if you did," she said.

"Your address," he said.

She pawed at his sleeve. "You're cute."

"Your house," he said.

"Mmm. 1402 Wellington," she said. Jake knew the area. He put the car in gear and lit out of the parking lot. It was a twenty-minute drive. Within two minutes, Nora had slumped over and started snoring. Her purse slipped out of her hand. It lay open on the seat between them. Jake looked down and spotted a nearly empty pint of vodka. He was glad it wasn't anything worse than that, though it was bad enough.

By the time he got Nora home, she was fast asleep in his front seat. She lived in a small brick ranch in an older neighborhood. A gray cat sat in the front window staring at Jake.

"Nora?" Jake said. He gently nudged her shoulder.

Smiling, she opened her eyes and stretched. "You coming in?" she asked.

"Not tonight."

"Are you mad at me?"

"No."

She burst into tears. "You don't know how to have fun, do you? That's what I was worried about. That's why some of the girls were telling me I shouldn't waste my time. Maybe they were right."

Jake gritted his teeth. "Maybe they were. Come on. Let's get you inside." He reached over to undo her seatbelt. She jerked away from him.

"I can do it myself," she said. "I don't need your help."

Nora grabbed her purse, then started to gag. Before Jake could react, Nora threw up all over the dashboard and sprayed the floor.

"I'm ... I'm ..." Nora fumbled with the door handle, staggered out, then ran up her sidewalk. Jake waited to make sure she got inside, rolled down all his windows, and tried to plug his nose with one hand as he drove the rest of the way home.

SEVENTEEN

Two days of fumigating, and Jake had the truck cleaned out. He sent one text to Nora asking if she was okay. She never answered. He debated telling Gemma what happened. But he opted to keep his weekend private. If Nora had the kind of problem he suspected she did, he didn't want to be the one to say anything. At least not yet.

The sucker punch Kyle Russell gave made his lip swell twice its size. By Monday morning, it looked downright ugly. He got a few sideways glances heading into the office, but nobody pried into his business.

Birdie's lead at the Kitty Club panned out. The bouncer she'd met gave her Morgan Prater's phone number and her current employer. Morgan worked as a cocktail waitress at the Broadway Casino just outside of Dayton. Jake called her, and the girl agreed to meet with him just before her evening shift on Monday night.

He pulled into the parking lot of the casino and spotted the blue Honda she'd described over the phone. Jake parked just beside it.

Morgan Prater wasn't alone. She had a mountain next to her in the driver's seat. He glared at Jake and rubbed his thick, red beard. Then he leaned over and whispered something in Morgan's ear. She held a hand up, seeming irritated.

Jake got out of his vehicle. He wore his badge around his neck today. He flashed his credentials. The couple had another heated exchange, then Morgan finally rolled down the passenger window.

"I have fifteen minutes before my shift starts."

A light drizzle began. Jake squinted. He'd stand out in the rain if he had to. But he hoped that wasn't necessary.

"Is there somewhere quiet we can talk?"

"You can talk to her right here!" her companion said. It was then Jake noticed he wore a black vest over a white dress shirt with a bowtie. The uniform of a card dealer.

"Jess, it's fine," Morgan said.

"It's not fine. It's bad enough you told this guy to come here. What if somebody besides me sees you talking to him?"

"Nobody's in trouble tonight," Jake said. "I just have a few questions. Like I told you on the phone. I'm investigating a murder down in Worthington County. A friend of yours told me you might be able to help me."

"Some friend," Jess the card dealer said.

Morgan ignored him and got out of his car. "Go inside," she told him. "Tell Marty I'll be in in a few minutes if he asks."

"You better be," Jess said. But surprisingly, he dropped any further protest. Instead, he pulled the keys out of the ignition and exited the vehicle, slamming the door behind him.

Jake waited a moment while Jess walked out of sight. Then he turned to Morgan.

"I appreciate you making time for me."

"You came all this way," she said. "And you said Joey's dead. Did somebody really shoot her?"

"They did."

"Come on," she said. "We'll talk in your car. You're not planning on kidnapping me, are you?"

Jake smiled. "I'll leave my keys on the dashboard if that makes you feel better."

"It kinda does."

Morgan was pretty. Jake could see Jaxon Waters had a type. Brunette. Well-endowed. But short. The girl was maybe five foot one in heels. Joey DeSilva had been five foot one. Samantha Blanco was about the same.

Morgan walked around Jake's car and got in. He slipped behind the wheel and put his keys on the dashboard between them.

"Did she suffer?" Morgan asked, her voice going quiet.

Jake thought for a moment. Then answered honestly. "Yes. I think she did. She was shot in the thigh. Kept running. Then she was shot in the back. Coroner thinks it took a minute or two for her to bleed to death."

Morgan squeezed her eyes shut. "I'm sorry for that. Joey was all right, you know?"

"She introduced you to Jax?"

Morgan nodded. "I knew her from back home. She's from Westeridge. I'm from Pennington. We both ran track. I raced against her a couple of times in the 400 meter. She was fast. I was faster. Anyway, she and Jax came into the Kitty Club where I worked a couple of times. Paid for a private dance. They were nice. We got to talking."

"How long did you work for Jax?"

"Look, I'm not part of that life anymore. I make good money here. More than I ever did stripping."

Jake knew she was lying. Odds were, Morgan had been taking johns as recently as a month ago.

"That's good," he said. "But I'm not here to get in your way or jam you up on how you pay your bills. I'm trying to find out who might have had a reason to put bullets into Jax Waters and Joey DeSilva. I had a long conversation with Marcus Ekon. You remember him?"

Morgan's eyes got wide. "You talked to Marcus? He's out?"

"He's out. He's working not too far from here. He was pretty torn up when he heard about Joey. He said he was afraid something like this was going to happen to her. He didn't think Jax was capable of protecting the girls who worked for him. Turns out Marcus had a point."

"He's a good dude," Morgan said. "Marcus. Things were different when he was around. Better." She got a far-off expression on her face. If Jake had to guess, he'd say she was reliving some trauma.

"Did somebody hurt you, Morgan? Somebody Jax sent you to?"

"I don't think I can help you."

"Marcus thinks you can. And he's worried about you. That you don't have enough protection now."

"Jess protects me."

"He didn't always though, did he?"

"What is it you want from me?"

"Tell me how things were working for Jax. Who did he answer to? Who did you answer to?"

"I don't know. I was never involved in that side of the business. That was all Jax and Joey."

"She recruited the girls."

Morgan nodded.

"You. Samantha Blanco. Was there anyone else?"

Morgan shook her head. "Nobody else that I knew."

"How did you find out about your dates, Morgan?"

She shrugged. "I'd get a text. An address. A time. Joey or Jax would tell me what to wear. If there were any specials. You know, that kind of thing."

"Specials."

Morgan sighed. "Don't pretend you're naïve, Detective Cashen. You know what I mean."

"Fine. Did any of these specials involve you getting hurt?"

"Not when Marcus was around, no. But since then, sometimes things could get a little out of hand. But when that happened, I would tell Joey. That would be the end of it. They never made me go out with somebody I didn't want to."

"You had regulars?"

"Forget it. I'm not a rat. I don't have to tell you anything like that."

"Did you ever hear anybody threaten Joey or Jax? Were either of them afraid of anyone?"

She shook her head. Jake didn't buy it.

"Did they ever send you to work with anybody in Blackhand Hills?"

She turned to look at him. Something flickered behind her eyes.

"I'll take that as a yes," Jake said. "Morgan. Were you working in Blackhand Hills too?"

"Jax was expanding operations there, yes. That's what Joey said. A lot of the clients Jax was interested in cultivating liked the area. It's remote. But getting posh, you know? And nobody really bothered us out there. He was trying to get a foothold."

"How many times did he send you on dates in Blackhand Hills?"

"I don't know. Five or six maybe. I'm guessing it was the same for Sam. It was just the two of us. For starters. Jax wanted to bring in a few more girls. Some of the ones he had didn't want to travel that far. But I liked it. And more for me, you know? If nobody else wanted to leave the Dayton area. I think that's shortsighted."

"When did this all start? Jax moving things into my territory?"

"That's what he called it," Morgan said. "His territory. He said we were gonna have the market cornered in this new tourist town."

"Why did he move his base of operations?"

"I don't know."

"Yes, you do. Who was he scared of? Who forced him out of Dayton?"

"I don't know. I swear. That part of the business wasn't my business, you know?"

"So, it went smoothly? Your transition to Blackhand Hills?"

She shrugged. "Mostly."

It was then Jake noticed the makeup on her neck didn't quite match the tone of her face. The setting sun hit her full on as the clouds parted.

"Somebody hurt you," Jake said, his voice taking a hard edge. "Recently. I can see the bruises on your neck. Did Jess, your new protector, do that to you?"

"No! God, no. Jess just looks scary. He wouldn't even kill a spider if it crawled on him."

"Somebody put their hands around your neck hard enough to leave those bruises. That happened while working for Jax, didn't it?"

"Yes. Okay? Yes."

"Who was it? When was it?"

"I don't want to say."

"Do you want me to find out who killed Joey?"

She blinked rapidly, holding back tears.

"Yes. I really do."

"Then help me."

"Things were fine, okay? Just like Jax said they'd be. Only, this one guy he sent me to, he got too rough. It happens sometimes, okay? But I handled it."

"You handled it. Morgan, you could have been killed. I think you know that. I think that's why we're sitting out here in this parking lot all the way back in Dayton and you're working at a casino now. You wanted out if Jax couldn't protect you. Or he told you to lay low for a while."

"He said he would handle things. Yes."

"He was going to talk to this guy who hurt you."

"Yes."

"Was it somebody in Blackhand Hills?"

"Yes."

"I need a name."

"He was important, okay? Jax said it was important that I showed him a good time. No matter what. I tried. But it just got out of hand."

"How?"

"He ... this guy. He didn't want to pay. He said he needed me to send a message to Jax. That we shouldn't be in his backyard. He said I should tell Jax that he was encroaching on the territory of the Hillbillies or something."

"Hillbillies?" Jake said, his gut clenching. "Could he have said Hilltop Boys?"

"Yes! That's it. Hilltop Boys. He said you don't want to be messing in the backyard of the Hilltop Boys. He made me repeat it. Then he hit me. Knocked my tooth loose. He put his foot on my back and held me down. I thought he was going to kill me. Or worse. When he let me up, I tried to just get my things and go. That's when he told me he could make me a better offer."

"What kind of offer?"

"He said I had two choices. Either I leave Blackhand Hills and take my pimp with me. Or I could stay, and he'd put me to work for him. For these Hilltop Boys. Said he could help me expand my horizons, whatever that means. Well, I told him where he could shove his horizons and I ran out of there."

Jake took out a pad of paper and pencil from his center console. He handed it to Morgan.

"Who was he? Where did you meet?"

She shook her head.

Jake took out his phone. He pulled up a picture of Joey lying in the woods. He turned the screen so Morgan could see it.

"Oh Jesus," she said, covering her eyes with her hand. "I don't need to see that."

"Yes, you do. And you need to tell me who Jax sent you to that he thought was important enough to almost strangle you to death."

"Will you leave me alone if I tell you?"

"I'll leave your name out of it if I can."

"Do you really think this could have had something to do with what happened to Joey?" Morgan pointed to her neck.

"I think you think it. So yeah. I think it's important too."

She let out a hard sigh and took the pencil from him. She scribbled a name and handed the pad back to Jake.

"We met at one of the cabins up there. Near this creek. I think it's called Secret Pines or something."

She was describing the second cabin on Ed Lattimore's property. One of the ones that had been vacant when Joey and Jax were murdered.

She'd written the name Dusty Riff. Jake let out a breath. Though he'd had no personal dealings with anyone by that name, he knew some Riffles who were cousins of the Bardos and known affiliates of the Hilltop Boys who worked on Rex Bardo's crew. Jake folded the paper and slipped it in his pocket.

"Do you mind if I take a picture of you? Your bruising?"

Morgan shrugged. She pulled her collar down. Jake snapped a picture with his phone.

"If I can identify the guy who did this to you, will you press charges?" he asked.

"No way," she answered. "I want nothing to do with him, that town, or going to court."

"Morgan," he said. "How old were you when Joey and Jax approached you?"

"What does that matter?"

"Is there somebody out there who's missing you?"

"What?"

"Your mom? Your family?" He thought about Raymond DeSilva. Though Jake couldn't say why, he had a feeling about Morgan. Like Joey and Samantha Blanco, she was clean. No track marks. Good teeth. She'd come from somewhere. From someone.

"There are people who can help you, you know. I'm one of them. If you're running away from something ..."

"You don't know me."

"Yeah," he said. "I think I do. Is there somebody I can call for you?"

"Why are you asking me that?"

"I told you, Marcus Ekon's worried about you. He told me you were different. Special. And that you didn't belong in this life. That he tried to get you to call your family. Tried to talk you into going home. It's not too late for that. It's never too late for that."

"Just go back to Blackhand Hills, Detective."

"I could get a message to someone for you, at least. Let them know you're okay. It's up to you if you want to reach out after that."

"You could do that for me?"

She was crying now. Silent tears that spilled down her cheeks.

"Of course."

She took the pencil back from him and scribbled another name and phone number. She handed it to Jake.

"That's my sister," she said. "Maybe if you could tell her I'm doing all right. Give her this number. She can call me. If she still wants to hear from me."

"Morgan!"

The shout came from the back door. Jess was back.

"I gotta go. I'm already late."

Before Jake could convince her otherwise, Morgan opened the car door and vaulted out. She ran toward Jess. He put his arm around her and walked her into the building.

"Keep her safe, man," Jake said.

He pulled out the first note she'd scribbled for him.

"Son of a bitch," he muttered. He sent a text to Birdie.

Morgan Prater had a run-in with the Hilltop Boys. This thing was getting stickier by the minute.

Damn, was Birdie's reply.

Jake put his key in the ignition and started the long drive back to Blackhand Hills.

Eighteen

"You gonna tell me I should see the other guy?"

Birdie didn't miss a trick. She was in the office all of thirty seconds before she noticed Jake's swollen lip. It was worse today than yesterday and had scabbed over where Kyle's ring had made contact.

"Jake," she said when he didn't respond. She leaned in close and grabbed his chin.

"Good lord. What happened?"

"It was a misunderstanding," he answered. "And I'd rather not talk about it."

He'd ignored two texts from Meg asking him how his date with Nora had gone. He drove Grandpa's truck into work the last two days while he aired out the puke smell from his date.

Birdie sat at Majewski's desk but kept her gaze locked with Jake's.

"I'd rather talk about how my interview with Morgan Prater went. She gave me a name. Sort of."

Jake described the gist of his conversation with Morgan up to and including her run-in with the man she claimed was connected to the Hilltop Boys.

"That's bad," Birdie said. "Jake, that's real bad."

"You ever heard anyone talk about this Dusty Riff?"

"I've heard the name Riff out there. I'm assuming he's one of the Riffles. Bardo's cousin. But she's sure the guy was trying to poach her?"

"She knows what she heard."

"Still. You've never known that crew to dabble in prostitution, have you?"

"Not while Rex Bardo was still fully in control."

Bardo was doing fifteen years to life on a drug trafficking charge in federal prison. By all accounts, he was still running the family business from behind bars, but there was only so much he could keep tabs on.

"We've already seen his brother Floyd try to expand operations without Rex's approval."

"And we know how well that went. Do you think this warrants you paying King Rex another visit? He's been helpful to you in the past."

"I don't know that I'd call our interactions helpful. Rex tells me things when it suits his purposes. And if what happened with Morgan was sanctioned in some way, I'm not going to win any points by going to him with this. I need to take the temperature in town first. I'd only go to Rex to confirm something I already mostly know the answer to."

"Good point. You don't want to owe him favors. And if he didn't sanction this, and your intel is the first he's heard of it, he's sure as hell not going to let on."

"Family comes first with him," Jake said. "That's a lesson I can't ever forget."

"So Floyd," she said. "I gotta be honest. I don't see him being brave enough to do something behind Rex's back if that's what it is. He's had his wings clipped already for trying."

It's what Jake had been turning over in his mind for the last few hours. This didn't feel like it had Rex's fingerprints on it. And Floyd Bardo had been smacked down hard enough not to get up for a while. At the same time, somebody out there was throwing around the Hilltop Boys' name. None of their people would be dumb enough to do that without permission.

"What are you thinking?" Birdie asked.

"Kyra," Jake said. "We both know Rex's niece has more brains than her father. Rex trusts her. He told me as much. I think she and I need to have a conversation today."

Birdie nodded. "I got the same impression when we dealt with her on the Red Sky Hill murder. She's a player. She's a better successor to the Hilltop Boy empire than her father Floyd is. And King Rex is shrewd enough to know it. You want me to come with you?"

"No," he said. "Not this time. Kyra and I have a rapport, I think."

Birdie smirked. "A rapport. I guess you could call it that."

"What do you mean?"

Birdie shook her head. "That girl knows how to play guys like you."

"Guys like me?" He tensed at the phrase. Nora had said that the other day, too.

"Yeah."

"What's that supposed to mean?"

"The rule followers," Birdie said. "The honorable ones."

Jake laughed. "Okay. Whatever you say. I just mean she was willing to talk to me last time. And I don't want to make this seem like a bigger deal than it is. If I show up there with you, it's gonna look like we're sending in the cavalry. This just needs to be a casual conversation. Besides, there's something else I'd like you to look into in the meantime."

Jake pulled out his notepad. He flipped to the page where Morgan had written her sister's name. He handed the pad to Birdie.

"Morgan Prater's young," he said. "Just twenty-one. She said Joey DeSilva's the one who recruited her a couple of years ago."

"When she was underage?"

"Maybe. I talked her into giving me the name of somebody who might be out there wondering what happened to her. I couldn't stop thinking about Joey's dad. She says that's her sister. At some point, I'd like to get word to her that Morgan's okay. For now, at least."

"Is this all she said? Did she have any theories on who might have wanted to kill the Waters?"

"Nothing beyond this run-in with Dusty Riff or Riffle. It was the only thing out of the ordinary to her since she and the other girls started taking jobs here in Worthington County. She confirmed they've been using Lattimore's properties as meeting places."

"Oh boy. That's gonna go over well when it goes public."

"Let's try to keep it under wraps as long as we can."

"Of course."

Jake grabbed his suit jacket and keys off the desk. "All right. I'm gonna head out to Bardo Excavating. Kyra Bardo will be there."

"You're not gonna call first."

"No. Let me use the element of surprise."

"Something tells me nothing surprises that chick. I'd lay odds she already knows you'll show up at some point."

"You're giving her too much credit."

Birdie's expression was pure annoyance. "And you're not giving her enough. Mark my words. I'm right. She's gonna make you a mile away."

Jake shook his head. He wouldn't let Birdie's paranoia affect his judgment today.

NINETEEN

Birdie was right. As Jake walked into the small trailer office on the Bardo Excavating property, Kyra Bardo seemed to already be expecting him. She leaned over her desk looking at plans. She wore a black suit that might have been painted on, three-inch red heels, and earrings that sparkled.

"Thanks, Gil," she said to the man standing beside her. He looked like a college kid barely able to grow a beard. He mooned over Kyra as he folded up the blueprints and turned toward Jake.

"He doesn't have an appointment, Ms. Bardo."

"It's fine." Kyra smiled. "Detective Cashen won't be staying long."

"I won't need long," Jake agreed.

"Shut the door behind you, Gil."

Gil hustled out of the trailer, shaking the thing as he nearly fell down the steps leading to the yard.

Kyra took a seat behind her desk. Actually, it was her father's desk. This whole office belonged to him. It was Floyd Bardo's name on the outside of the door. But Jake knew Kyra was really running the day-to-day. She had two brothers. The older one, Knox, should have been Rex's heir apparent after Floyd, but only Kyra had so far shown the steely-eyed temperament to run things the way her Uncle Rex wanted.

"I'm not going to pretend you don't know what I'm working on," Jake started.

Kyra crossed her arms in front of her. Her eyes darted over Jake's face. She kept just the hint of a smirk on her ruby-red lips, but didn't answer.

Jake reached into his jacket pocket and pulled out two crime scene photographs. One of Joey DeSilva face down on the creek bed. The other of Jaxon still in the hot tub. The second one was more gruesome, of course, but tame compared to the ones taken after Dr. Stone's crew pulled him out of the water.

Kyra never bothered to look down. She kept her eyes on Jake.

"In the course of running down a lead, a name came up that I think might mean something to you."

No response. Not the slightest falter of her smile.

"Dusty Riff," he said. "I know he works for you."

"For me?" she said. "Jake, nobody here works for me. That's my father's crew out there. You want an employee list? I'm happy to give it. It's not very long."

"You need me to tell you what Jaxon Waters's business was in Blackhand Hills?"

"Enlighten me."

"Sex trafficking. High-end escorts. Guy was trying to get a

foothold in the region. You want to pretend you didn't know about it?"

"My family runs a legitimate business here. I wouldn't know about anything else."

"Right. Well, one of Waters's girls had a run-in with someone who called himself Dusty Riff. He threw around the Hilltop Boys' name and yours. It got rough. He put his hands on her. She's got bruises around her neck to prove it. It was a message. One I'm trying to find out who sanctioned sending."

"I wish you all the luck with that. But like I told you, that has nothing to do with me. Maybe you should talk to my father."

"Sure. Only he's not here. He's never here, is he?"

"His name's on the door."

So, she wanted to dance.

"Here's what I know," Jake said. "Your family has never dirtied their hands with something like sex trafficking. Rex steered clear of that for a reason. Same reason he steered clear of harder drugs. It's bad business. The kind that ends up with people shot to death in hot tubs. But Dusty Riff is out there using the Bardo name. Trying to poach Jaxon Waters's girls at worst. Or at least sending Waters a message that nobody uses your backyard without paying rent."

Kyra narrowed her eyes and her smile dropped just a little.

"The thing is," Jake went on. "I don't really care about any of that. But if your turf war led to two people getting shot, then it becomes something I've got to get involved in. I'm going to find out who killed those people. Because I'm that good. Your uncle understands that. And I'm guessing whoever Dusty Riff is, he didn't have permission to use Hilltop Boys currency. He got sloppy."

"What is it that you think I can help you with, Jake?" she asked. Kyra leaned forward, resting her forearms on her desk. It gave Jake an unobstructed view of her cleavage. He knew that's what she wanted. He looked away. The girl was a knockout and she knew it.

"I need to talk to this Dusty. What's his real name? Where can I find him?"

"I told you. Whoever Dusty is he doesn't work for me."

"He might not be on your formal payroll. But you know who he is."

It was his turn to lean forward. He met Kyra's eyes and didn't back down.

"If he's out there hurting women, that's not good for business. And you know your Uncle Rex will be the first to tell you that."

No reaction.

"You're in over your head, Kyra. I'm offering you a life preserver if you're smart enough to grab it."

There. It was subtle. But she blinked. Jake knew he was right. Whoever Dusty Riff was, he'd gone off script. Hurting Morgan Prater wasn't supposed to happen. He got scared or cocky or both.

"He's not worth it," Jake said. "Dusty's putting your family business at risk. So, you need to decide what kind of boss you really want to be. The Feds are hitting the human trafficking cases hard. Do you really want them sniffing around here?"

At that moment, Kyra finally looked her true age. Jake knew she couldn't be much more than twenty-five or twenty-six. She was playing a grownup's game. Was she smart enough to know the rules?

"Here's the smart play," Jake said. "You tell me where I can find Dusty. And you tell him when I come looking for him, he should cooperate."

Anger flashed in her eyes. She sat back. "Or. What?"

"Or? When I find him anyway, I make sure the word gets out that you can't protect your people. That you really are in over your head and Uncle Rex put his trust in the wrong Bardo."

Jake rose. He pulled out his business card and tossed it on Kyra's desk. She didn't pick it up in front of him, but instinct told him she would the second he walked out.

"That's my personal cell phone on the back. I expect to hear from you within twenty-four hours."

He didn't wait for her to answer or to throw him out. He turned his back on her and walked out of the office, confident that soon enough, his phone would ring.

TWENTY

The next morning, Jake and Birdie took a trip down to Westeridge to talk to Raymond DeSilva again. Armed with Morgan Prater's story about how Joey recruited her, Jake hoped DeSilva would remember more details about conversations he'd had with his daughter in recent months. When they arrived at DeSilva's home address, DeSilva's neighbor stopped them before they could knock on the door.

"He's not home," she said. An elderly woman wearing a pink-and-blue-quilted housecoat stood on her porch next door. She stepped down, picked up a rolled newspaper off the sidewalk. She held it in front of her as she walked up DeSilva's driveway.

"I'm Detective Cashen," Jake said. "I've been working on Mr. DeSilva's daughter's case. We made arrangements to speak this morning."

"You won't find him in there," she said. "Ray's in the hospital. He tried to take his own life last night."

Jake's heart dropped.

"My God," Birdie said. "Do you know what happened?"

"I've been getting his mail for him," the woman said. "Ray's not been himself ever since what happened to poor Joey. I check in on him every night. Sometimes I bring him supper. Last night he wouldn't come to the door. I've got a key. So I went in. He took some pills. I found him passed out in his recliner. Don't know what might have happened if I didn't go in there when I did."

"It's a lucky thing you did," Jake said.

"Where did they take him?" Birdie asked. "We'd like to pay our respects if we could."

"County hospital. It's only two miles down the road. I was going to go visit him later today. He's on the third floor. Room 311. Not sure if he's allowed to have visitors yet. But I was gonna go anyway. They'll keep him for seventy-two hours, the paramedic said. He was a friend of Joey's, too. From high school. Everybody knows everybody around here."

"I know what that's like," Jake said. "Thank you."

"If you see him, you tell him Mrs. Harvey's gonna bring him some chicken soup later. The food in that hospital is the pits."

"We'll tell him," Jake said.

Birdie and Jake climbed back into the car and followed Mrs. Harvey's directions to the county hospital. Just as she said, Ray DeSilva was admitted into room 311 on the psychiatric floor. He wasn't alone. Dale Halsey sat at his bedside. DeSilva himself was fast asleep.

Halsey saw Jake and Birdie and quietly left DeSilva's side. He closed the door behind him.

"There's a common room just down the hall," Halsey said. "It's got nice big windows and a view of the whole town from there. I tried to get Ray to take a walk with me down here earlier. So far, he won't really get out of bed."

Jake and Birdie let Halsey lead the way. He was right. The sitting area overlooked the entire town of Westeridge. He could see a church steeple in the center of town and the river that ran through the northwest section.

"Do you know what happened?" Birdie asked. "We ran into his neighbor, Mrs. Harvey."

Halsey smiled. "She's a trip. Into everybody's business, that one. Though in this case, that was a good thing. But I don't think Ray took enough Xanax to actually kill himself. At least that's what they said in the ER last night. It was more of a cry for help."

"Poor man," Birdie said.

"If he can just hang on," Halsey said. "We can help him through this. I've got members of Lean On Us daisy chaining their visits with him today. We're all taking shifts."

"He's lucky to have friends like that," Jake said.

Halsey shook his head. "I don't know. You should have seen him the other day at Joey's funeral. He collapsed at the gravesite. I'm kicking myself for not staying with him. I offered. We've all offered."

"Grief can take your breath away," Birdie said. "But I suppose you're the last person I have to tell that to."

Halsey looked at her. Worry lines creased his face. "You know something about that, Deputy Wayne?"

Birdie gave him a slight smile. "Yes. I know something about that."

"Ray said the two of you were gonna come down to ask him more questions. I asked him if he wanted support with him for that. He said he was okay. It's important to him to do everything he can to help with your investigation. I'm afraid he's just not up to it right now."

"I understand," Jake said.

"Do you have any new leads?"

"A few," Jake said. "I've talked to another friend of Joey's. A young woman who didn't live too far from here. She's followed a similar path as Joey. I tried to talk her into getting in touch with her family down here. She wasn't willing to go that far, but she gave me a note and asked if I could get it to her family. Maybe you can help with that."

Jake took Morgan Prater's note out of his pocket. She'd written her sister's name in looping cursive along with the phone number, probably a burner, where she could be reached. Jake showed it to Halsey.

Halsey took his readers out of his shirt pocket and read the name. His hand went over his mouth.

"Mallory Prater," he said. "You found Morgan?"

"You know her?"

"No. Not her. Not personally. But Mallory's been part of Lean On Us for about a year. Actually, Ray encouraged her to join. Morgan went missing about two years ago. You're saying Joey knew where she was this whole time? I don't think she ever told her sister that. She's all right? Morgan's alive?"

"Yes," Jake said. "I was afraid her circumstances were something like you're describing."

"Is she in trouble? In danger? Do you think whoever did this to Joey could be after Morgan, too?"

"I'm not certain," Jake said. "For the moment, I don't think Morgan's in immediate danger."

"Mallory will be so relieved." Halsey handed the letter back to Jake. "I can get word to her. Will Morgan see her? Will you tell Mallory where she is?"

"First she wanted me to make sure her sister got this number. Morgan's over eighteen. I can't force her to see Mallory if she doesn't want to."

"Sure. Sure." A shudder went through Dale Halsey. "I'm just so grateful you were able to talk to her."

"And it sounds like Mallory's also lucky to have you for a friend."

"I wish I could do more. Morgan got caught up in something bad. Just like Joey. Just like a lot of the young girls in this region. Mallory said it all started when they were in high school."

"That's what Morgan said as well," Jake said. "But I got the impression maybe her home life wasn't ideal."

"I don't know. Brad Prater, her father, is about as straight-laced as they come. He's an electrician. Volunteer fireman. Delivers Meals on Wheels in his spare time. And he's got three daughters. Mallory's the oldest. Then there's Michelle. Morgan was the baby. None of them ended up like Morgan. They almost lost her like I lost Lena. It was about four years ago. Morgan OD'd. Brad got her into rehab. We were able to prosecute the dirtbag who sold her the stuff."

"Do you remember who that was?" Jake asked.

"Will that help? I mean, do you think that crowd had something to do with killing Joey?"

"I don't know. But the more I can find out about Joey's associations, the better."

"He was a college kid. A med student she was dating. Seth Jarvis. He flipped on his supplier. They were responsible for two deaths the weekend before after selling fentanyl-laced product. It was a drop in the bucket, but at least we got some convictions out of it."

"We?" Birdie asked.

"Lean On Us has worked with law enforcement over the years. We've helped put some of this scum behind bars. But it's like one of those hydra monsters. You cut off one head and another one grows in its place. Sometimes stronger with a larger reach."

"We do what we can," Jake said.

"Yes," Halsey said. "We do what we can."

"If I can help you in any way, I'd like to," Halsey said.

"I'll keep that in mind," Jake said. "And I may need to take you up on it the further we get into this. Right now, I think the best thing you can do is stick by your friend in there."

Halsey nodded. "You think you'll never find your way out of the dark. When you lose a child. It's not like any other kind of grief. I lost a sister. Car accident when we were teenagers. My parents. Even Ray. When his wife died, it gutted him, of course. But Joey kept him going. Even after she left him. Just knowing she was out there. That there was always hope. I was so mad at her when she took off. I thought, how could she leave Ray like that? They went through his wife's illness together. I don't know. I guess the pain of it was too much for Joey. Maybe Ray was a reminder of that for her. It's just so sad."

"He's got a chance," Birdie said. "You found a way to turn your loss into something that helps people."

"Made it so Lena didn't die in vain." Halsey gave a sad smile. "That's what people always say. I don't know. I hope that's true."

"Mr. Halsey?" One of the nurses peeked around the corner.

"Is he waking up?" Halsey asked.

She nodded. "He's asking for you."

"Do you want to come with me?" Halsey asked Jake.

"Not yet," Jake said. "I think Ray needs to focus on getting better right now. I'll be in touch in a few days."

"Okay. I'll tell him you stopped by. If he feels up to a conversation, I'll help him make the call."

"That's good. Thank you." Jake still held Morgan's note.

"Do you think you could make sure Mallory Prater gets this when you see her?"

Halsey took the letter. "I hope it brings her comfort. I hope she's not planning on dumping all over Mallory if she calls."

"I don't think she is," Jake said. "She seemed genuinely concerned about letting her sister know she was okay."

"I hope she is," Halsey said, pocketing the note.

"I hope so too," Jake said.

"We can only save the ones who want to be saved," Halsey said. "The rest? Hard as it is. Sometimes we have to just let them go."

He turned and walked back down the hallway to Ray DeSilva's room.

"She didn't want to be saved," Birdie said.

"Who?"

"Joey DeSilva. She wasn't looking to be saved, Jake. Part of me is just mad at her, you know? Look what she's done to that poor man in there. I can see why Halsey's worried Morgan Prater's reaching out might do more harm than good."

"Joey DeSilva didn't ask to be shot," Jake said.

"I know. Maybe that didn't come out right. I don't mean to be insensitive. But this town. It's just ... it feels cursed. All these young girls. It's no wonder so many of them tried to get out."

Jake couldn't help feeling the opposite. If only more of them had stayed. They'd be safe tonight. And Joey DeSilva might still be alive.

TWENTY-ONE

J ake and Birdie didn't make it back to Stanley until after three o'clock. Ray DeSilva never woke up enough to have a meaningful conversation. But he had Dale Halsey by his side until a few other members of the Lean On Us support group showed up. Heartbreaking as it was to watch DeSilva let grief hollow him out, Jake thought with the support he had around him, he might make it to the other side.

The plan was to switch cars and punch out. But when Jake and Birdie headed down the hallway to his office, Sheriff Landry stood in front of the doorway, looking anxious.

"You're back," she said, breathless. "I wasn't sure we'd see you again."

"Things were a little dire in Westeridge," Jake said. He briefly explained the condition they'd found Ray DeSilva in.

Meg's face fell. "My God. I just can't imagine the pain he's in. If something like this happened to Paige, I don't know how I'd put one foot in front of the other."

"Let's hope you never have to find out," Jake said. "Thanks for coming down there with me, Bir ... er ... Erica."

"No problem. You know that. Anyway, I'm gonna head out and ..."

"Before you do that," Landry said. "The reason I was hoping to catch you both. I just got off the phone with ONIC. They finished the analysis on all the phones found at the Waters' crime scene. They sent a courier with the flash drive. The file is huge. It's going to take some time for you to go through all of it. Ten burner phones. But I'd like you to get started on it tonight. I figured you'd want to anyway. Your overtime's already approved. For both of you."

Landry smiled at the end. Getting overtime for Birdie had been a bear for the last two weeks.

"That's great," Jake said. "I'll have some sandwiches sent in. We didn't eat lunch."

"Already taken care of," Landry said. "I've got pizzas on the way. Hope you like pepperoni."

Jake slipped out of his suit jacket. Landry handed him the package containing the flash drive. Birdie hesitated at the door.

"You coming?" he said. "We're gonna have to divide and conquer on this one. It's ten phones. We need to look for patterns. Most frequently called numbers. Reverse lookups. Build a timeline. Ramirez said the ONIC analysts will do a bunch of the legwork on this. We just need to pick out the data important to our case."

Birdie's expression was odd. For a moment, anyway. Then she found a smile.

"Let's get cracking then."

"I'll get out of your way," Landry said. "Paige has a choir concert in about an hour. I'll be home after that. If you find anything, you call me. I don't care how late it is tonight. I want to know what you know when you know it."

"Sure thing," Jake said. But he was already distracted, firing up his laptop and slipping the flash drive in.

He hadn't been kidding. This would be a divide-and-conquer proposition. Jake made a copy of the flash drive for Birdie. He'd handle one half of the reports and she'd do the rest. As Jake started looking through the PDFs, one of the younger deputies came in with two pizza boxes.

Jake thanked him and had him set the pizza boxes on the table near the coffee maker. Jake scarfed down two slices as he poured over the data.

It became quickly clear that two burners in particular had the most call traffic. He surmised Waters was using those himself. The others were likely given to Joey and the other girls working for them. He went to the transcripts of incoming and outgoing text messages. Birdie had set herself up at Majewski's desk. They worked in silence together.

"Looks like business was booming," she said. Jake looked up. It was the first either of them said in almost two hours.

Jake pored over the data. As time went on, he started to understand some of the code words Waters used.

"Star," Birdie said. She was with Jake step for step, understanding the data.

"I think Star must be Joey," she said. "Here's a text from a local number arranging for a meetup four days before the murders. It's hitting the tower closest to Lattimore's cabin."

"He's sending her out to meet with johns while they're telling everyone else they're on some romantic getaway. It's getting harder and harder to feel sorry for the way Jaxon Waters met his end."

Birdie's own cell phone went off. She got up and took the call out in the hallway.

Jake thought Birdie's guess about Star was probably right. The other names used most frequently were Diamond and Pearl. He could reach out to either Samantha Blanco or Morgan Prater again to confirm. Ekon said Morgan went by Pearl on the MOCA app. And Morgan had already told him she hooked up with a john at the cabin nearest where Joey and Jaxon stayed the week before the shootings. Sure enough, he found a text message back and forth from Pearl to someone identifying himself as Rocko during the same window of time.

Birdie came back to the office. Her face was flushed but she smiled and went back to the printouts.

"I know Pearl is Morgan Prater," Jake said.

"Do you see anyone else? He's got Joey, Morgan, and Samantha working the region in the week before the shootings."

"I'm looking for repeat business," Jake said. "I'm seeing maybe half a dozen regular customers. Both Samantha and Morgan claim they never knew real names."

"It would have been bad business if they did," Birdie agreed.

"I want to find this Dusty Riff," Jake said. "He would have been communicating with Morgan."

"Pearl," Birdie said. "Did she give you a timeframe of when she saw this guy?"

"Just a rough one."

"And you got nowhere with Kyra Bardo?"

Jake put his pages down. "I wouldn't say nowhere. I think we came to an understanding."

Birdie smirked. "I'll bet you did."

"What's that supposed to mean?"

"Are you sure she didn't just play you? Tell you what you wanted to hear to get you out of her hair?"

"I think she's a little smarter than that. If she's dabbling in prostitution, she's doing it without Uncle Rex's sanction. That's a pretty dangerous position for her to be in."

"Or could it be more her dad Floyd's new pet project? And Kyra's left once again trying to clean up his mess."

"Maybe. I don't know. The vibe I got from her. I tend to think after Floyd's last screw-up, he's effectively been benched. His name's on the letterhead just for show, you know?"

"Maybe," she said. A text came through on Birdie's phone. She looked at it, frowned, then returned it.

"Everything okay?" Jake asked.

"Everything's fine. These are a lot of texts to go through. Landry can't possibly think we're gonna pull an all-nighter here."

"If you've got somewhere else you need to be, I won't stop you."

"I'm fine," she said, but Birdie definitely seemed distracted. It wasn't like her. Jake went back to the lines of texts. Most of it was mind-numbing and mundane. Even on the burners, Jaxon Waters and the girls were careful about what they said. It was just simple times, dates, meeting places. A few times, Jake found disagreements over fees.

"There was a lot of money changing hands," Birdie said. "Five thousand for the full night. A thousand bucks an hour."

"There are a few here where Jax had these women accompanying their dates to certain events."

"Anything local?"

"Not so far as I can tell. This one here sounds like a fundraiser in Columbus. It's on the seventeenth of June."

"That'll be pretty hard to pin down," she said. "Is there a meeting place listed?"

"Hilton Hotel," Jake said. Birdie wrote it down on her notepad.

"It's worth doing some checking. Just see who might have been there."

"Sure."

Birdie's phone rang again. "I'm sorry," she said. "I have to take this one."

She excused herself again for a few minutes.

Jake focused in on the texts relating to Morgan or Pearl. What he said to Birdie about Kyra Bardo, he believed. At the same time, he had a kernel of doubt of his own that she might have been playing him.

"Where are you hiding?" Jake said. He combed through the texts. Nothing jumped out at him. Just mundane details about when and where Morgan would meet for particular dates. Everything was consistent with what she'd already told him.

The evening of the shootings and even the night before were actually fairly quiet on the cell phones. He found a text from Samantha Blanco the morning of. It matched her story. She was trying to get a hold of Joey to arrange a money drop. This was after

Joey was already dead at the creek bed. Samantha's texts got increasingly agitated.

Birdie came back into the office. "Jake," she said. "How long do you think you want to work tonight?"

"What?" He hadn't paid attention to the time. It was after six now. They'd been at this for almost three hours.

"Do you have to go somewhere?"

Birdie took a breath. "Yes, actually. I didn't know we were going to end up getting into all of this tonight. I can stay. It's important. And I know Landry went out on a limb to get my overtime approved. It's just ..."

Jake sat back. This was extremely uncharacteristic of Birdie. She went just as hard as he did when she was on a case.

"What's going on?" he asked.

Birdie blushed. "I have a date, all right? I don't want to make a big deal about it."

"A date? It's gotta be a big deal for you to turn down all this." He spread his hands wide, gesturing toward their growing mountain of paperwork.

"It could be," she said. "It's actually a third date. We've got reservations at Emmerson's in an hour. I stink. I'd like to be able to go home and take a shower. Shave my legs."

Alarm bells went off. Third date. She wanted to shave. Emmerson's? That was the most expensive restaurant in town.

Jake could almost feel Ben Wayne's spirit rising up beside him. "Hold on. This isn't a date, date. You and this guy ... who is he?"

"You don't know him," she said. "He lives in Athens. We met at the gym."

The gym. Travis mentioned she started dating someone from the gym. But that was a couple of weeks ago.

"The gym?" Jake said, his tone turning harsh. "That's only slightly better than meeting some guy in a bar, Birdie. What do you know about him?"

"He's nice," she said. "We hit it off. And he's the first nice guy I've found worth my time since I moved back to Blackhand Hills. Now I can cancel. If you think ..."

Jake put a hand up. "No. I've got this. It's just ..."

"Just what?"

He couldn't think of a good answer. But once again, he could practically hear Ben in his ear.

"You've brought him around Travis?" Jake asked.

"That's none of your business," Birdie snapped. "I'm not asking for your permission to go on a date. I'm asking for your permission to punch out."

He wanted to tell her absolutely not. But that was Ben talking.

"Are you meeting him there?" he asked. "I'd rather ..."

Birdie's eyes got wide. "You'd rather? Jake ... as much as you ... you're not my brother."

"I didn't mean ..."

"Yes. You did. And you still haven't answered my questions. Are you okay if I skate? I'll be back by six tomorrow to dive into this again."

"Fine," Jake said, harsher than he wanted to. "Just ... be careful."

Birdie's posture changed, becoming more relaxed. There was a twinkle in her eye.

"Always," she said. "I'm sorry I snapped at you. I appreciate that you look out for me. But my dates can't be any worse than yours lately."

Birdie grabbed her jacket off the chair. He found himself seething. He distracted himself by diving back into the stream of text messages.

He should have cut out like Birdie had. It had been a long day already. He'd be fresher in the morning.

Another hour went by. He was just about to pack it in when he saw a single line on a text from the phone he believed Waters used the most.

"I'm not fucking around. You like to take pictures? That kind of thing can come back to bite you."

"Not here. You can't do that. Promises were made."

"All bets are off. You want this shut down, it'll cost you five grand."

Shut down, Jake thought. Pictures. Christ. Jaxon Waters was blackmailing someone. The recipient's number stopped Jake cold. It was a local area code. He grabbed his laptop and did a reverse lookup.

"No," Jake said. "No way. He can't be that stupid."

He scrolled through the texts. The same number popped up over and over.

"Shit," Jake said. "You are that stupid."

He checked the clock. Landry should just be coming back from her daughter's choir concert. Jake folded the pages he was looking at, stuffed them in his pocket, then grabbed his car keys.

Twenty-Two

J ake pulled into Landry's driveway just as Phil Landry parked their Chevy Suburban in the garage. There was something afoot. Paige, Meg's seventeen-year-old daughter, slammed her car door as she got out and began to stomp inside the house. She was thwarted by a locked door.

Jake hated to interrupt what was obviously a tense family moment, but Meg had insisted he apprise her of his findings as soon as he had them.

"Paige!" Meg shouted as she got out of the car. It was then she saw Jake. Her face fell. She looked at Paige.

"Jake!" Paige said, brightening. Whatever was going on, it appeared his presence was a welcome distraction for at least one Landry.

"Hey, Jake," Phil said as he climbed out of the driver's seat. He shot a stern look at Paige then unlocked the garage entrance to the house.

"Come on in," Meg said.

"Sorry," Jake said. "I see I've maybe caught you at a bad time."

"By the look on your face, I'd say there's no good time for what you came to tell me."

He couldn't argue with her. Instead, he followed her in. Phil had a hand on Paige's shoulder. Whatever he'd whispered to her made her eyes well up with tears. The girl quickly recovered as Jake walked in.

"You look nice," Jake said to her. She wore a maroon velvet, floor-length dress. Her choir ensemble, no doubt. He couldn't remember the last time he'd seen Paige wear anything other than black. Today she wore heavy black-eyeliner.

"I hate this thing," she said. "It's hot. But Mrs. Schuler goes to a lot of trouble hand-making them for everyone. I'd just like something a little more modern."

"Well, it's nice on you," Jake said.

"Go wash your face," Phil told his daughter. "We'll have dinner as soon as Mom's done talking with Jake."

"You can join us," Meg said.

"That's okay. Still full of the pizza you ordered at the office."

"Come on," Meg said. "We'll go to my study."

Meg's study was at the front of the house. Jake said a quick apology to Phil. He really hated disrupting their family time.

"Don't worry," Phil whispered to him as Jake walked by. "Gives me a break from hearing those two scream at each other for a few minutes. Seriously, think about joining us for dinner. It might be the only way I can get any peace tonight."

Jake slapped Phil on the shoulder. "You're on your own with that one, buddy. But head on down to Gemma's bar after work next week. It's her grand opening. I'll save you a table."

"I'll take you up on that," Phil said. He went into the kitchen and busied himself with a delicious-smelling roast cooking in a crockpot.

Meg waited for him in the study. She kicked off her heels and sat in one of the leather chairs in the corner. She motioned for Jake to take the other one.

"How bad is it?" she asked.

Jake sat down. "Not great." He reached into his back pocket and pulled out the copy he'd made of the pertinent text exchange off Jax Waters's burner phone. He handed it to Meg. She reached for a pair of readers she kept on her desk and slid them on. She took a moment to scan the texts.

"Okay," she said. "So Waters branched out. Added blackmail to his entrepreneurial adventures. Sounds like a good way to wind up with a bullet between the eyes."

"Right," Jake said. "I traced the second number. That's why I'm sitting in your house right now instead of just calling you on the phone."

Meg put the pages down and took off her glasses.

"Who?"

"Willis Bondy."

She blinked. It took a moment for the name to register. When it did, she pinched the bridge of her nose.

"County Commissioner Willis Bondy?"

"Yep."

"Christ, Jake."

"There are a series of texts and calls from Bondy to Waters's burner phone over the last six weeks. I don't know for sure which of Waters's girls he was spending time with. My guess is Samantha Blanco. He called her Diamond. And she took photos."

"And Waters decided to use them to blackmail Bondy?"

"That's the gist. Yes."

"This is awful. It's going to blow up."

"It could. I'm hoping Bondy can be persuaded to cooperate."

"Cooperate how?"

"I want to talk to him. Give him a chance to come clean."

"I have half a mind to go find him tonight and wring his damn neck. I've got Rob Arden storming into my office, threatening to pull more funding if we don't handle things exactly to his liking. Meanwhile, his bro is out there paying for hookers and getting blackmailed over it. Jaxon and Joey Waters's names have been out in the press for days. Bondy doesn't see fit to get ahead of this and contact you straight out?"

"It doesn't look good on any level. But let me talk to him. He's an idiot. But he's got to be scared."

"He won't be hard to find," she said. "That statewide commissioners' conference is still in full swing at the rec center for another couple of days."

"Fantastic," Jake said, his voice dripping with sarcasm.

"What do you need from me?"

"Nothing yet. If Bondy refuses to cooperate, then we have a different set of problems. But let's just take it one step at a time."

Above them, a door slammed. Meg inhaled sharply through her nose. Her closed eyelids fluttered. She found a fake smile on the exhale.

"Do yourself a favor," she said. "Slip out the back door before Mount St. Paige erupts again."

Jake laughed. "Good luck with that."

"You sure you don't want to stay for dinner?"

"I'm good. Thanks."

Jake took his leave just as Phil Landry slouched his way up the stairs to fetch his daughter.

Twenty-Three

The next morning at eight a.m., Willis Bondy surprised Jake by willingly showing up in his office. Bondy had been a county commissioner for over a decade. Before that, he'd served as Navan Township Supervisor. He had a wife in town and two grown children who'd long since moved away from Worthington County.

Jake set him up in the interview room and offered him a coffee, which he declined.

Jake sat down across from him and put a thin file folder between them containing the offending texts and photographs.

"Thanks for coming in," Jake started. "Do you know why I wanted to talk to you?"

Bondy sat with his arms folded in front of him. He was a solid, square-shaped man with hair thinning in an unusual pattern, with a bald oval at the back of his head. His gray-blue eyes stared straight at Jake. His only movement was the rise and fall of his chest.

"Mr. Bondy, I know you know what I'm working on. So why don't we both save each other some time and you just tell me what you know about Jaxon Waters."

"I don't know a damn thing."

"Okay. Here's the situation. I confiscated a pile of cell phones at the crime scene where we found Waters. We've run forensics on those phones. I'm giving you a chance today to tell me your side of what was going on."

"I don't have to tell you anything."

"No. You don't. At the same time, you've left a pretty big swath of digital evidence behind. I know about your dealings with Jaxon Waters."

"And I know all about you." Bondy's tone turned dark.

"Me?"

"Yes. Your uncle warned me about you."

"Did you tell my uncle you were coming to talk to me today?"

"I'm here as a courtesy to you. Because like it or not, we both work for the county."

Jake reached for the file folder and opened it. He'd highlighted some of the more damning text messages. He slid them in front of Bondy.

"I need you to explain what this was all about."

Bondy briefly looked at the pages. His eyes flickered and he swallowed hard.

"Do you want a water now?" Jake asked.

"I don't want anything."

"Okay. So, I know what Waters was doing in Blackhand Hills. Which means I've got a pretty good idea what your association with Waters was. At least initially. But you can see what those texts spell out."

No response.

"Waters had pictures of you. You were with one of his girls. She called herself Diamond. I believe her real name was Samantha Blanco. She betrayed you and sent pictures to her boss, Jaxon Waters. He turned around and tried to put the squeeze on you with them. Now Jaxon Waters is dead with a bullet to the head. I'm trying to find out who did it. I've got a double homicide I'm trying to clear."

"Boy," Bondy said. "Your uncle wasn't exaggerating. You really are a prick."

"Are you kidding me? This doesn't have anything to do with my uncle." Jake slapped a hand on the photos. "I'm not the one who put you in this situation. You did that all by yourself. Whether you get it or not, I'm trying to give you the opportunity to help yourself now. You know. Seeing as we're both public servants."

He couldn't hide the sarcasm in his last sentence. But he no longer cared. Other than willingly coming into the office, Bondy had signaled his lack of cooperation loud and clear.

"What is it that you want from me?" he asked.

"We're in a help-me-help-you situation. I don't really care what you got up to with Samantha Blanco. I'm not looking to embarrass you with any of this. I have no intention of making any of this public if I don't have to. You have my word on that. But I've got two dead people out at that creek. I need to find out who did it and why."

"I didn't kill anybody."

"I'm not saying you did. But I need to clear a few things up."

"Like what?"

"Do you own a firearm?"

Bondy shifted in his seat. "There's nothing illegal about that. I know my second amendment rights."

"Excellent. I'm all for you exercising them. But that's not an answer."

Bondy stared at the wall. Arms still crossed in front of him.

"Can you tell me where you were on July 17th between say eight p.m. and noon the next morning?"

"You want me to account for my whereabouts in a sixteen-hour period?"

"That's exactly what I want you to do."

"I'd have to check my calendar."

"I can wait."

"Is there anything else?"

"This," Jake said, picking up the file again. "Why don't you tell me your side?"

"I'd say you've already drawn your own conclusions."

"Sure. I'd say it's pretty clear Jaxon Waters was a grade A asshole."

"He was a criminal!" Bondy shouted. It seemed an odd point to make seeing that so was Bondy himself. But Jake decided not to make that particular observation just now.

"He sure was," Jake said. "But the fact remains he's also a murder victim and I have a duty to find out who killed him. Are you going to get in the way of that?"

"I have nothing to do with this. I'd like to leave now. You said I was free to go whenever I chose."

"That's right. But maybe you need to fully understand what's about to happen if you won't cooperate willingly."

Bondy's eyes narrowed with unabashed hatred. Undeterred, Jake leaned forward to get into his face.

"It would be good if you agreed to let me search your phone. It would also be very good if you could give me the specifics about any firearms registered to you. I can find out anyway, but if you make me go through extra hoops, that would not be good. And it would be excellent if you could write down for me where you were on July 17th. And I mean everywhere. Where you went. Who you talked to. What you did."

"You know what I think would be good?" Bondy said, sliding the file back toward Jake. "I think it would be good if you would just go to hell. I didn't kill those people. What I do in my private life is nobody's business but mine. End of story. I don't have to give you access to my private phone. I don't have to tell you jack or shit. Now I'm late. I have work to do."

Bondy stood. He wore an expression of disgust that made Jake briefly think he was about to spit in his face. He curled his fists out of reflex. But Bondy simply marched out of the interview room.

Less than an hour later, Jake had Landry briefed about how the interview went. Birdie had watched everything from the adjoining observation room.

"So that didn't go so well," Landry said.

"He's a moron," Jake said.

"What's next?" Landry asked.

"Warrants," Jake answered. "I need his phone yesterday. I'd bet my next paycheck he's going to spend the next hour trying to delete stuff from it. Which is only going to make his life worse."

"Step ahead of you," Birdie said. "I've already written everything out. I'll get Judge Cardwell to sign off on them. He gets off the bench in an hour. I'll be right outside his chambers waiting."

"Good."

"Jake?" Landry said. He knew she could sense something in his face.

"Sheriff, I'm sorry. But this has to be now. I gave Bondy the chance to do this the easy way. You heard it all. He's giving me no choice. I've got to serve that warrant immediately. As soon as Cardwell signs them. You know where he's headed."

Landry looked back down the hall in the direction Bondy had just stormed off.

"I can try to be discreet," Jake said.

"No," Landry said. "Screw that guy. You gave him his chance. If you need to waltz right into that commissioners' conference and serve him with his continental breakfast, so be it. He made his own bed. It's like you said. We've got two murder victims and you're not the one who put him in this position. He did it all by himself."

"All right," Jake said. "Then I guess we giddy up. You understand there's gonna be blowback."

"Yep," Landry said. "Let it rain."

TWENTY-FOUR

"Do you think he'll just come out?" Birdie asked.

"I friggin' hope so." Jake walked to the front desk in the lobby of the Blackhand Hills Resort and Convention Center. The only true luxury resort in Blackhand Hills so far, the resort was nestled in near Whisper Hollow with private access to some of the best walking trails in the region. This had caused no end of controversy with the locals who resented out-of-towners enjoying the natural wonder of the hollows and cave systems. The main hotel was fabricated to look like a rustic lodge with a giant fieldstone fireplace in the center of the lobby and rotunda. Behind it, a life-size diorama had been built featuring stuffed game and wildlife native to the region. The focal point was a record-breaking, fourteen-point white-tail buck overlooking the guests as they checked in.

Jake didn't have to ask the concierge for help. The sign in the lobby pointed toward the Buckeye Room. The county commissioners' convention was currently in session there.

"Sir!" A man in a three-piece suit hustled out from behind the desk as he saw Birdie in uniform and Jake with his badge clipped to his belt. "How can I help you?"

"I need to get in there," Jake said, pointing to the closed double doors of the Buckeye Room.

"It's a private event," the man said.

Jake put his hand on his hip, drawing further attention to the badge. "I'm here on police business."

The man looked helplessly toward the desk. Jake was done worrying about him. He gestured to Birdie and they opened the Buckeye Room doors. The speaker on stage was using slides featuring mountain climbers and blathering on about how to motivate teams.

"There," Birdie whispered. Willis Bondy was seated at a table near the front of the room along with the rest of Woodbridge County's commissioners. Uncle Rob sat two people away from him.

Jake steeled himself for the commotion he knew was coming but hoped to avoid. He walked up to Bondy and whispered in his ear.

"Mr. Bondy, I've got the search warrant I promised you. Let's just quietly walk out into the lobby."

Bondy turned purple. "I most certainly will not walk anywhere with you. I know my rights." He said it loud enough to draw the attention of the tables closest to them.

"Let's just step outside."

"Deputy Cashen, what's this about?" Rob got to his feet. The speaker paused.

"I have some business with Mr. Bondy," Jake said, keeping his tone low. "I'm sorry to disturb your event but this can't wait."

"Oh, I'm sure you're not sorry," Rob said.

"Do you see what goes on here?" Bondy shouted. "I have a room full of witnesses."

"Sir," Birdie said. "This doesn't have to be a scene."

"Apparently that's how he wants it. Mr. Bondy, I have a warrant to confiscate and search your cell phone. If you'll just relinquish it willingly ..."

"You've got a hell of a lot of nerve," Bondy said.

"I asked you to do this in my office two hours ago," Jake said through gritted teeth. "The only reason there's a scene is because you're insisting on it."

Jake took Bondy by the arm. "Are you arresting me?"

"Not yet," Jake said. "Now let's go outside."

Bondy put his arms up. "You can all see that I'm cooperating!"

"For Pete's sake," Birdie muttered. Bondy made a show of following Jake out into the lobby. When Rob Arden and two other commissioners tried to follow behind them, Jake shut the Buckeye Room doors in their faces.

Jake pulled out Bondy's copy of his warrant. He slapped it against Bondy's chest.

"Your phone," he said. "You'll need to hand it over. And this?" He took out the second warrant. "This gives me permission to search your house."

"I'll fight this," he said. "I'll have my lawyer file a motion this afternoon."

"Knock yourself out," Jake said. "In the meantime, that's a court order. You seem bound and determined to make all of this worse than it needs to be. Would you like to accompany us back to your house?"

"I will do no such thing. If you want to arrest me, put the cuffs on. Do it right here in front of witnesses."

A few of the conference attendees spilled out of the Buckeye Room, including Uncle Rob. None of them tried to intervene. They just stood slack-jawed watching the show.

"That ends my duty to you for the day," Jake said. Birdie held an evidence bag. Bondy dropped his phone into it. Then they left Willis Bondy and the rest of the state's county commissioners stunned in their wake.

J ake wasn't sure how to answer the text he got from Landry.

> How did it go?

Jake showed his screen to Birdie. She rolled her eyes. Jake texted back.

> He wanted the circus.

> Okay. Keep me posted. Are you heading to serve the warrant at his residence?

> Yes

> Fair warning. My office has already taken calls from local media. Someone's tipped them off that Bondy's a person of interest.

Jake swore under his breath. He showed the phone to Birdie again.

"I don't get it," she said. "We've got the guy dead to rights in terms of his um ... peccadilloes. Why is he acting like he's being persecuted or oppressed?"

"Don't know. Don't care. I'm just hoping he gave his wife a heads-up that we were on the way."

He checked his GPS app. Bondy's house was in the northern part of Arch Hill township. A twenty-minute drive from the convention center. Though Jake now had Bondy's phone, he could still do the decent thing and make a call. Though it would be the first decent thing the man had done all morning.

Twenty minutes later, Jake learned that Willis Bondy had in fact not told his wife, Addie, that Jake was coming. Or why.

"You can't come in here!" Addie Bondy stood in her front door with a salon cape wrapped around her shoulders. Her hair was festooned with foils. Her hairdresser trailed behind her.

"Addie, you need to get back under the dryer," she said. "You've got ten more minutes."

"Sorry to disturb you, ma'am," Jake said. "I was hoping your husband would let you know what's about to happen today."

"He most certainly did not!" Addie Bondy had just as much attitude as her husband. In her case, Jake felt bad. There was no good way to hear what he had to tell her. He handed her a copy of his search warrant.

"That's a court order," he explained. "I have permission to search the home and confiscate evidence."

"Evidence of what? Has my husband been charged with a crime?"

"Not yet," Jake said. "Are you going to let me in?"

Addie stepped back. Her hairdresser, a blonde girl in her mid-twenties, took her by the shoulders. Jake stepped over the threshold bringing Birdie right behind him.

"Addie, come on," the other girl said. "Let's at least get you rinsed. Can we do that? Can I take her to the sink?"

"By all means," Jake said.

Addie Bondy was in tears now. She went to the kitchen at the back of the house. Jake stood by for a moment while her friend quickly removed the foils, rinsed her head under the sink, and wrapped her with a towel.

"Mrs. Bondy," Jake said. "I need to know where your husband keeps his firearms."

"What?"

"His guns," Jake repeated.

"Th-they're in his study. In the safe."

"Do you have the combination?"

"Yes."

She led them into a room off the kitchen. Bondy had a large gun safe in one corner next to his desk. Mrs. Bondy opened the safe and stepped aside.

"Will you please tell me what this is all about? What's Will done?"

"Laptop and an iPad on the desk, Jake," Birdie said.

"Bag 'em," Jake said.

"I demand to know what this is all about?" Addie stomped her foot.

"Mrs. Bondy," Jake said. "I really wish your husband would have called you after I had a conversation with him this morning. I would have given him the chance to tell you all this himself. But if you'll read the warrant, I'll ..."

"No," she said. "You tell me. Right now. What is Willis accused of?"

Jake took a breath. "Your husband exchanged a series of texts with one of my murder victims that have made him a person of interest. He had ... um ... a liaison with an associate of my murder victims. All of that is what has given us probable cause to search this house and confiscate these items."

"Liaison?"

There was a sharp knock at the door. "Addie?"

Jake tensed. He recognized the voice as none other than Tim Brouchard. Former prosecutor. Current county defense lawyer most likely to become a pain in Jake's ass.

"Stay with her," Jake said to Birdie. He went to the front door.

"Jake," Tim said. "You should know I represent Willis Bondy ..."

"Of course you do," Jake said, stepping onto the porch. He produced another copy of his warrants and handed them to Brouchard. Brouchard quickly glanced at them, but Jake got the impression none of this was a surprise. So Bondy took the time to call his lawyer but didn't bother telling his poor wife what was going on.

"This isn't how I wanted this," Jake said. "Your client came to my office this morning. He was texting with my victim, Jaxon Waters. I have reason to believe Waters was blackmailing him with photos he had of Mr. Bondy in a compromising position with a prostitute under Jaxon Waters's employ."

"Yeah," Brouchard said, clearly already apprised of the damning situation.

"I asked your client to cooperate and hand over his phone. I asked him to quietly come out and talk to me. He refused all my requests. He wanted a scene. So, he's getting one."

No sooner were the words out of his mouth before a Channel Nine news van pulled up and parked in front of Bondy's house.

"Just great," Jake said. Brouchard looked over his shoulder and swore. Jake could see Bethany Roman in the passenger seat.

"I won't be making any comments to them," Jake said. "You are free to say whatever the hell you want."

"Jake, Bondy screwed up. He should have called me first. We could have handled this without all the drama."

"That would have been better," Jake said.

"He wants to cooperate now."

"I'll bet he does. Right now, I'm gonna finish serving my warrant. Are you going to try to impede me from doing that?" Brouchard's eyes flashed. Part of Jake hoped he'd say yes.

"No," Brouchard said. "Mr. Bondy wishes to cooperate fully. He knows he's got plenty to answer for, but he's got nothing to hide."

Behind them, he could hear Addie Bondy sobbing into her hairdresser's shoulder.

"He should try telling that to his wife," Jake muttered.

"I meant what I said," Brouchard said. "My client wishes to cooperate. He understands the seriousness of your investigation."

"Then you tell your client to answer my questions."

"We can arrange for that. At your convenience, of course."

"My conven—" Jake took a breath. "My convenience would have been this morning when I gave him the chance to avoid all of this."

"You know how to get a hold of me," Brouchard said. "I'll produce my client for an interview down at the station."

"Deputy Cashen!" Bethany Roman had gotten out of her vehicle. She hustled up the sidewalk. Her cameraman was already filming.

"Don't take another step," Jake shouted. "Not unless you want to walk into an obstruction charge, Ms. Roman. You're free to stand in the street."

"Is it true you've arrested Commissioner Bondy in connection to the Blackhand Creek murders?"

"No comment," Jake said. He turned his back on her. Tim Brouchard broadened his chest and got in between Bethany Roman and Willis Bondy's front door.

Jake turned his back on both of them. What should have been a routine search warrant was about to turn into a spectacle that would make statewide news.

TWENTY-FIVE

Two nights later, Cashen's Irish Pub had its official grand opening. Gemma was a nervous wreck and trying to cover. Grandpa Max wasn't helping matters. He was nervous too and coped by sitting at his copper top and shouting orders to Gemma and any of her servers that passed by. Jake got there an hour later than he was supposed to. The place was packed. Virgil, Bill, and Chuck took the same table as they had during the soft opening and gestured to Jake to come on over. He never got there. Gemma grabbed him by the shirtsleeve and pulled him into the kitchen.

"You have to do something about him. If he keeps this up, half of my wait staff is going to quit after tonight. He's been running them ragged. He accused my lead bartender of weak pours. He thinks he's John Taffer or something."

The kitchen door swung open and Jake could see Gramps flagging down one of the waitresses. She plastered a smile on her face, but it looked forced.

"I'll see what I can do. It's good though. You've got a line out the door."

"Will you keep an eye and an ear out? See what people are saying about their food and service and everything?"

Jake peered out the door again. "Gemma, all I see are people smiling and having a good time. Try to relax. Some hiccups are to be expected. It's opening night."

"I can't afford hiccups!"

Okay. He'd said the wrong thing. She was a powder keg of emotions.

"I'll do a walkabout," he said. Leaning in, he kissed his sister on the side of her head. "It's good, sis. Everything's going to be fine."

"You always say that," she muttered. "Because I'm always the one who runs around and makes sure it's fine."

He patted her arm and walked away. Behind them, one of the chefs swore up a blue streak. Jake was worried his sister might actually have an aneurysm before the night ended.

He made his way over to Grandpa Max just as he was about to chew out one of the busboys for having gum in his mouth. It was a fair point, but not one Max needed to make.

"Hey," Jake said, sliding into the chair next to him. "How about you just enjoy the night as a regular patron? You're driving Gemma off a cliff."

"She's lucky I'm paying attention," Max scoffed. "These kids are gonna rob her blind if we don't stay on 'em."

"She's gonna kick you out," Jake said. "Both of you just need to relax."

Ryan bussed the table next to them. He caught his uncle's eye and shook his head as if to say, "You're wasting your breath."

"Have a beer," Jake said to his grandfather.

"I need to stay sharp."

"Gramps," he said. "You're more on edge than Gemma is. It's no good. Do us both a favor and zip it."

Grandpa opened his mouth to argue, but something miraculously stopped him. Gemma had moved behind the bar. She was coiled tight as a rattlesnake. To anyone else she might look happy, smiling, joking with one of the patrons. But Jake knew better. So apparently did Grandpa Max. Even from this distance and with his lousy eyesight, Gemma's posture spoke volumes.

"This is her thing," Jake said. "Not yours. She wants you to enjoy things as a spectator. If she fails, she fails. It's on her. Not you."

Jake could swear he saw the glisten of a tear in the corner of Max's eye. Was it pride?

"She's doin' all right. Isn't she?" he asked.

Jake smiled. "She's doing great."

"I want this for her. That kid's had a tough road. No thanks to the no-good deadbeats she gravitates toward."

"She doesn't need 'em," Jake said. "She's got us. So, let's work on helping her tonight, okay? Not getting in her way." The old man nodded. He could be sweet in his own way and that's what this was.

Ryan came by and collected Grandpa's empties. "Good work, kid," Grandpa said. Ryan looked stunned. He turned to Jake. Jake made a downward gesture with his hand.

Don't make it a big deal.

One of the waitresses came by and took Jake's drink order. He asked for a draft beer and left it at that. Now that Grandpa was temporarily settled, he got up to do what he promised Gemma. He made his way around the restaurant, scanning for trouble.

He found none. It was just as he'd told her. Her customers were enjoying themselves, the food, and the drinks. Any delays or mishaps seemed quickly rectified and everyone stayed in good spirits. Half the town turned out. Jake said hello to Lieutenant Beverly's wife and neighbor at one end of the bar. Beverly's daughter, Carly, was one of the servers tonight and doing a good job of it. A group of deputies had taken over the pool room in the back. It was there he ran into Birdie and a guy he'd never seen before. Big. Muscular. Handsome in that gym rat sort of way. Birdie waved. She motioned for him to come join her.

"Jake," she said. "This is Keith Ingram."

Jake extended his hand. Ingram grabbed it in a forceful shake and offered to buy Jake another beer.

"Erica's been telling me all about you," Keith said.

"I apologize in advance," Jake said.

"Naw, naw. Only good stuff. She's having a blast working on this case with you. Isn't that right?"

Erica looked a little sheepish as she sipped her beer. "Blast isn't the word I'd use."

"Oh no," Keith said. "I didn't mean anything bad by that. Poor choice of words, man. I didn't mean to seem insensitive."

"It's fine," Jake said. "I know what you meant."

"Good. Good. I really respect what you do, man. All of you. I don't think I could do it. You know. Seeing the worst of everybody all the time."

"So what do you do?" Jake asked. Birdie gave him a wide-eyed stare.

"I'm into exercise science," Keith said. "A personal trainer. I started out working for one of the chain gyms, but now I take private clients exclusively. I could give you a discount if you're looking for something. I always do it for cops and the military. Frontline workers."

"That's good of you," Jake said. "We have a gym at the sheriff's department. That's really all I have time for."

It was a lie. Jake primarily worked out at the high school facilities with the wrestling team he helped coach.

"Oh sure, sure," Keith said. "That's great that they have that for you guys. I mean, it's so important for you to be able to blow off steam in a healthy way in your line of work."

Jake tipped his beer mug, hoping that would put an end to the topic of his workout regimen.

"I'll be right back," Birdie said. "Ladies' room." She gave Keith a peck on the cheek and shot Jake a wink.

Jake took a generous swig of his beer, wishing for something stronger. Making small talk with Keith the personal trainer wasn't high on his list of goals tonight.

"So how long have you known Erica?" Keith asked.

"Forever," Jake answered, needing to shout over the growing crowd. "Since she was in diapers, practically."

"Yeah. I guess maybe she told me something like that. You knew her brother?"

"Yes," Jake said, his tone coming out a bit edgier than warranted. "Ben was my best friend. He was like a brother to me."

Keith nodded. "Awful what happened to him? Erica doesn't like to talk about it much. But I know it eats at her."

"How long have *you* known her?" Jake asked.

"A couple of months. She doesn't like to work out at the sheriff's department. She was coming in to Fitness World where I've got a couple of clients. It looked like she could maybe use some pointers with her routine so I struck up a conversation."

Jake nearly spit out his beer. Birdie was a former Army MP. Before that, she'd been an All-State softball player. He highly doubted she needed any pointers on how to do squats or whatever the hell it was from anyone.

"We just really hit it off," Keith continued. "She's funny as hell. She's led an interesting life. She's just so easy to be around."

"You know she's basically a single mom now, right?"

"Oh. You mean Trav? Great kid. Yeah. We get along great."

Travis was currently in the other corner of the bar bussing tables with Ryan.

"Well," Jake said. "It's like I was saying. Ben Wayne was like a brother to me. Bird ... Erica might as well be my little sister. Do you get what I'm saying?"

"You're close. You go way back, yeah. I'd love to hear some stories about how Erica was as a little kid. I bet she was hell on wheels."

"Ben's not here to look out for her," Jake said. "But I am."

He gave Keith a pointed stare. He could feel Ben's presence in a weird way. He missed him tonight. The two of them would have undoubtedly sat in a corner comparing notes about Birdie's taste in men.

"Are you guys serious?" Jake asked.

Keith narrowed his eyes at Jake. "Why are you asking me that?"

"I'm just trying to make conversation. Erica's ... she ... she matters, okay? So, I'm asking you, are you serious?"

Keith leaned forward. "Are you serious?"

"Yes."

"Yeah. I don't know what you want me to say."

"Erica's got a lot of people looking out for her," Jake said. "You understand me, right? Those four deputies playing pool over there? Consider them her brothers too."

"You don't like me much, do you?" Keith said. "I'm just trying to be nice, man."

"I get that. But it's like I said. We look out for Erica around here."

"You think I don't."

"I don't know you."

"Maybe you should try to get to know me. You're friends with Erica. She's a great girl. She's more than just some chick I'm boning, okay? I actually give a shit about her."

Jake tensed. "That's how you talk about her? You're boning her?"

"That's none of your business, man."

"You just brought it up. Not me."

"I was trying to make a point. I'm saying she's *not* just some chick I'm boning. I mean, it started out that way. But now ..."

"You maybe ought to quit while you're ahead," Jake said. "I'd say I'm getting tired of hearing the words chick and boning in the same sentence as Erica."

"Man ... you need to relax. You know how it is."

"I do? How is it, Keith? Explain it to me. Maybe talk slow so I understand."

"You're a real asshole, you know that?"

"Everything going okay over here?" Birdie asked. She could clearly sense tension between Jake and Keith. She slid into her chair next to Keith and put an arm on his shoulder.

"Yeah," Keith said, giving Jake an icy stare as he lifted his beer bottle and took a drink. "It's all good."

"Any chance this seat's empty?" Jake froze. The voice behind belonged to Bethany Roman. She didn't wait for Jake's answer before plopping down on the seat beside him. She reached across the table and introduced herself to Keith, shaking his hand.

"Hi again, Erica," she said. "This is a fantastic turnout. You must be so proud of your sister."

"I am," Jake said, looking around to see if he could get the attention of one of the servers. He could use another beer right about now.

"You've been avoiding my calls again," Bethany said.

"Now's not really the time or the place for this," Jake said.

"You have to talk to me sooner or later."

"Do you guys want some privacy?" Keith asked. He put a protective arm around Birdie and kissed her neck. Birdie blushed.

"No!" Jake said. "Stay right where you are. Bethany won't be staying."

"You don't have to be rude, Jake. We're old friends, aren't we? Some people say we're more than friends." Bethany leaned in and kissed Jake's neck the same way Keith had done to Birdie. Jake went rigid. He took Bethany's hand off his knee.

"Ah," Keith said, nodding. "I see how it is." He whispered something in Birdie's ear. She gave him a tight-lipped smile.

"You made a heck of a spectacle at the county commissioners' convention the other day. The whole town's buzzing. Are you planning on arresting Willis Bondy?"

"Bethany, I meant what I said and I'm trying really hard to be polite. I'm not going to comment on work. I'm here at my sister's grand opening, trying to enjoy myself. That's all."

"So am I. It's a public place. You can't avoid me forever."

"I can avoid you tonight," he muttered.

She wasn't taking no for an answer. Instead, Bethany draped her arm around Jake. He froze.

"Are you two a thing?" Keith asked.

"She's just leaving," Jake said.

Bethany ran her fingers over Jake's ear. He felt it turning red. The woman was trying to get a rise out of him. He wouldn't take the bait.

"I've missed you, Jake," she said.

"Maybe you better just move along," Birdie said.

"Oh, *I* see how it is." Bethany laughed. Jake could smell the alcohol on her breath. He decided to give her the benefit of the doubt that that's why she was acting as bold as she was.

"Have it your way," she said. "But you will have to talk to me about this case sooner or later."

"You know where you can get your information," Jake said. Then Bethany leaned in again and kissed his cheek. Jake gripped his beer mug so hard he hoped it would shatter.

She hopped out of her chair and disappeared into the crowd.

"You okay man?" Keith asked. "That was weird."

"All good," Jake said, taking another drink.

"Can I get you another round!" The voice behind him came out pointed and harsh. A chill went up Jake's spine as he slowly turned. Nora Corley stood there holding a drink tray. She glared at Jake so hard he got ready to duck in case she lobbed the tray right at him.

"Uh ... we're fine," Birdie said. "Anybody need any refills?"

Jake waved a hand over his beer mug.

"I'll have another Heineken," Keith answered. Jake wanted to punch him for doing anything that would bring Nora back to the table.

"You sure you're good, Jake?" Nora hissed.

"Hey, Nora," he said. "How have you been?"

"Peachy, asshole. Just peachy."

She picked up Keith's empty and spun on her heel away from them.

"What in the fresh hell was that all about?" Birdie asked.

"It was …" Jake started. Then he didn't know how to finish. He realized there was no good answer to that question.

"I think I'm gonna call it a night," he said. "Gemma seems to have everything well in hand here."

"You might wanna try slipping out the back," Birdie whispered.

She was joking. But the idea had merit. Jake looked behind him. Nora was standing between him and the main exit. Bethany had made her way over to the bar.

The service door near the alley and dumpster was the cleanest getaway he was likely to make tonight.

He didn't hesitate to take it.

TWENTY-SIX

The next morning, Jake sensed something was wrong. Birdie got to the office before him. She hunched over the table, working on a mass of spreadsheets generated from the burner phone forensics. She'd been working on cross-referencing all numbers and locations. It was a pile of work and the kind of mind-numbing detail that drove Jake insane. Birdie had been a godsend with it.

But today, she barely acknowledged him as he walked into the office. He got one-word answers and grunts if he tried to ask questions or make small talk.

At one point, Darcy stopped by to drop off some messages that had been left for him. She, too, seemed to sense the friction. As she started to leave, she shot Jake a look that seemed to say "What did you do?" Jake shrugged.

After a good hour, he'd had enough.

"Birdie," he said. "Is something wrong?"

She straightened. She gave a little smirk but otherwise ignored him.

"Birdie," he said. "What gives? You've seemed pissed at me all morning. If you are, it's not like you to keep your mouth shut about it."

She whirled on him. "Yes, Detective. I'm pissed at you."

"Okay. Why?"

"Why? You really need to ask me why?"

"Yes. I really need to ask you."

"Jake, you were an asshole last night. I can't believe you don't know that."

"What are you talking about?"

She put the spreadsheets down. "You managed to make Keith feel like dirt. Like a loser. And you did it in about fifteen minutes so I can at least give you credit for having talent."

"I don't know what you're talking about," he said.

"Yes, you do. Jake, you had no right to give my boyfriend the third degree like you're some psycho dad from the fifties."

"I did not act like some psycho dad."

"So you didn't ask him whether he's serious about me? Did *you* seriously ask him what his intentions are?"

"I didn't say it like that."

"You didn't low-key threaten him and tell him you'd send a roomful of deputies after him?"

Jake opened his mouth to answer, then shut it. His opinion of Keith just slid down a few notches. Turns out he was a sniveling snitch on top of everything else.

"He's your boyfriend now?"

"Jake!"

"Look, you seem to think I owe you an apology. I don't agree. I'm your friend. You're like my sister so …"

"No!" she shouted. "I am not your sister. I do not need you to act like my brother. If Ben were here …"

"Ben's not here. That's the point. I am."

"I am a grown-ass woman, Jake. I've been on my own since I was eighteen years old. I've lived all over the world. Fought in two damn wars. I don't need you giving every guy I date a hard time like that. It's insulting."

"Well, I didn't mean to insult you."

"And you still don't think you did anything wrong."

"Well," Jake started. "No."

"That is exactly the problem. You're not my brother. My friend, yes. My colleague, definitely. So, do me a favor and for right now? Let's just stick to that, okay. Just … keep your mouth shut when it comes to my personal life."

"I didn't …"

"Jake?" Darcy was back at the door. Somehow, her timing seemed deliberate. Her tone was certainly insistent.

"What is it, Darcy?"

"You have a visitor. Tim Brouchard just showed up with his client. Willis Bondy. Brouchard told me to come tell you that Bondy is willing to cooperate. I've set them up in the interview room. Brouchard says he'll only talk to you."

Darcy shot a sheepish look at Birdie. Birdie waved it off. "By all means," she said. "I've got my hands full here."

Darcy mouthed a "sorry" to Jake. He doubted she was.

He grabbed his suit jacket off the chair. "Well, you could knock me over with a feather," he said.

He followed Darcy out into the hall. She shut his office door behind them.

"Whatever you did," she said. "I'm telling you. Tell that woman you're sorry."

"I didn't do anything," Jake said.

"Right," she said. "Say it anyway. Trust me. You'll thank me later."

Jake grumbled instead of answering. As they walked toward the interview room, he took some consolation in the prospect of taking his frustrations out on Tim Brouchard and whatever bullshit he'd shown up to peddle today.

There was no bullshit. Shocking as it was, Brouchard was cordial, downright polite as Jake walked into the interview room. Bondy was a mess. Sweating profusely, great dark stains had soaked through the armpits of his blue dress shirt. He dabbed at his glistening forehead with a handkerchief.

"Good morning, Jake," Brouchard said. "Sorry to drop by like this. But I was certain you'd want to hear everything my client had to say as soon as possible."

"I'm listening," Jake said.

"First of all," Brouchard said. "Mr. Bondy is deeply sorry for not coming to you immediately after he became aware of the identities of the victims out at Blackhand Creek. I can only say that the distress of this perhaps impaired his better judgment a bit."

"A bit," Jake said.

"I didn't kill those people," Bondy blurted. "You have to know that. I had nothing to do with whatever happened out there. Nothing. My only failings were moral ones. And the only victim to that failing is my wife. This should have been nobody else's business."

"Right," Jake said.

Brouchard reached into his briefcase and produced a thin stack of papers. He slid them across the table to Jake.

"My client's alibi you'll find is ironclad. For the past two weeks, he's had a suite at the Blackhand Hills Resort. The first week, he entertained various county commissioners from different parts of the state. Those who arrived ahead of the conference to vacation here with their families. For the past week, as you know, he's been involved in the conference itself."

"What is this?" Jake asked. Then he glanced at the paperwork. He'd been handed copies of credit card statements and receipts. Most were associated with the Lodge itself. A bar tab. Four different meals. Confirmation of a tee time at the resort's golf course.

"On the evening of July 17th, Mr. Bondy entertained four commissioners from Cuyahoga County. They had dinner at the Maple Restaurant inside the resort. Then drinks at the bar after. You'll see receipts backing that up. I've spoken to security at the hotel. They will provide footage from their cameras showing Mr. Bondy returning to his room directly from the bar at one a.m., the night of the murders. Then he emerged from his room at eight the next morning. His wife will confirm she was with him the entire time. Then Mr. Bondy had breakfast and made his eleven fifteen tee time. He was on the course as your bodies were discovered. The gentlemen he dined and golfed with are also willing to provide affidavits confirming they were with him."

"Okay," Jake said. "But let's not pretend your client has clean hands in this."

"I'm not a murderer!" Bondy shrieked.

"What you are, is a material witness," Jake said. "You had dealings with Jaxon Waters you failed to disclose. At a minimum, you could face obstruction of justice charges."

"I most certainly did not obstruct any justice," Bondy said. "I've broken no laws."

"You sure about that?" Jake said. "Look. I'm out of patience with you, Bondy. You know what's going on. Drop the act. The way I see it, you've got one chance to get yourself out of deeper trouble. I think your lawyer knows that too. That's why he brought you here. And I'd bet money he told you to answer my questions. All of them."

Bondy cast a desperate look at Tim Brouchard. Brouchard patted him on the back. "We're here to cooperate," Tim said. "Mr. Bondy understands that now."

"I want to know what your dealings with Jaxon Waters were. All of them. How you met. Where you met. What you did, said. Every detail. Names. Dates. Conversations. Start from the beginning."

Jake grabbed a pad of paper from the end of the table and a pen from his pocket. He put both of them in front of Bondy.

Brouchard nodded at Bondy. Bondy picked up the pen and slowly wrote down four names. Jake could read upside down. He recognized all four names. One, Alan Grimes, was a lawyer in Marvell. He was currently running for Probate Court Judge. Another name was one of the county commissioners there. Pete Gerwick. The third name, Ned Blackmun, sounded familiar to Jake but he couldn't place it. The final name, Andy Zielinski, was a prosecuting attorney in Cuyahoga County.

"I was looking for companionship," Bondy started. "That's all. I'm not proud of this. But Addie and I were struggling a bit. I did something I shouldn't. I confided in someone I thought was a friend. Alan Grimes."

"Go on," Jake said.

"Alan suggested I try this app he uses. MOCA. Again, I was just looking for someone to talk to. A woman. I realize now that even considering something like that is an emotional affair. But ... I met someone. Connected with her. She called herself Pearl. We talked for a while. Private messaged on the app. This went on for a week or two. Then we arranged to meet. Pearl suggested the time and place. This was all consensual."

"All right," Jake said. "Where did you meet?"

"At the cabin out at Blackhand Creek. We had a date there. You can understand it was important that Pearl be discreet. I didn't want people getting the wrong impression, you see."

"Sure."

"Well, I met her out there. More than two months ago. I believe it was June 20th or so. We had dinner. We talked. We had a few drinks. She was ... easy to talk to. We really hit it off, I thought. Anyway, one thing just naturally started to lead to another. And we ended up ... we ... had carnal relations."

"You had sex with her," Jake said.

"We had sex. But I'm telling you, it was consensual. And I'd been drinking. If I hadn't been, it might not have gotten to that point."

"Right," Jake said.

"You're judging me," Bondy said. "Don't think I can't read your tone."

"I think you need to concern yourself less with my tone and more with telling me everything that happened."

"That was it. The next morning, I got up to leave. At that point, Pearl insisted that I pay her. We never discussed money before that."

"You thought you'd just charmed her with your personality," Jake said.

"Detective," Brouchard said. "I'm not sure if that's productive."

"I made a mistake," Bondy said. "I didn't know she was a ... call girl. I told her I would not condone that. And I left."

"You stiffed her," Jake said.

"I was not going to pay her for sex. Absolutely not. And I thought that would be the end of it. But a day later, I started getting calls and texts from a man I later learned was Jaxon Waters. He insisted I pay him the money for Pearl. Only now he wanted five thousand dollars. I refused."

"How'd that go?"

"He began to threaten me. He sent me pictures. Pearl had apparently recorded our ... dalliance without my consent. Mr. Waters told me if I didn't give him five grand, he was going to send those to my wife. Post them on the internet and ruin me. So ... I met with him."

"Where? When?"

"The morning of July 16th."

"The day before he was murdered?"

"I had nothing to do with that. But yes. He asked me to come back to the cabin, so I did. I never got out of my car. He came to the window. I gave him cash. He gave me a flash drive and swore he'd kept no copies of the video. I had to just pray he was telling the truth. I realize how foolish I was. But that man was alive when I left."

"Was he alone?"

"I only spoke with him briefly in the driveway of the cabin. I think there was a woman inside. I could see her from the window. I know it wasn't Pearl. This woman was also a brunette. I couldn't give you a positive ID on who she was though."

"Okay," Jake said. "These names. You've told me how Alan Grimes fits in. What about these other three?"

"It is my belief that they have all … um … partaken of the services of Jaxon Waters's … er … employees."

"They've paid for sex from these girls. From Pearl? From the same app?"

"Yes. I regret that I referred Commissioner Gerwick to it. This was before my physical encounter with Pearl."

"Naturally."

"You don't believe me?"

"No," Jake said. "I think you're an idiot, but you're not stupid, you know? You knew what you were looking for on MOCA. Your boys here knew what they were looking for."

"I don't know what they were looking for. I only know I was looking for companionship. And it got out of hand."

"Right now, I don't give a rat's ass what you want to tell yourself. You want to call this cooperation? Then stop lying to me."

"Detective," Brouchard interjected. "Does it matter at this point? You have Mr. Bondy's story. He's given you names. Potential witnesses. It's up to you to investigate them further if you see fit. You have Mr. Bondy's cell phone. I'm sure your analysts will be able to confirm the timeline he's laid out for you along with the places he's identified. For now, I don't see that there's anything more we can add. We need to end this interview."

"Fine," Jake said. "But here's how this is going to go. You don't leave the county. You remain available to me. I'm going to have more questions. Bet on it."

"Of course," Brouchard said. "If you'll indulge us. Let Mr. Bondy have a few minutes to collect himself. Jake, why don't you and I step outside?"

Bondy started to cry in earnest. Jake couldn't stand the sight of him anymore. He got up and followed Bondy out into the hall.

"He's a mess," Brouchard said. "But what he's told you is the truth. I hope it helps."

"I meant what I said. He stays local. He stays available. I have to verify your timeline, Tim."

"Of course. But I have a favor to ask you. Mr. Bondy will be making a statement to the press later resigning his commissionership. I would appreciate it if your office could also release a statement indicating that Willis Bondy is not a person of interest with regard to the killings out at Blackhand Creek. That he's not being charged with anything."

"That's not my call," Jake said. "You'd have to talk to your former buddies at the prosecutor's office for that."

Brouchard smiled. "I already have."

Of course he had. Jake knew Brouchard was a good enough lawyer not to have made this trip to his office without having his ducks in a row.

"Fine," Jake said. "But I don't give statements to the press. I'll give Landry a heads-up though."

"That's all I ask," Brouchard said. They weren't in a handshaking place. Brouchard knew it.

Birdie walked out of the observation room next door. She'd clearly witnessed his entire interview with Bondy. Brouchard stiffened. He and Birdie had had a few run-ins in the past. Brouchard usually wound up on the sharp end of those.

"I'll just collect my client," Brouchard said, excusing himself.

Jake handed Birdie the notepad with Bondy's four names on it. She looked at it, recognizing the ones Jake had.

"Well," she said. "This just got a bit messier."

"Just a little," Jake said. "Their contact numbers are gonna be in Bondy's phone. Can you start trying to check 'em against what we've got from the burners?"

"On it," she said. As Jake was about to thank her, he got a text of his own. He pulled his phone out. Birdie managed to see the caller ID. She gave him a sharp look, then went back down the hall.

It was Kyra Bardo.

We have a mutual acquaintance I think you'll want to speak with. Four o'clock tomorrow after your shift. Truck stop off County Road 14. The Roundtable. Do you know it?

Yeah.

Be there. Dusty's a redhead.

Jake pocketed his phone. In the span of an hour, he'd just gotten five new murder suspects. He realized each one of them could cause a bomb to detonate right in the middle of Blackhand Hills.

TWENTY-SEVEN

The Roundtable Diner's claim to fame was a giant, thirty-foot-high statue of a medieval knight visible for about a mile toward exit 20 off County Road 14. The statue had fallen into a state of disrepair. Its left hand had cracked off along with the tip of his sword.

Jake parked right out front and walked inside.

Dusty Riff was easy to spot. He leaned over the counter, chatting up one of the waitresses. She gave him a polite smile but looked uncomfortable. She recoiled as Riff tried to reach for her arm.

"Dusty Riff?" Jake said, letting his voice boom. Riff smacked his gum. He stood up, giving the poor waitress a chance to make a clean getaway back into the kitchen.

Jake flashed his badge. There were only two other tables that filled in the whole place.

"Why don't we have a seat back there?" Jake said. He spotted an empty booth way in the back. They could talk without being overheard.

Jake didn't wait for Riff to answer. He made his way to the booth and took the seat facing the doorway. Riff took his time, then slid onto the opposite bench.

"Thank you for agreeing to meet with me," Jake said, though he knew Riff didn't have much of a choice. Whether it was Kyra, her father, or maybe even Uncle Rex ... he knew Riff had been given the order to talk to him. Whether he would cooperate was another matter.

Jake put his cell phone on the table. When a different waitress came to take their order, Jake just ordered a coffee. Riff ordered a Western Omelet and a large orange juice.

"I'll cut to it," Jake said. "I won't pretend you don't know what I'm here about. You understand I'm investigating a double homicide out at Blackhand Creek."

"Which has zero to do with me."

Jake opened his phone and pulled up Morgan Prater's profile picture on MOCA. He showed it to Riff.

"This girl," Jake said. "Tell me about your encounter with her."

Riff leaned in and squinted as he looked at the picture. "She looks sorta familiar. Is she dead too?"

"No. She's not dead. I know you met with her. Tell me your side of what happened."

"What's she saying?"

"Never mind what she's saying. I'm asking what you're saying. And that's the third time I've asked."

Riff shook his head. "She's a whore. You can't trust a damn word she said."

"Dusty, you're not here because you wanna be. You're here because the people you work for know it's in their best interests that you talk to me. And it's in your best interests if you tell me the truth. Now, I don't give a rat's ass if you paid this girl for sex. I'm not looking to give you a hard time about that. But you met with her. I have a pretty good idea when and where. Here's your chance to get your side out."

"She's. A. Whore!" Riff said. "Which means she's also a liar."

"Fine. What happened when you met with her?"

"Look, this girl? Bad news. I caught wind of the fact that there was some funny business going on out in those cabins. So, I decided to go out there and see for myself. What I found was as bad as I'd been hearing."

"Which was?"

"You may not want to believe this, but you and me? On this? We're on the same side."

"Oh yeah? What side is that, Dusty?"

Dusty leaned in and whispered. "This guy was out there advertising. Using MOCA to lure guys up there. Pimping his whores out in our backyard. We can't have that. You give them an inch they're gonna take a mile. So yeah. I met with her. We had a little fun. There's nothing wrong with that."

"Sure. How are we on the same side again?"

Riff sat back. "We don't want these girls being trafficked up that hill any more than you do. It's bad news. Word starts getting out. Draws the wrong kind of people into Blackhand Hills. Like when the cartel tried to move in. We shut that shit down."

"*We* did?"

Riff waved Jake off. "I did you a favor. I made sure that girl knew to tell her boss we weren't gonna stand for their ... encroachment into our territory."

"How'd you do that?"

"I told her who I was. But listen... this was me being freelance."

"You want me to believe you were acting all by yourself? Taking real initiative to try and run the likes of Jaxon Waters right out of town?"

"Damn straight. I told you. We're on the same side with this. We both know damn well the kind of bad element that kind of operation attracts. We can't have it. No way. Zero tolerance. And that's what I told her. Pearl, she called herself. Nice girl. Not the brightest knife in the shed."

Riff tapped his temple, impressed with his own intellect.

"That's it?"

"That's it," Riff said. "We had a little fun. You said you're not looking to jam me up about that. So can I level with you? Fine. Yeah. We partied up there. But I made sure she understood what to tell her boss when I left. That if he tried moving his operations here on a permanent basis, that wasn't gonna work out for him."

"You threatened her?"

"No, man. No threats. Just delivered a message."

"Did you use your fists to do that, Dusty?"

"What? Is that what she's saying? Nah. No way, man. I don't hit girls. Alls I did was tell her to tell her boss that he'd have to answer to the Hilltop Boys. Told her to say that specific thing to him. That was the end of it."

Jake picked up his phone. He scrolled to the picture he'd taken of Morgan with the bruising on her face. He turned the screen so Riff could see it.

"Was this part of your message?"

Riff squinted again. He reared back. "Nope. I didn't do that. Whoever thumped that girl, it wasn't me. She's in a dangerous line of work. It could have been anybody."

"Dusty, I need to know where you were from July 17th through the 18th."

"Like an alibi?"

"Yeah. Like that."

"Gone. Way gone. I got family near Fort Myers. I was down there the whole week for a reunion."

"Can you prove that?"

Riff took out his own phone. He fiddled with the screen for a moment then turned it so Jake could see. He'd pulled up the Delta Airlines app.

"My plane tickets," he said. "See that? Flew out on July 14th. Didn't get back until the 21st. I wasn't here, man. I told you. I partied with that girl, Pearl, up at the cabins. But it was way before any of this. Maybe a week at least. I never met her old man. Never heard of that guy you found shot up there. Didn't even know his name until it showed up in the news. Your shootings had nothing to do with me."

"You're telling me you threatened Pearl? Or told her to deliver a threat on behalf of the Hilltop Boys."

"No. That's not what I said. I'm telling you. I was flying solo. Just trying to check out what was going on up there. I heard rumors."

"What kind of rumors?"

"Just that some asshole was running whores up there. So like I told you. I went to check it out. See what was what. That's all. Just me. And there was nothing wrong with that girl when I last saw her. So if she's telling you something different, she's lying. Straight up."

"And *you* wouldn't lie to me."

"I've got no reason to. I wasn't even in town when those people got shot. I just proved that. I'm doing the right thing here."

"Good Samaritan," Jake muttered.

"Look, Kyra told me to cooperate. To give you whatever you needed. You've met that chick, right?"

"I have."

"Yeah, well. She's got a set of brass balls on her. Bigger than her old man's, that's for sure. I know better than to piss her off. The Bardos have been good to me. They gave me a job when I got outta jail. Took a chance on me cuz we're cousins. I drive a loader out at the quarry. It's hard work. Steady pay. That's all. You can run my record. I've stayed out of trouble. All the stupid crap I've done I did when I was young and dumb. No more. This town means something to the Bardos. Having that kind of trash moving into Blackhand Hills? That's no good for anybody. Definitely not for you. So yeah. I took it upon myself to tell that girl to tell her boss they should clear out. Apparently, he pissed somebody off way bigger and way worse than me. Bad enough to get a bullet in his head for it. But you got my alibi. And you got the truth from me. That's all I got to say."

The waitress delivered Riff's omelet. He wasted no time digging into it. Jake put a twenty on the table.

"Make sure she gets the change," Jake said, gesturing to the waitress. "Enjoy your breakfast, Dusty."

"Yeah," he said, his mouth full. He sprayed small bits of egg onto his chin. "You're welcome, by the way."

Jake got to his feet. Dusty Riff was lying about everything except one of the most important things. He was nowhere near Blackhand Creek when Jax and Joey Waters were killed. But he'd roughed Morgan Prater up. Tried to poach her from Jax. And there's no way he'd done any of that all on his own.

Which meant Kyra Bardo was making moves that could cause trouble for Jake down the road. He just hoped the heat from the Waters' murder would force her to rethink her plans to expand the Hilltop Boys ventures into prostitution.

Jake slid behind the wheel. Three texts came in while he talked to Dusty. Meg wanted a status update. And she wanted Jake back at the office as fast as he could get there. The final text was from Dale Halsey. It read simply, Call me when you can.

Jake punched in his contact and called him back. He answered on the third ring.

"Mr. Halsey?" Jake said. "This is Jake Cashen."

"Oh, Jake. Thanks for calling me back. I didn't want to bother you."

"It's okay. How's Ray DeSilva?"

Jake braced himself for the answer. "Doing better," Halsey said. "He's been released from the hospital. I've got him staying with me, actually. We're all keeping an eye on him. He's coming around. We're gonna go to a ballgame tomorrow. He seems to be looking forward to it."

"That's great news. So what was it you wanted to talk to me about?"

"Oh. Yeah. You asked for help finding Morgan Prater's family. I was able to get a hold of her sister, Mallory. Delivered the message she sent. It was a real relief to her, as you can imagine. Turns out she hasn't heard from her in almost five years. She said she called the number on that note, but it was out of service. She was hoping you could maybe put her in touch with her. Do you think she might be willing to see Mallory?"

Jake pulled out of the parking lot of the Roundtable Diner and hit the on ramp going south.

"I can try," Jake said. "I've asked her to stay available. I'll pass along the information. But you might want to tell her sister not to get her hopes up. She could change her mind about wanting to see her."

"Believe me, I know how this goes. I told Mallory the same thing. The thing about Morgan ... about a lot of these girls. There was some abuse from her father. It's why she ran away. Sometimes ... well ... there's a lot of blame to go around, you know?"

"I know," Jake said. "So I'll leave it up to Morgan. She's got to feel safe reaching out. Do you have contact info for her sister you could send me? Let's start there. Put the ball in Morgan's court if she wants to get in touch."

"Sure thing. That's what I was hoping you'd say."

"Thanks, Mr. Halsey," Jake said. "It's a good thing you're doing. Both for Ray DeSilva and for Morgan's sister."

Halsey grew silent for a moment. Jake thought the call dropped. Then Halsey took a great breath and let it out.

"It's just ... it's what I would want if my Lena were out there somewhere. You know?"

"I understand," Jake said. He wished he could do more for the man. And he wished he could do more for DeSilva and Morgan Prater, too.

TWENTY-EIGHT

S he was pacing. That was never a good sign Right after he hung up with her, Gemma called to ask him to come to the bar to pick up Grandpa and Ryan. He got the impression Gramps was driving her nuts again.

"Do we have a new problem?" Meg asked as he walked in and took a seat in front of her desk.

"With Riff? I don't think so. He's gonna alibi out. He didn't kill the Waters couple, but he lied about everything else. I can't prove it, but I think Kyra Bardo is one hundred percent trying to branch out into running prostitutes. Riff claims he hooked up with one of Waters's girls to send a message to him. That Blackhand Hills is Bardo territory. The girl said he tried to poach her. I believe her. She doesn't have a good reason to lie."

"Terrific. I swear sometimes I think my life would be easier if Rex Bardo were released from prison. I can't believe he'd sanction human trafficking in his backyard."

"I don't think so either. But unless the Court of Appeals loses its backbone, he's in there for life. That's a hard thing for a man to process. So either Kyra's got more stones than I realized and isn't afraid of Uncle Rex, or Uncle Rex is deliberately looking the other way. For now, it's not our immediate problem. The Waters' murder has put heat on the situation Kyra Bardo doesn't need. She's smart. She'll cool her heels on this for a while."

"Small blessings," Meg said. "What about Bondy's list?"

"Birdie's running down alibis for the men Bondy identified. It's gonna get sticky. We can keep things under wraps for a while, but word's gonna get out."

"Even if what happened out at that creek was a one-off, people are going to start thinking Blackhand Hills is corrupt. God. This plays right into Tim Brouchard and Ed Zender's hands. They're gonna lay this at my feet come November."

Jake didn't have a good answer for her on that.

"Sorry," Meg said. "I know the optics aren't your problem. Whatever it is, I'll just deal with it. You *will* find out who did this."

"I'll try to get 'er done before people start going to the polls."

She stopped pacing and put a hand on her head like it would pop off. "You really think it'll take that long to clear this one?"

He'd meant his comment as half a joke. He regretted it now. She was strung tight enough as it was.

"No," he said honestly. "I don't think it'll take that long. But right now, I don't have a solid lead. Jaxon Waters probably had a dozen people he pissed off enough to want him dead. I can't find a single person willing to come forward for him. I think Joey was the only person on this planet who cared to spend time with the guy. It's making it impossible to build a background on him. He's got no ties to anyone or anything. He was a two-bit pimp and as far as I can tell, he was freelance. I'm not finding a bigger fish here."

"Keep casting," Landry said. Her cell phone buzzed on the desk. She picked it up and frowned. "I gotta cut this short. Parent/teacher conference."

"Anything bad? It's summer break?"

"No. Just honors classes crap. They want more parental involvement with the junior class."

"She's doing okay," Jake said. "Paige. She's a good kid."

Meg smiled. "I know she is. She's just gonna drive me to drink and turn my hair pure white before I'm sixty."

Jake's phone buzzed next. Gemma again. Her ringtone was Wagner's "Ride of the Valkyries." Everyone in the department knew it.

"Sounds like you've got your own family drama."

Jake let it go to voicemail. A moment later, Gemma texted.

"She wants me to take Grandpa Max off her hands. He's been hanging out at the bar all the time. Which is what Gemma wanted."

"She didn't really think that through, did she?" Meg smiled.

"Not at all."

"Get out of here. Keep me posted."

Jake gave her a salute and left her office.

J ake made it to the pub just after six. Gemma didn't officially open until six thirty during the week, which meant Gramps was probably making a nuisance of himself with the staff again.

He found Ryan and Travis picking up trash in the parking lot.

"What kind of mood is she in?" Jake asked. Ryan shrugged. "She's just amped up like she's been for the last two months. The old man likes to get a rise out of her. I wish she could see that's what he's trying to do."

Jake smiled. "It's been like that since we were kids. She falls for it every time."

"Well, good thing you're here. You mind taking me out to Maudeville? Ashley Polhemus's mom is getting all new furniture. She's got a couch she wants to give me."

"You bet," Jake said. "Let me deal with those two. How much you got left to do out here?"

Ryan looked at Travis. "Twenty minutes? Maybe a half hour," Ryan answered.

"Perfect."

Jake walked into the bar. He found Grandpa sitting at his regular copper top. Gemma was behind the bar, counting inventory.

"You call this clean?" Grandpa shouted to one of the poor waitresses wiping the tables and pulling the chairs down. Gramps waved a ketchup bottle in the air. He had the lid off.

"Get me some hot water from that coffee pot," the old man said. "Pour it into one of those big salad bowls. Then you take off the caps of every ketchup bottle in this place and soak 'em for at least twenty minutes. That'll get the gunk off. And you gotta do that every night."

"There's no time to soak ketchup caps," Gemma said. "We open in a half an hour."

"Then have 'em do it tonight after close. This stuff matters."

Gemma caught Jake's eye. He gave her a nod.

"Hey, Gramps," Jake said, sliding onto the stool opposite him. "How about I spring you out of here before Gemma opens? You can help me sort Ryan out. We'll pick up that couch from the Polhemus's barn."

"Don't they provide furniture in that dorm you're spending a million bucks for him to live in?"

"He gets a loft bed and a desk," Gemma said. "There's a common area where the kids can set up furniture. Jody Polhemus is giving it to me for free. We like free."

Gemma seemed more agitated than usual. Jake watched her wipe down the same six inches of counter space three times. She kept looking at the clock above the exit sign.

"She's been like that for an hour," Grandpa whispered. "I don't know if she's got the constitution for all this."

"She's doing fine," Jake said. "The place has been packed for two straight weeks."

"Novelty," Grandpa said.

"The food's good. Her prices are reasonable. Word of mouth has been great. Admit it, things are going better than you expected."

"Hmmph."

It was as close to agreement as Jake knew he was likely to get.

"Jake?" Gemma said, flinging her towel over her shoulder. She walked with purpose and the fire in her eyes told him he was about to get a lecture.

"Did you do something to Nora Corley?"

"Do? Like what?"

"She was furious the other night after she waited on your table. She's shown up late the last two shifts. She was supposed to be here an hour ago and now I can't get her to answer her phone."

"Yeah," Grandpa said with a twinkle in his eye. "He took her out on a date. That's what your brother did."

"You what? Christ, Jake. When were you gonna tell me?"

"She asked me out," he said. "I thought it would be harmless."

"What did you do?" Gemma said.

"I didn't do anything. It didn't work out."

"Did you sleep with her?" Gemma whipped him in the arm with the towel.

"Ow! No. It never got that far. She was in no condition to ..."

"You should have talked to me," Gemma yelled. "Cleared it with me. She works for me, Jake."

"Take it easy. Listen, I didn't want to say anything. But Nora might not be the greatest hire."

"Oh fine. You took her out. It didn't go how you wanted. Now you're bashing her?"

"Does that seem like my style? Gemma, listen. I think the woman has a drinking problem. That's what happened. She ordered one cocktail from the bar at the Brass Bell. She went to the bathroom and came back sloshed. She had a pint of vodka in her purse I think she was drinking from. It got ugly. She picked a fight I had to finish. I took her home. She puked all over my truck."

"Sounds like a winner," Grandpa said.

Jake wished Gemma would hit *him* with the towel.

"Anyway, like I'm saying. Now she's showing up late for shifts or not at all. I'd say there's something bigger going on with her. And it doesn't give me any pleasure to have to tell you."

Gemma stared at the ceiling. "Great. Just great. She was my server with the most experience."

"I don't know. Just talk to her. See where her head's at. I'm not looking to get her fired. But I care more about you than I do her, okay? I probably should have said something."

"Yes. You should have," Gemma said. "You seem to have a knack for keeping your mouth shut when you shouldn't and opening it when you shouldn't."

Gemma turned on her heel and went back to furiously scrubbing the same spot on the counter.

"What's that supposed to mean?" Jake asked, even though he knew it was probably better to leave it alone.

"I heard you stuck your foot in it pretty hard with Erica, too."

"What?"

"You heard me. You put your nose where it doesn't belong with her new boyfriend."

"She told you that?"

"She didn't have to. Half the bar heard you."

"Half the bar did not hear me. I was discreet. It was in the very back of the pool room where we were sitting. And I didn't do anything wrong. I just wanted to see what kind of guy he was. I have to be honest. He didn't impress me."

"Get mad at ya, did she?" Grandpa Max grinned like the Cheshire Cat.

"You stay out of it," Jake said.

"Oh, she got mad all right," Gemma said. "She had good reason. I'd have knocked your block off."

"You wanna come at me about *your* taste in men?" Jake said, then wished he hadn't. He knew he'd just poked the bear.

"You're both lousy at it," Grandpa said, being the rare mediator between Jake and Gemma's argument. "Shoulda sent her to the convent and you to the seminary and saved us all the trouble."

"Oh, pipe down," Gemma said. "Jake, do yourself a favor. Apologize to Erica."

"I will not. I didn't do anything wrong. I didn't do anything Ben wouldn't have done."

"And he would have been wrong too!" Gemma said.

"Save your breath," Grandpa whispered. "She'll ask for your advice, do the opposite of what you tell her, then ask you for your help after the thing you told her was gonna happen, happens."

Jake wanted to agree, but Gemma stared right through him.

"All righty," Jake said. "I'd say it's time to cut our losses and get outta here. The boys should be finished up out there. Let's get over to Jody's and get that couch off her hands before dinner."

Miraculously, Grandpa didn't argue. He just scooted off his stool and headed for the door.

"Hot water," he said. "All the ketchup bottle caps. Every night."

Gemma waved a dismissive hand over her head. Jake took Grandpa's arm and led him toward the door. They walked out into the bright sunlight. Travis and Ryan were just heaving the last garbage bag into the dumpster beside the building.

"She's right about one thing," Grandpa said. "Do yourself a favor and just tell Erica Wayne you're sorry even if you're not. It's just easier sometimes."

"I'm done talking about it," Jake said. "That guy she's with gives me a bad vibe. That's all I'm saying." He kept his voice low so Travis wouldn't hear. No point dragging the boy into it or risk him repeating what he'd said to his aunt.

Jake opened the passenger door on the truck so Grandpa could climb in. As he started to walk around the back of it, another car pulled up alongside.

Jake's whole body went rigid as Rob Arden got out of his Tesla and slammed the door.

"Figured I'd find you here," he said.

"I don't have time for you right now," Jake said. "Boys! Let's load up!"

Ryan and Travis hesitated as they started walking toward the truck.

"You have no right to hassle Willis Bondy. I know what you're trying to do. I've known that man for thirty-five years. You're trying to ruin him. Over what?"

Arden got a little too close to Jake.

"You're gonna wanna step back. In fact, you're gonna wanna get in your car and just drive away."

"Or what?" Rob spat. "I've had enough of your crap. What you did at that convention. In public. It was uncalled for. At least now the whole county knows what you're about. But I will not stand by while you ruin a man's reputation."

"I haven't ruined anything. And you might want to rethink how well you know Willis Bondy."

"I know him like a brother. Whatever you think he's done, you're wrong. And I'll be the first one in line to take you down for this."

"You sure about that?" Jake said. "I mean, are you really sure how well you know Bondy? I'm gonna give you a piece of advice you probably don't deserve. Stay clear of Willis Bondy. Trust me. You're not gonna want his stink on you. I'm not in the business of ruining people."

"You're a liar. You peddle in filth. I know who you are and soon enough everyone else will, too."

"That's enough outta you!" Grandpa climbed down from the truck. "Do what my grandson said and crawl back in that overpriced piece of crap car of yours and head on outta here. You're not welcome."

Rob took a step back. It almost seemed as if he hadn't realized Max Cashen had been in the truck the whole time. Jake had no idea when the two men had last breathed the same air.

"Of course you're gonna defend him. Cover up what he is. That's what you do, isn't it?"

"Shut your mouth!" Max said. Spit flew from his lips and his face turned bright red with rage. The old man was shaking. For a moment, Jake worried he might keel over.

The commotion was loud enough that Gemma came out of the bar. She stopped short when she saw Rob with Grandpa. Something about her posture stirred something in Ryan. He rushed forward. Travis was right behind him.

"Get out of here," Max seethed. "Don't ever come back. My son told you to back off. You don't want your secrets spilled? You just keep on driving."

Son, Jake thought. It was a slip of the tongue. He had to have meant grandson.

Rob Arden's face turned white. He opened his mouth but seemed incapable of sound. Finally, he found his voice.

"How dare you."

"You know exactly how I dare. Now leave!"

Arden staggered backward and fumbled with the handle on his car door. He got it open and practically fell into the driver's seat. He put the car in gear and sped off, spraying gravel all over the side of the truck.

"You okay?" Jake asked his grandfather.

Grandpa Max's face was still contorted with hatred. But he turned and climbed back into the truck.

"Mom?" Ryan asked. Gemma stood slack-jawed near the front entrance. She recovered when she heard the sound of her son's voice.

"Better get going," she said. "Jody's expecting you."

Jake wanted to interrogate his grandfather about what just happened. There was some undercurrent of vitriol between Rob and Max that seemed out of proportion to the event. But he knew his grandfather well enough to know he'd get nowhere. Max sat with his fists clenched and his jaw hard set. When Jake climbed behind the wheel. Grandpa thumped the dashboard.

"Let's skedaddle," he said, coming back into himself.

Whatever happened, the moment had passed. Ryan and Travis got into the backseat. Jake waved to Gemma. Cars had started to fill the parking lot, waiting for her to open.

He left her to it. It was all he could do.

Twenty-Nine

Birdie seemed fine the next day. Despite both Grandpa Max and Gemma's advice to apologize to her, Jake still didn't think he'd done anything wrong. Looking out for friends was always the right thing to do. Period.

If anything, Birdie was eager to see Jake as he tossed his backpack in the corner and went for the coffee.

"You want the good news or the bad news first?" she asked.

He eyed her over his coffee mug as he downed the first palate-burning sip. "You pick."

"Well ... I've managed to run down every one of Willis Bondy's burn list. Gerwick and Grimes were both at a seminar in Columbus during the timeframe of the murders. They're smarter than Bondy, or at least they listened to good advice. Both have given us consent to search their phones. These other two, Zielinski was having a hip replacement the week of July 10th. He was in a skilled nursing facility from July 11th to the 18th. This last one, Blackmun. He doesn't have an ironclad alibi, but I think we can safely rule him out anyway."

"Why's that?"

"He's another attorney over in Beacon Township. But, the guy's blind. He lost both eyes in an accident involving a propane grill when he was a kid. He never would have been able to pull off that hit."

"Is that the good news or the bad news?"

"Well, I guess you can take your pick. Good in the sense we can clear them. Bad in the sense we're no closer to finding out who did this."

"It's good work, Birdie. Excellent."

"Bondy's giving his press release this morning." She looked at the clock on the wall. "Probably right about now. I know Darcy fielded some phone calls from the media, but so far, the thing hasn't blown up. I think Willis Bondy was never a particularly popular guy around town. He's kind of a dick. Tessa Papadopoulos says he stiffs her waitresses every time he comes in. She's threatened to ban him from eating there."

"She'll carry through on that now once she hears what he's been accused of."

"Well, no love lost anyway. The county's better off not having him representing anybody on the commission."

Darcy poked her head into the office. "Hey, Jake," she said. "I've got a woman out here you're gonna wanna talk to. Both of you."

"Yeah?"

"Yeah. She came in with this printout of the Crime Stopper page we uploaded on Jaxon Waters."

Jake and Birdie exchanged a look.

"Who is she?" Birdie asked.

Darcy shrugged. "She says she's Jaxon Waters's girlfriend."

Jake got to his feet. "Put her in the interview room."

"Already done."

Jake grabbed a notepad. Birdie had her tablet. That was one difference in the way they worked. Jake preferred pen and paper. He had notes scattered all over the place. Birdie used a tablet with an attached Bluetooth keyboard. She followed him down the hall.

The woman in question sat at the table sipping from a Styrofoam cup. Darcy had already taken the liberty of getting her a coffee.

She was pretty. Brunette. Big brown eyes and full lips. When she turned and got up to shake Jake's hand, he was struck by something. Whoever she was, she looked an awful lot like Joey DeSilva.

"Thank you for coming in," Jake said. "I'm Detective Jake Cashen. This is my partner, Deputy Wayne. You are?"

The woman sat back down and tucked her hair behind her ears. "My name is Mariah. Mariah Ortiz."

"My clerk said you're here about my murder investigation?"

"I'm here about Jaxon Waters," she said. "I'm hoping you can clear something up for me."

Ms. Ortiz took a folded piece of paper from her purse. She smoothed it out on the table. As Darcy described, it was a picture of Jaxon Waters with the Crime Stopper number below it. The photo was from Waters's bogus company website.

"You knew Mr. Waters?" Jake asked.

"Can you promise me something?" Ortiz said.

Jake caught Birdie's eye. It was a strange thing for the woman to ask. Jake started to get the sense he might be dealing with a crackpot.

"What is it you want from me?" Jake said.

"Proof," she said. "Are you absolutely sure Jaxon's dead?"

Jake folded his hands. Birdie got out her tablet, poised to type.

"Yes," Jake said. "There's no doubt. The coroner was able to identify Mr. Waters from dental records. He's dead."

Mariah Ortiz's entire posture changed. Her shoulders sank with relief. Tears glistened in the corner of her eyes. "Good," she said. "Thank God."

"Ms. Ortiz," Birdie said. "Maybe you could tell us how you knew Mr. Waters? We've not been able to find out very much about his background. He had no next of kin. No family has come forward to claim the body."

"That doesn't surprise me. Jax said his parents died a long time ago. He didn't have any brothers or sisters. I never heard about any aunts or uncles. And that's really the only reason I even bothered to drive all the way down here. Just in case ..."

"Just in case what?" Jake asked. "Ms. Ortiz, what was your relationship with Jaxon Waters?"

"You promise me he's dead?"

"Yes."

She nodded. "Okay. Okay then. It's all right now. Jaxon and I were ... well, we were engaged for a very long time. We were going to get married. I thank God every day I never went through with it. I can't imagine what my life would be if I had."

"You were his girlfriend," Jake said. "When was this?"

"We were engaged for over five years. We broke up four years ago. I suppose it's been ten years now since I met him. For the longest time, I prayed I could go back in time and change that day. Called off work. That's how we met. I was a waitress at this little bar in Beavercreek. Jax came in and sat in my section. If he hadn't, so many things would be different. There's just one reason why I wouldn't change it. And that's Javi."

"Javi?" Jake asked.

"Javiar. My son. My son with Jax. That's why I'm here. I was hoping you could tell me. Is there ... did he leave anything behind? Any money? Not for me. But for Javi."

"Jax has a son?" Jake said.

"He doesn't know," Mariah quickly added. "I was scared to death he was gonna find out. Jax was ... he wasn't a good man."

"That's been my impression," Jake said.

"He was a charmer. Oh, in the beginning, you'd never know the kind of guy he really was. He could fool you. He fooled me. And he made so many promises. Looking back, I can see what an idiot I was. And I know how this is probably going to sound to you. Like I'm some gold digger showing up only after he's gone. Asking whether he left any money behind. But I can prove everything I'm saying. Javi is Jax's. I'll do DNA. Whatever it takes."

"I'm not questioning your story," Jake said. "As far as whatever assets Jax left behind, I'm going to have to recommend you talk to a probate lawyer. I don't know how all that will work out. Jax's business dealings ... they weren't exactly legitimate."

"I know about his business dealings. That's one of the reasons I decided to come here. What Jax put me through? What he did to me? If there's anything left over. If there's any good to come out of this for Javi, then I deserve ... *he* deserves to have it."

"What exactly did he put you through?" Birdie asked.

"He was a mean, mean man," Mariah said. "I told you. At first it was all sunshine and roses. He was romantic. I fell for him. Hard. Then little by little he changed. His temper. And he took over my life. Dictated what I wore. How I did my hair and makeup. Who I could talk to. After a while, I couldn't talk to anybody but Jax. He cut me off from my friends. My family. And I let him. I hate myself for that. But it didn't happen all at once. Like I said. Little by little until there was nobody in my life but Jax, and I'd do anything for him. Anything to keep him from getting angry."

"He hurt you," Jake said.

Mariah wiped away a tear. "He hurt me real bad." She looked up and smiled, displaying a row of straight white teeth. She ran a finger across them.

"These are all fake now," she said. "He threw me down once. I hit the edge of the table. Knocked out five of my front teeth."

"My God," Birdie said. "How awful for you."

"I'm lucky to be alive. Jax made me feel like dirt. That's how he operates. Makes you think you're nothing. That everything you are you owe to him. And you're his property. It took me a long time to find myself again. But I did. One night, I'd finally just had enough. I left in the middle of the night with nothing other than my driver's license and a hundred bucks I stole from the nightstand. But that was my money too. I earned it. He made me earn it."

"He sent you on ... dates," Birdie said.

Mariah nodded. "He pimped me out. That was never the life I sought. I've done a lot of work on myself to try to figure out how I could let that happen. How I could get messed up in all of that. But I've put it behind me. I started over. Only a few weeks after I left Jax, I found out I was pregnant. I knew it was his. There were others. I won't lie about that. And I don't owe you or anybody else the details, but just trust me. I know. Javi is Jax's son."

"He never knew," Jake said.

"No. And I told you. I got out. I got away. I stayed with a cousin of mine who was nice enough to let me crash with her until I got back on my feet. And she helped me take care of Javi. I thought about getting rid of him. Having an abortion. But I just couldn't do it. No matter who his daddy was, it's not Javi's fault. And he's part of me, too. In fact, he's all me. He's got nothing of his father in him. He's sweet. Considerate. He's a good boy."

She took a photo out of her purse and slid it across the table. It was of an adorable little black-haired boy sitting on a pony. He was grinning from ear to ear.

"He looks so sweet," Birdie said.

"He is. And he's smart too. He's already starting to read a few words. He's only three and a half."

"That's amazing," Jake said. "So you haven't seen Jax since before your son was born?"

She shook her head. "No. That's the other thing I thought I'd come talk to you about. About four months ago, Jax just showed up. I rent the house next to my cousin now. She still helps me look after Javi. I don't know how Jax found me. But he just showed up. I was terrified. He came pounding on the door. Thank God Javi wasn't home. He was at preschool that day. Jax didn't seem to notice the toys lying around in the yard. He didn't ask. He came because he wanted his ring back. The diamond ring he gave me when we got engaged. He said it belonged to him and that I was a thief for leaving with it. I told him if I gave it back, would he promise to go away and never come back? He just laughed at me. Pushed me out of the way and barged into my house. He went upstairs and started ransacking the place even though I told him where the ring was. I was keeping it for Javi. I thought someday I'd sell it to help pay for college or something. I never wore it."

"I can see why not. What happened after he found it?" Jake asked.

"He tried to scare me. Just laughing at me the whole time. Making fun of me for putting on a few pounds. I had a baby! Of course, I couldn't tell him that. And he brought this girl in with him. Paraded her in front of me. She was pretty. Thinner than me. He told me he'd upgraded. He pawed at her. Kissed her. I could tell it was making her uncomfortable. He was treating her like property. Like he owned her. Like he used to do to me. And she just stood there and took it. She was afraid. Like I used to be afraid. Only I'm not anymore."

"Mariah," Jake said. "Do you know who the girl was? Did he introduce her?"

She nodded. "He said she was his wife. He called her Joey. Man, I felt for her. I knew what he was doing to her. Making her do. And I'm telling you. She was scared to death. Laughing, you know, but it was fake. Just to make herself feel safe when he was acting so awful. Like a pig. Like always. He took the ring. But I just felt so awful for that girl. For his wife. Joey. I could tell she was terrified of him. I could see it in her eyes. I was her. It put me right back there. All of it."

"That must have been absolutely terrifying," Birdie said. "I'm so sorry that happened to you. Did you ... did you have a chance to talk to Joey at all?"

It was then Mariah Ortiz began to cry in earnest. She slowly nodded.

"What did you say to her? Or what did she say to you?" Jake asked.

"He was strutting around. Jaxon. Just looking through my fridge. Taking things. Helping himself to things. Like he wanted to make sure I knew that no matter what. All the time that had passed. That he could still take from me, you know? And it was awful because here was this poor woman. This new wife of his. And she had to have felt so bad. Like she's his *wife* now and here he is trying to show this other woman ... me ... that he still thinks he owns me in some way. I was just so scared. And so was she. He went upstairs. You know. To get the ring. I told him it was in my dresser. I was going to go get it, but he pushed me down. Made me sit on the living room couch. And for those ten minutes or so, it was just the two of us. Joey and me. And so I told her. I warned her. I told her honey, you have to get away from him. He's no good. And I was going to call the police, but she begged me not to. She said all the things I used to tell myself. That she's got it under control. That he's not as bad as people make him out to be. That he loves her. That he takes care of her. It was all just the lie she tells herself to feel safe. The way I used to. And I gave her a card. I had this card with me that somebody else gave me once when I was in a grocery store with Jax, and this lady saw the bruises on my face. It was a battered women's shelter. I never called them myself, but it always stuck with me how nice this woman was and how she was the first person who ever tried to help me. So I kept that card. And that day, I gave it to Joey. And I wrote my own number on it. I told her if she needed help, I could help her. I made her swear never to tell Jax. I knew that was risky. But that look in her eyes. The fear. And she seemed so grateful. She latched on to me at one point. Grabbed on to my arm and I swore I didn't think she was gonna let go. I asked her, I said honey, do you have people? Someplace she could go to. A brother. A dad. Well, that's about when Jax walked back down with that ring. Joey was slick. She put that card in her back pocket and acted like not a thing was wrong. Jax ... he grabbed me. That bastard. He grabbed me right in front of his wife and he put his hands between my legs. You know, grabbing me. Possessive.

Reminding me and her what he thinks he owned. Then, my cousin and her husband came home. Thank God for that. I don't know if anything else would have happened, but Jax wasn't looking to stick around. They left. I'll never forget that look on Joey's face just before they drove off."

"That was very brave of you," Birdie said. "And kind. To try to help her."

"That's the thing. I didn't think I'd ever hear another word about it. I started making plans to move. Cuz Jax knew where I was now. I was lucky that time cuz Javi wasn't home. But maybe he'd try to stop by again. So I told my cousin I was gonna start looking for a new place. And I don't know. Maybe a week later, I got a phone call on this number I didn't recognize. It was Joey. Jax's wife. She just … she just wanted to talk."

"When was this?" Jake asked.

"Three months ago. Like I said. A week after he came to my house that time. She just … she didn't say much. She just asked me about my life. I was worried at first. Like maybe Jax had put her up to it. To pump me for information. So I was real careful not to say anything about Javi. Then she just started spilling. Just how her life wasn't turning out how she thought it would. That she felt lonely. She asked me how I did it. How I got away. I was guarded. How do I know whether Jax put her up to it or if he was monitoring her calls? So I was real tight-lipped that first time."

"First time?" Jake asked. "There were other calls?"

"Yeah. Three more. Over the next maybe two weeks, she called three more times. Same stuff. Just asking how I found a job. Whether my family still wanted to talk to me. She seemed real afraid of that. Thinking that her family wouldn't want nothing to do with her because of how she lived her life now. That she was no good. And I know that's all Jax. Putting those ideas in her head.

He tried to do that with me. So I told her it was bullshit. That if her parents loved her, they still loved her. That it wouldn't matter to them if they were good people. She was still their little girl. That made her cry. I mean, full-on sobbing. I told her. Call your mom and dad. Reach out at least."

"That was good advice," Jake said. "I think she took you up on it."

"I'm glad to hear that. I really am. I hope she reconnected with them, you know. Before everything else that happened ..."

"Mariah," Birdie said. "During your time with Jax, can you think of anyone who might have wanted to hurt him? Or something that might have caught up with him that led to his murder?"

She shook her head. "Who knows? Jax had run-ins now and again with these thugs. One time when he had me out on a date with another guy ... some other guy showed up trying to get me to tell him where to find Jax. This was like six years ago. Jax came back to our hotel and he looked beat up but he told me not to ask questions. Said he'd taken care of it. I never saw that guy again and never had any other hassles except from Jax. So no, I can't tell you anything or anybody specifically. Except for this. When I finally came home, it was my brother who wanted to kill Jax. When he saw me and realized what had been going on all that time. But I don't wanna give you the idea I think Roberto did anything to Jax. He didn't. My brother lives in Tennessee. He was nowhere near any of this. I'm only saying it because if Joey did get back in touch with her family. If they found out what he'd been doing to her like he was doing to me, well, I think they'd have wanted him dead. But I don't know anything. I just know the kind of lifestyle that man lived. Who had a reason to want him dead? Well, I sure as hell did. And every woman he ever mistreated. And the list is long. He'd have deserved whatever he had coming to him. I'm not saying I had anything to do with this. I mean, why would I even show up here if I did? I just needed to be sure he was really dead. You understand."

DECLAN JAMES

"Of course," Jake said.

"So, if there's a form I gotta fill out. You know. To make a claim against Jax's estate or whatever."

"Again," Jake said. "That's the kind of thing you'd need a probate lawyer for. You should get one. And I hope there is something for you. For your son."

Mariah put her purse strap over her shoulder. "That's all I came here for. Thank you. You say nobody's come to claim him? His body?"

"Not so far."

She curled her lip and nodded. "I suppose I should think that's sad. You ask me? It's karma. He died alone with nobody to care. I don't think I'm ever gonna tell Javi a damn thing about his daddy. I haven't so far. I don't know if there's heaven or hell. But there can be oblivion. Let Jax rot there."

She shook Jake and Birdie's hands and let herself out of the room.

"What do you think?" Birdie said once Mariah Ortiz turned the corner down the hall.

"I get what she's saying," Jake said. "Ray DeSilva was back in communication with Joey. He knew what was going on. He was scared for her. And if Jax was the only victim ..."

"DeSilva had the ultimate motive for murdering Jaxon Waters. Only ... his own daughter? Could he have killed her too?"

"I can't fathom it. I just can't."

"Me either. But what do we really know about DeSilva and his relationship with Joey? Every time we've tried to talk to him he's been a mess. If Dale Halsey wasn't there holding him together, he barely could have given us his name."

"I think we need to know more about both Joey and Ray DeSilva."

"His grief is real," she said. "I'm not denying that. But what if ... Jake ... we never ran Ray DeSilva's phone. We don't know for sure where he was when these murders took place. I'd hate to think it. It would be ..."

"Yeah," Jake said. "But I think it's at least worth a trip back to Westeridge. I need one more conversation with Ray DeSilva just to be sure."

"I think it's a good idea."

"And I want you to come with me. What you said about their dynamic. While I'm talking to Ray, maybe you could go into town and ask around. See what people think of Ray. Of the whole situation."

Birdie's face lit up. "I'm ready to go whenever you are."

THIRTY

This time, when Jake knocked on Raymond DeSilva's front door, a woman answered. She introduced herself simply as Flora and explained that she came from DeSilva's church.

"Is he home?" Jake asked.

Flora opened the door wider to let Jake inside. "He's in the back. Sitting by the pool. It's the first bit of sunlight he's had on his face in weeks."

"That's good. And I'm so sorry. I don't want to disturb him."

"If you're here about Joey, he'll want to see you," Flora said. "And I was just about to get going. It's good he'll have somebody else to sit with him. Tell him there's a chicken casserole in the fridge. Lasagna in the freezer for tomorrow night. He's got fresh sheets on the bed and his laundry's done. Someone from his support group is supposed to be coming later this evening to have dinner with him. If he'll let them."

"That's so kind of you," Jake said. Flora let herself out. It left Jake in DeSilva's house alone for a moment. He walked through the living room and into the kitchen. There was a family room at the back of the house and a sliding door leading to the deck around DeSilva's upground pool.

Jake stopped short. All along the wood-paneled walls of the living room were pictures of Joey. School pictures. Thirteen of them. From kindergarten all the way through her senior year.

It struck Jake how much Joey really did look like Mariah Ortiz. It was hard to reconcile the vibrant, beautiful young woman Joey was with the body Jake had watched zipped into a bag and taken out of that creek.

He ran his hand over a certificate on the wall. Joey DeSilva had been a scholar-athlete, just like Ray told them. Ray had her high school cap and gown displayed in a shadow box. Several braided, multi-colored tassels marked her participation in various clubs, the honor roll, and varsity track.

"Flora!" Ray called out. "You still here?"

Jake went out the slider.

"Good morning, Ray," Jake said. "Flora let me in. She just left."

Ray wore a Hawaiian shirt unbuttoned to show his beer belly. He had on a pair of red swim trunks. He sat in a lounge chair by the pool and sipped from a tall glass of lemonade. Presumably Flora had made it. A pitcher sat on a round metal table beside him.

"It finally stopped raining," Ray said, his voice a bit distant. "They told me I should get some sun on my face. I was thinking about taking a dip in the pool later."

"It's a good day for it," Jake said.

Ray got up. He had an umbrella on a stand behind him. He worked the handle to open it, casting the deck into the shade.

"There's some extra chairs folded up there against the side of the house."

Jake saw where he pointed and grabbed another lawn chair. He set one up in the shade next to Ray's.

"Thanks for having me out here again," Jake said.

"You have something to tell me?" Ray asked.

"I have a few more questions," Jake answered.

Ray's face fell a bit. "I figured you would. I know I wasn't much help to you when you came out last time."

"It's understandable. You've been through one of the worst things a person can go through."

"You want some of this?" Ray asked, pointing to the lemonade pitcher. "I just gotta scare up another glass. Flora made it fresh. A little too much sugar for my liking, but it's still good."

"That's okay. I don't need anything."

Ray took another sip of his drink then put it down on the table beside him.

"What can I help you with, Detective?"

"Mr. DeSilva ..."

"Ray. Nobody calls me that. It's just Ray."

"Of course. Ray. I'd just like to ask you a few more questions about your conversations with Joey in those weeks before she passed away."

"Passed away," he said. "It sounds pretty, doesn't it? Like she just floated off on a cloud. But you and me? We know that's not what happened. We know she hurt. We know she was cold and scared trying to run away. I keep thinking about that. You know. What the last thing was she might have seen before everything went dark. Her own blood? That swampy dirt you found her in?"

Jake gave him a moment. Ray DeSilva got a faraway look in his eyes. He seemed a bit in a fog and Jake guessed the man was now on heavy antidepressants.

"Mr. DeSilva, can you walk me through it again? When did Joey reach out to you? You hadn't spoken to her in years, is that right?"

He nodded. "Four years. No contact. I only knew about her from what I saw online. What she posted on social media. I had a fake profile. If she knew it was me, she might have blocked me. I didn't want to fight with her anymore. That was the thing. I didn't have any of that left in me. I just wanted her in my life again. I learned my lesson."

"What do you mean?"

"Everyone tells you having toddlers is the hardest part. It isn't. It's when they are teenagers and trying to become adults. It's brutal, Detective. You have to stand by and watch them make all these mistakes. My Joey had the world at her feet. Every advantage I could give her. But none of it mattered because she didn't believe in herself. I don't know why that was. I think it had to be because of her mom. Losing her the way we did. It wasn't my fault. It wasn't anybody's fault. But I think because Joey was so young, she blamed herself somehow. Like maybe she thought if she'd tried harder, her mama wouldn't have left. But she didn't leave. She just died. The cancer took her. But ... I don't know. It was just different for Joey after that. She became a different person. And I never got my sweet little girl back."

"I can't imagine how difficult that was for you. For both of you. But she tried to come back to you?"

DeSilva nodded. "She did. She finally did. I don't know what happened. You know ... that's what everybody always told me. If you love someone, set them free. I tried to set her free. Tried to accept that she had to make her own mistakes. That it was part of growing up. God knows I made plenty of my own when I was a young guy. But it's hard, you know? It's different for girls. And I watched her get hooked up with these losers. One right after the other. Each one treating her worse than the one before. As a father, it kills you to see that."

"But she reached back out to you? She was the one who initiated that?"

DeSilva's head snapped back. As if the sound of Jake's voice brought him back to earth.

"What do you mean?"

"I mean you said she'd had no contact for a number of years. And that it was only recently you started talking again. Was she the one who reached out to you? Or was it the other way around?"

"What difference does that make?"

"I'm just trying to get a sense of what was going on in Joey's life in these last few months. If I can understand her mindset. Who she was talking to."

"She texted me," DeSilva said. "It was out of the blue. Maybe three months ago."

His phone sat on the table next to the pitcher of lemonade. He picked it up and started to scroll through it. "Yeah. Back in April. I got a text from a number I didn't recognize. But it was Joey. See?"

DeSilva handed Jake his phone. "Do you mind if I ..."

"Take it," DeSilva said. "Read it. Read all of it. If you think it will help. I'm sorry. I should have given all of this to you that day at the morgue. If it can help you now. I just … I wasn't myself. I don't know who I am anymore. Can I tell you? A part of me is so angry with Joey. I'd lost her. I hated that I'd lost her. But in a way I'd made some kind of peace with it. Then she started to come back to me. I almost wonder if I'd never known. If she'd just truly … passed away. I could have lived my life pretending that she was just out there somewhere. Angry with me or not wanting me in her life. I could have maybe been able to bear it. Maybe it would have been better if she'd never reached out that last time. She was never going to leave that man. She was never going to be that beautiful, brilliant young girl of mine again. But why did she do this? Why did she have to say she was going to come back to me? Give me hope that I could have her again?"

He cried softly, burying his face in his hands. Jake looked at his phone screen and did what Ray DeSilva had given him permission to do. He read it all. These were texts he'd never seen before. They didn't come from Joey's iPhone nor any of the burners.

"She texted you from different numbers?" Jake asked.

"Yeah. That wasn't unusual. I told you, I hadn't heard from her in years. But even back then, I'd just start getting these calls or texts from random numbers. I never knew if it was really Joey. I suspected Jax was monitoring her calls. Half the time I wondered if maybe he was texting pretending to be her. Just to mess with me. I don't know. I don't know anything anymore."

"I see," Jake said. He'd only seen a short exchange from Joey to her father on her iPhone a few days before she died. He'd called her mija and told her he loved her. But this exchange, going back four months ago from a different number, was completely new to Jake.

JOEY

> Pop. It's me, Joey. I just wanted you to know that I'm okay.

> I'm here, honey. I'm always here. You know that. Are you really okay? Where are you? Do you need something? Can I help you?

Several days passed before Joey texted back.

JOEY

> I'm okay. Are you okay?

> I'm fine. I'm over the moon to hear from you. Do you need anything?

> No, Pops. I have everything I need. I just wanted to see if you were okay.

> Can I call you? Can we talk?

Two days before a response.

JOEY

> Things are good. There's nothing I need.

> Please. Let me see you. I'll come to you. Wherever you are. Or just call me. I won't bother you. I just want to hear your voice.

> It's too much, Pops. Maybe soon.

A week went by before another response. Joey's next text came in one week before her murder.

JOEY

> I miss you, Pop. I think maybe I would like to see you again.

> Anytime. Anywhere.

I'm with Jax. You know he's my husband now.

> I won't say anything about that. Not anymore. You know how I feel. I just want to see you.

You'll try to make me come home.

> Not if you don't want to. I promise. It can be just us, right?

Jax isn't as bad as you think he is.

> Then let's not talk about him. I won't bring him up.

Okay. We can meet for lunch.

> Tell me where. Tell me when.

I want to bring Jax.

> Joey, please. Just us. You and me. Anywhere you tell me.

She responded two days before the murders.

I'll be in Blackhand Hills. Do you know the area?

> Yes.

I'll send you a pin. I'm staying here for the summer. There's a restaurant right off the highway. We can meet for lunch on Wednesday. Noon.

> Just us?

Yes. Jax will be out of town that day.

I'll be there. Oh honey. I can't wait to see you.
Can I bring you something?

She never responded. Joey never sent another text to her father from this phone. She'd used her personal iPhone for the next contact. That's the text Jake had already seen. And she never met him at that restaurant. Jake realized the day of their planned meeting ended up being the day DeSilva had to come down to identify his daughter's body.

Jake handed the phone back to him. "Thank you for sharing that with me."

"I was so happy. I tried so hard. She knew how I felt about that man she was married to. She knew. But I didn't push. Everyone told me not to push. If she agreed to meet with me, I was supposed to let it be on her terms. I was being so careful to let it be on her terms. Every time I'd ever tried to push her too hard in the past, she'd disappear. It took me a long time to learn that lesson. But that's something they tell us in group therapy at Lean On Us. I was afraid to even share any of this in group. I was the lucky one. I knew it. My daughter was still alive. Most of the others, their babies are all gone. Lost to drugs. I was feeling so lucky. Dale told me I shouldn't feel that way. That it was okay to be grateful that my Joey was still alive. And I can't help but think that God punished me. I kept thinking how glad I was that I wasn't like any of those other people in Lean On Us. It was my pride. I was boastful in my heart. I was going to get to see my baby girl and Dale could never see his. I thought that. But Dale told me I shouldn't feel guilty. That I should feel joyful that she wanted to see me. Oh, but I was so prideful in my heart and then God took her away."

"Dale was right. You shouldn't feel guilty that you were going to get to see your daughter. Mr. DeSilva, this wasn't your fault. Mr.

Halsey ... the parents in Lean On Us. They were right. It was okay for you to feel relieved or lucky that she reached out to you. There's nothing wrong with that. And you didn't cause this."

He wiped his tears. "I'm sorry. I can't tell you anything else. I don't know if that's helpful to you."

"It is," Jake said.

"Will you stay in touch? Let me know when you have something?"

"Of course," Jake said. He had more questions about Ray DeSilva. But none he could resolve this moment.

"Ray?" a male voice shouted from the front of the house. A moment later, another man walked around the back. Jake raised his hand in greeting.

"Thank you for coming," DeSilva said. "I meant what I said. If there's anything else I can do, you just let me know. Detective, this is Michael Perry. Mike lost his daughter like Dale did. A drug overdose just last year. "

"It's good to meet you, Mr. Perry," Jake said. "I'm very sorry for your loss."

Perry had a haunted look about him. "How are you doing today, Ray?"

Ray shrugged. Jake rose and offered his seat to Perry. Perry took it and put a hand on Ray's shoulder.

Jake thanked Ray. He got a text from Birdie. She'd made her way to a local watering hole. She sent the address and asked him to come there after finishing up with DeSilva. It was almost as if she could hear his growling stomach from there. Jake hadn't stopped to grab breakfast before they hit the road.

Perry started talking to Ray about mundane things. It seemed to take the man's mind off his grief, at least for a moment. Jake said his goodbyes and left the two men alone.

As Jake walked toward his car, he still had that nagging feeling that had refused to leave him since Mariah Ortiz's interview. Someone who had hurt Joey would have the purest motive to kill Jaxon Waters. Ray DeSilva was every picture of the grieving father. It was real. Palpable. But something he'd said stuck with Jake as he got behind the wheel.

It would have been better if she'd never reached out that last time. She was never going to leave that man. She was never going to be that beautiful, brilliant young girl of mine again.

Had Ray DeSilva killed his own daughter? Had he seen it as the only way to save her from herself?

As sick as it seemed, Jake knew he would have to rule him out once and for all. As he pulled away from DeSilva's house, he couldn't shake the knowledge that Raymond DeSilva might have been one of the few people who knew where Jax and Joey Waters were staying on the night they were shot down in cold blood.

THIRTY-ONE

I t took Jake a minute to find Birdie in the din of the bar called Blokes. It was a place he would have passed by without a thought. An ugly brick building painted black for some inexplicable reason. He might have thought it was a biker bar. But the heavenly aroma of beef brisket made his mouth water. A three-hundred-pound, ginger-haired cook with a handle-bar mustache worked a Clem's Cadillac smoker on the side of the building. Jake knew this place was something special.

"Jake!" Birdie called out as his eyes adjusted to the light. She was in the back of the bar near a few pinball machines. She sat at a long table surrounded by a group of other cops. Some in uniforms still, some in plain clothes. A barrel-chested man with a silvery buzz cut sat beside her, drinking from a twenty-ounce mug. As Jake approached, Birdie found Jake a clean mug and poured him a water from the pitcher at the center of the table.

"Glad you made it," she said. "Arnie, this is who I was telling you about. Jake Cashen. Jake, this is Detective Arnold Delacourt. Three days from now, he gets to retire. How long's it been, Arnie?"

"Thirty years," Arnie answered, lifting his mug. Birdie clicked her glass against his.

"Congratulations," Jake said.

"Have a seat,' Birdie said. "We've been waiting for you. You hungry?"

"Starving," Jake said.

"You gotta try the burnt ends," Birdie said. "Molly!" She got to her feet and waved toward one of the servers near the bar. "Can you bring that other plate when you get a chance?"

Molly gave Birdie a thumbs up. It had only been a couple of hours since he left her, but Birdie seemed to have endeared herself to Montgomery County law enforcement and the whole bar.

A few minutes later, Molly came back with a heaping plate of barbecued burnt ends that melted in Jake's mouth. Eating them felt like a religious experience.

"See?" Birdie said. "Told ya."

"Don't tell anyone else when you leave town," Detective Delacourt said. "The place'll be overrun."

"No doubt," Jake agreed. He tried not to make a pig of himself, but it was damn hard.

"So," Birdie said. She reached over and purloined one of the burnt ends from Jake's plate. "Arnie and I got to talking. I told him what we came down here for. It's worth hearing what he's got to say if you're not in a rush to get back to Blackhand Hills."

"If Molly over there keeps these coming," Jake said. "I might actually move down here."

"Oh, you haven't even tried the cheese curds," Birdie said. She slid a plate of those down the table toward Jake.

"You have a story?" Jake said to Arnie Delacourt.

"Arnie's pretty familiar with Ray and Joey DeSilva. He's been on a drug task force that's been going after a lot of the same people Joey got mixed up with."

"Things were always quiet here," Delacourt said. "Westeridge is a nothing little town. We were lucky for a long time. The worst thing that ever happened was kids smoking weed or underage drinking. Then about ten years ago, China White made its way here. It's ruined a lot of lives."

"You knew Joey DeSilva? The crowd she got mixed up with?"

"I know Ray pretty well. My sister lives a couple of houses down from him. Plus, everybody knows him. We all go into the hardware store he manages. Your partner here's saying you don't have much in the way of leads."

"It's not so much trying to find out who wanted Joey's husband dead, but who didn't want him dead. Did you have any run-ins with Jaxon Waters?"

"I didn't know him personally. But from what I can tell, he definitely matched Joey's type."

"That's kind of what I'm getting from her father. He says she fell in with a string of loser boyfriends. That she was a different kid once she started dating."

Delacourt ran a finger around the rim of his mug. He grimaced. Birdie caught Jake's eye. She raised both her brows. It seemed Arnie Delacourt might have a very different story to tell.

"You have any insight into Joey DeSilva different than her dad's?" Jake asked, sipping his beer.

"She's dead now. I read about what happened. It's a real tragedy. She was young. And yeah, she had a pretty lousy track record. Back when she was in high school she ran around with this grade A loser. Ricky Saul. The kid came by his criminal career honestly though. Ricky Senior got his start stealing cars and selling crack. He only went downhill from there. Ricky Junior never made it past the eighth grade. He got expelled. This kid was a monster. A bully. He's in prison now. Rape. Aggravated assault. Joey made quite a stir having him take her to prom. All the teachers were up in arms. There wasn't much they could do about it at the time though."

"Poor kid," Jake said. "Ray said Joey was always down on herself."

"Look," Delacourt said. He put his mug down. The three of them had the table to themselves now. The rest of the cops had migrated to either the bar or the pinball machines.

"Joey was a kid. And Ray's a dad who's now had to bury his daughter. I can't imagine what that's like. Whatever he's gotta do to sleep at night or live with it, it's not my business. But Joey? She wasn't just some good kid who got mixed up with bad ones. She was always trouble. Always a mean girl."

"How so?" Jake asked.

"That girl had a reputation. School officer was always having to pull her out of class. If there was a bullying incident, Joey was most likely at the heart of it. She had a pack of girls following her around. They made life hell for a lot of the rest of the kids at Westeridge High. She almost got expelled her senior year. She got in a fight and broke this other girl's jaw. Hit her with a broken bottle under the bleachers at the Homecoming football game. Joey DeSilva led a reign of terror in that district for a lot of years. Now I suppose none of that matters now. She's dead. But I'll be honest, when I read her name in the paper as your murder victim, it didn't surprise me. It seemed like karma. As much as I hate saying that.

I'm telling you, that girl was mixed up with some seriously bad people."

"I appreciate your candor," Jake said. "From what I've been able to learn, the guy she ended up with, Jaxon Waters? It may be that she met her match. He was turning her out. I've got another witness telling me Joey seemed pretty beaten down by him when she saw them together a few months ago."

"Damn," Delacourt said. "Ray did everything he could for that kid. Maybe that was the problem. When his wife died, he just didn't know how to go on. Joey got out of control and Ray was in such deep grief, he couldn't be much of a dad to her. To be honest, a lot of us thought her running off was probably the best thing for Ray. It ended the chaos for him for a while. He came back to the land of the living."

"She'd made contact again," Jake said. "About three months before the murder. They were texting with each other. He was going to meet up with her."

"I suppose that was a relief to him," Delacourt said. "But there wouldn't have exactly been a ticker-tape parade welcoming her back to town."

"I get that. From what I know, Joey ended up recruiting a bunch of other girls to work for Waters."

"That sounds more like the Joey DeSilva I knew. Man, I hate that it ended this way. But Ray's life was a lot better after Joey took off. He tried to report her as a missing person. There wasn't a whole lot I could do for him. Joey was over eighteen when she ran. But he came in almost every week for years, hoping we had some intel on where she was. It broke my heart to have to turn him away. We had a bit of a falling out over it. The sheriff's department just became a convenient place for Ray's blame."

"It was an impossible situation," Jake said. "You said you were on a drug task force. Were you ever able to bust some of the players? It's a long shot, but maybe somebody knows something. If Joey reconnected with some of that element. Or if she hooked Waters up with somebody."

"We made some arrests," Delacourt said. "Dale Halsey was a godsend for that. That man has been tireless. Getting the families of these kids together. Forming Lean On Us. Joey wasn't innocent. But most of the rest of those kids were. We mostly busted lower level dealers."

"Halsey's been helpful to me as well," Jake said. "And I think he's been the main thing keeping Ray DeSilva going."

"I don't doubt that. Halsey's suffered as much as any of them. It kills me that I was never able to bring charges in connection with Lena's death. That's one of those cases that just keeps you up at night."

"Halsey said she OD'd at a party," Birdie said.

"She died out in the woods in the south part of the county," Delacourt said. "There's an abandoned grain mill out there. Kids have been using it as a meeting spot for a couple of decades. It's remote. Rumor was there was a rave out there one night. Somebody spiked Lena's drink or something. She went into convulsions and nobody bothered to call 9-1-1. They were all too scared or gorked out of their minds. She could have been saved. Narcanned. It was such a waste. Halsey was a wreck. I literally pulled him off the ledge. He was gonna jump off the bridge. That was the turning point. After that, he got his shit together and formed Lean On Us. He never wanted another parent to feel alone like he did. He's lost so much, but he's saved so much more."

"You were never able to get a conviction?"

"Nobody would talk," Delacourt said. "Halsey went absolutely nuts for a while. The bridge was the end of it. But before that, he pretty much blew his life savings. Got mixed up with psychics even. Hired this douchebag of a private investigator. A real shyster. Halsey took out a second mortgage to pay him. He got fleeced."

"I've heard that kind of story before," Jake said.

"It broke him. Mentally and financially. I even tried to figure out a way to bring charges against the guy. Larry Lovell. Prosecutor wouldn't go for it. He's on my list though. Somehow. Some way. Karma's gonna catch up with that piece of crap."

"It usually does," Jake said.

Delacourt reached into his back pocket and pulled out a thick wallet. He thumbed through a stack of bent business cards. He pulled out a dog-eared one and tossed it on the table.

"This PI. The one who screwed Halsey over. Lovell's as seedy as they come," Delacourt said. "He's in bed with every lowlife in town. One of these days he and I are gonna have a reckoning. But he's the kind of guy who can't keep his mouth shut if you know how to play him. He's got an ego, if you know what I mean. He'd know more about the losers Joey DeSilva might have been hanging around with. Take everything he says with a grain of salt. I wouldn't take a damn thing he says as gospel. But if anybody would know how to put you in touch with whatever gang Joey was hanging around with, or if she got back in touch, it'd be Lovell."

"Where can I find him?" Jake asked, taking the card.

"You can't miss him. He's got a big-ass billboard on the highway as you're heading out of town. Just follow the literal signs."

"I appreciate this," Jake said. He slid the card into his suit jacket pocket.

"Try those cheese curds," Delacourt said, popping one into his mouth.

Jake did. He could practically feel his arteries clogging by the minute. It would almost have been worth it.

Delacourt, Birdie, and Jake made small talk for another half an hour. As the dinner crowd started to arrive, Jake and Birdie said their goodbyes.

"I appreciate your ear," Jake said, shaking Delacourt's hand.

"Anytime."

"If you can think of anything. A name. Somebody else who Joey DeSilva might have crossed."

"This list is long," Delacourt said. "But I can send over what I have. It's not much. Most of her transgressions happened when she was a juvenile. And I can't imagine anybody from here would have hunted her down in Blackhand Hills. Not after all this time. But like I said, maybe one of Lovell's informants might know something. If they'll talk."

Birdie and Jake exchanged a look.

"Arnie," Birdie said. "I have to ask you something. And I know it's gonna sound so awful. I hardly want to give it a voice. It's just ... Ray. You said he was better off when Joey was out of his life. Do you think? I mean, is it possible ... see ... we have information that Ray knew where Joey and her husband were staying that final week. I'm just wondering. If you think it could have been in him to, I don't know. Take matters into his own hand? I mean, if Joey was the chaos agent in his life ..."

"There's no if," Delacourt said. "But you think maybe Ray himself put a bullet in her back?"

"I don't know," Birdie said. "We're just … we're running out of road, you know?"

Delacourt whistled. "That's a wild theory. My gut? No way. At the same time, I guess you never know how far somebody can be pushed. Does he have an alibi?"

"We haven't gotten far enough into the theory to have him establish one."

"I mean … wow. That would be … man. I don't know. But like I said. We've all seen people get pushed enough to do some pretty awful things. I guess if I were you, yeah. I suppose I'd go through the effort of clearing him, too. If I can be of any help, you let me know."

"I will," Jake said. "And you already have been."

Birdie and Jake left. He got behind the wheel and found himself staring at the dimly lit marquee outside the bar. The "K" had fallen off the sign so in the night sky, it simply read "Bloes Bar."

Jake pulled out and headed south. He and Birdie sat in silence for a while, Delacourt's words burning through both of them. Ray DeSilva was better off when Joey wasn't around.

They got stalled behind a semi. Jake slowed to a crawl.

"Lovell," Birdie said.

"What?"

"Lovell," she said, pointing to the billboard ahead of them. "The PI Delacourt said fleeced Dale Halsey. There's the billboard Delacourt was talking about." Sure enough, a reddened, bald, grinning head stared down at them from the sign. Lovell's name was scrawled across the bottom of the sign with an arrow pointing to the next exit.

"Maybe we should pay him a visit," Jake said.

"I mean ... it's a sign," Birdie said. Jake groaned at the pun.

He checked the dashboard clock. It was just past six o'clock. The traffic jam stretched for miles. Jake wrenched the steering wheel to the right and drove onto the shoulder. The exit was only a quarter of a mile away.

THIRTY-TWO

The offices of Lovell Investigations were an old farmhouse off the highway next to a horse rescue sanctuary. At six o'clock on the dot, Jake and Birdie caught Lovell himself walking out the side door and locking it.

Jake pulled in next to the only other car in the gravel driveway, a clunker of a Town Car with a vanity plate that read "ISEEU2."

"This ought to be good," Birdie muttered.

"Mr. Lovell?" Jake called out. He stepped out of the car and pulled his wallet out of his jacket.

Lovell squinted and opened his own car door, throwing his briefcase on the front seat.

Jake got close enough to show Lovell his badge.

"Sorry to just show up on your doorstep like this," Jake said. "But we were in town and your name came up as somebody who might be able to help with a murder investigation I'm handling in Worthington County."

Lovell's gaze shifted to Birdie, then back to Jake. "Sure," he said, sounding decidedly *unsure*. "Come on in."

He shut his car door, fussed with his keys then led Birdie and Jake up the ramp along the side of the building.

The place smelled like mildew. The floorboards creaked as Lovell led them down a short hallway and into a back room. His office. He had files stacked haphazardly all over the room. One giant fern in bad need of water on a tripod planter blocked the path that Jake had to step around to get to the chairs in front of Lovell's desk.

"Have a seat, Detective," Lovell said. "I was just about to head out and grab some dinner."

"I won't keep you long," Jake said.

"You said you had a murder? What's that got to do with my neck of the woods?"

"As I said, I spent some time in town. One of the detectives there said you've had run-ins with mutual witnesses in my murders."

Lovell looked dubious. His billboard photo was badly out of date. The man in front of Jake looked to be about fifteen years older, heavily jowled. He had a set of bad dentures that made him whistle his "S"s.

"Jaxon Waters and Josephina DeSilva were my victims," Jake said. "Both shot to death at a cabin in Blackhand Hills."

"Oh. Yeah, I did hear about that. Kinda wondered if somebody might start asking me questions."

Birdie and Jake looked at each other. "Why's that?" Birdie asked.

"Cuz I've known Ray DeSilva for about thirty years. I offered to help him track down that girl a couple of times. Gratis. He was torn up when she went missing. Damn cops down here wouldn't take him seriously. Wouldn't try finding her. The usual song and dance about her being an adult, not a runaway, that kind of thing."

"Sure. I guess I wasn't aware Mr. DeSilva went to those lengths to find her. He didn't mention it."

Lovell seemed nonplussed by the contradiction. "Ray's a funny guy. Not funny like he makes you laugh. Just odd. Kinda gave up on life after the number that kid ran on him."

"That's kinda what I've heard," Jake said. "Losing her like this has pretty much broken him."

Lovell shrugged. "Yeah, I guess so. You ask me, horrible as this might sound, I think he's better off without her."

"You're not the first person to say that," Jake said. "I spent some time talking to Detective Delacourt."

Larry Lovell had a lousy poker face. He scrunched up his nose and rolled his eyes.

"I understand you've had run-ins with him."

"What's he saying about me?"

"Well, it's not so much what he ..."

"Oh, I know what he says about me. Every time I walk in there he treats me like I'm something he just scraped off his shoe. We're all on the same side, you know? I've had a good relationship with law enforcement my entire career."

"I'm sure you have ..."

"He's got an attitude. That's what. And it's not just me saying it."

"We're talking about Delacourt? Or DeSilva?" Jake asked.

"Arnie. He's on a power trip. And I'm not saying all cops are bad. Like I told you. I've had a good working relationship with most of the cops in this county and the neighboring ones. You can ask around. But Arnie Delacourt's had a hard-on for me for about ten years."

"Gotcha. Well. Um. That's unfortunate. But I was hoping I could bend your ear a bit about Joey DeSilva. I was under the impression you've crossed paths with some of the people Ms. DeSilva tangled with while she still lived here. That's essentially what Detective Delacourt passed along."

Lovell sat back. He was red-faced now, completely worked up by whatever beef he and Arnie Delacourt had. Jake wondered why Delacourt even bothered sending him here.

"It's a pretty small town," Lovell said. "It's true that my bread and butter mostly comes from defense attorneys. That's Delacourt's main problem. He's the kind of cop that thinks all defense lawyers are scum. I hope you're not another one."

"I'm not," Jake said. "I assure you, I'm only trying to get some background information on Ms. DeSilva or anyone else she might have hung around with. She was murdered, Mr. Lovell. The more I can understand about the people in her life ..."

"Yeah. Yeah. You don't have to pussyfoot around it. You're asking about dealers. Pimps. The underbelly of our little town. Well, I can tell you plenty. I know everybody. All their little secrets. But I find it real funny that Arnie's out there badmouthing me. But when somebody like you comes to town, who does he send them to? Me. That's right. Cuz he knows I'm good at what I do."

"Mr. Lovell," Jake said, trying not to let his exasperation with the man show. "Detective Delacourt said you might know some of the people Joey DeSilva was connected to when she lived in Westeridge. We're just trying to be thorough with our background work. You understand."

"Sure," Lovell said but he eyed Jake with suspicion. "You're telling me Arnie Delacourt wants me to rat out some of my informants?"

"I'm not saying that at all. But this girl was murdered. I'm just trying to piece together what might have happened. Starting from the beginning. From when she started to get into trouble."

Lovell snorted. "How much time you got?"

"Plenty," Jake said. "I've gotten a lot of information from Dale Halsey. I understand he's helped with information that led to several arrests involving dealers around here."

"That man is a goddamn saint," Lovell said. "Dale Halsey has done more to put a dent in the Montgomery County drug trade than Arnie Delacourt ever could. They ought to pay Dale half of Arnie's salary. It would be a better use of taxpayer dollars."

"Detective Delacourt sounded very appreciative," Jake said. "I got the impression Lena Halsey's death is one of the big regrets the guy has in his career."

"Regrets? Arnie doesn't regret anything. He'd have to be able to feel in order to have regrets. The only thing Arnie Delacourt cares about is how soon he can punch his time card and go home. He should have retired five years ago. He's a drain on the county budget."

Jake could see this was going nowhere fast. Part of him was ticked Delacourt sent him on what was turning out to be a wild goose chase.

"Oh, I clocked that the minute I sat down to talk to him," Birdie chimed in. "All bluster. A blowhard. I bet you run circles around him in terms of real detective work."

Lovell pointed a finger at Birdie. "Honey, I could tell you stories."

"I know the type. It's guys like him who make it hard for people like me. We've got the same thing in Worthington County. Old guys don't know when to step off so people my generation can move up. So I'm out here doing all the work on a deputy's pay while they're making six figures."

"They ought to have taken his badge just for what he did to Dale Halsey alone."

"He said Halsey hired you to look into what happened to his daughter," Jake said.

"Because Delacourt was too damn lazy to go the extra mile. Now he sits there while Dale hands him gift-wrapped intel. He makes arrest after arrest on Dale's hard work. And mine."

"Well," Jake said, picking up Birdie's lead. "I had a hunch I'd come to the right place to get real answers."

"I'll do what I can," Lovell said. "Between you and me, I don't know why Dale even still talks to Arnie. If it were me, I'd have gone to the attorney general's office over what he did."

"What he did?" Jake asked.

Lovell looked annoyed. "Halsey."

"What Halsey did?" Jake asked.

Lovell rolled his eyes. "No. What Delacourt did *about* Halsey. Or rather, what he didn't do."

"You looked into Lena Halsey's death for her father," Birdie said. "We understand Dale paid you a lot of money. That's I think what Arnie Delacourt was sore about."

"And I delivered," Lovell spat. "I earned every penny of my fee from Dale Halsey. He'd be the first one to tell you that."

Lovell pushed himself back from his desk. He started rummaging through the pile of dog-eared files stacked all around him. He licked his finger as he thumbed through pages. Finally, he pulled out a thick file and slapped it on his desk.

"Right here," he said. "Talk about gift-wrapped. Dale was smart enough to come to me. I've been in this business a long time. I've made a lot of contacts. People trust me around here. Yeah. It means I've gotta rub elbows with some unsavory elements from time to time. But the ends justify the means. And it did for Dale Halsey. You looking to place blame? I'll send you right back to Arnie."

"You found out who sold drugs to Lena Halsey?" Jake asked.

"Yeah. And I found out who stood by and watched her die. A lot of good that did. Halsey tried to take it to Delacourt. He wouldn't touch it. Told him some bullshit about the DA refusing to prosecute. Saying it wasn't enough for probable cause. I've got four witnesses. Their stories were consistent. Delacourt wouldn't even bother running their phones. They'd put them in those woods. And two of these people were willing to go on record. I had it all set up."

Lovell pushed the file closer to Jake. Jake picked it up. At the very top were the witness statements Lovell yammered on about. Birdie slid her chair closer so she could read along with Jake.

It was a party in the woods by the grain mill, just like Delacourt had described. Drinks were passed around. One of the witnesses watched Lena Halsey take something out of a blue plastic cup. A few minutes later, she began to foam at the mouth and started convulsing. Most of the party-goers scattered. But one stayed with her. The stories were consistent in that. Her friend, they thought. A girl who yelled at all the rest of them to run before the cops came. They all thought, because she promised them, she was going to call an ambulance. And she'd brought a new boyfriend with her.

An older guy. He had been the one handing out the blue plastic cups.

Jake's heart raced. Two names. Four accounts. And they were all consistent.

Joey DeSilva and a man they identified only as J.

"Joey DeSilva," Jake said. "You're saying Joey DeSilva and her boyfriend were the last people to see Lena Halsey alive?"

"Yeah. None of these kids would come forward at first. They were too scared of getting in trouble. And they all said it was Joey who made them leave. She was gonna take care of Lena. And the boyfriend, nobody had ever met him before. They just described him as tall, dark-haired. And she called him J. Sometimes Jack, I think."

"Jack," Jake said. "Or Jax?"

Lovell shrugged. "Beats me."

"She never called an ambulance," Birdie said. "She just ... she let Lena die?"

Lovell took the file and tossed it back on the pile. "Halsey said Delacourt said my witnesses weren't reliable. That's bullshit. And *all four* told the same story. Delacourt wouldn't pursue it."

"Delacourt told you this," Jake said. "You talked to him?"

"That's not how I work. This was Dale Halsey's work product. Arnie and I have our differences. I wasn't looking for glory. We both knew it was better coming from Dale."

"Mr. Lovell," Birdie said. "Does Raymond DeSilva know this? Does he know his daughter and Jax could have been implicated in Lena Halsey's death?"

"That would have been up to Dale to tell him. Not me. He's a bigger man than me. How those two managed to stay friends, I don't know."

"You've never asked," Jake said.

"Who, Dale? That's none of my business. My job ended when I delivered this report to Halsey. I don't go around spreading information like this. What my clients choose to do with their business ... is their business. Halsey's not the type of guy that would have held this against Ray DeSilva. I can tell you that much."

Jake bit his tongue to keep himself from saying what he wanted to say. Lovell had just spread the information right to Jake and Birdie.

"Do you mind if I have a copy of those statements?" Jake asked.

Lovell shook his head. "Sorry, man. Can't do it. Not without a court order."

"Can I trust that you'll keep that file safe?" Jake asked.

"You think I'd bury it? Why would I do that? Why would I even show you in the first place? I'm just saying. Arnie Delacourt can kiss my ass if he's out there saying I'm the one who took advantage of Dale Halsey. He's the reason there was never an arrest or prosecution to come from Lena Halsey's death."

Lovell rose. He'd decided the conversation was over. Jake's head spun. He had more questions than answers, but Larry Lovell had said all he would say today.

"You'll hear from us again," Jake said, extending his hand to shake Lovell's.

"Sorry I couldn't be more help," Lovell said. "Joey DeSilva's a tragic case, but predictable. She was a bad seed and she played with fire. For Ray's sake, I'm sorry things ended up this way. If you see him, you give him my condolences."

"Of course," Jake said. He and Birdie walked back out to the car. He felt like he was walking in a zombie shuffle as his mind raced through the information Lovell had just given them.

Jake started the car and backed out.

"Jake," Birdie said. "Joey DeSilva killed Lena Halsey. Or is responsible for her death. And we don't know for sure. But J? Jack? New boyfriend? Jax was with her that night. My God. That's what he's saying. Why didn't Arnie Delacourt tell us that? Why would he lie about not being able to bring an arrest for Dale Halsey?"

"I don't think he was lying," Jake said. "I mean, did you get that vibe? Because to me it felt very much like a salty old cop feeling bad about the case he could never crack."

"That's what I thought too, but ..."

Joey DeSilva recruited Samantha Blanco and Morgan Prater. Both girls didn't live far from here. Joey DeSilva and Jaxon Waters gave Lena Halsey drugs that killed her. Joey DeSilva prevented Lena Halsey from getting the medical care that could have saved her life.

"Call him," Jake said. "Do you have his card?"

Birdie already had her phone out. She put it on speaker as she punched in the number on Arnie Delacourt's card. He answered right away.

"Detective Delacourt," Birdie said. "This is Deputy Erica Wayne again. I'm sorry to bother you at home. But you wrote down your cell so ..."

"What do you need, Erica?"

She looked at Jake. "I was just hoping you could clarify something for me. Did you ever tell Dale Halsey that you wouldn't be able to bring charges against Joey DeSilva or anyone else in connection with the death of Lena Halsey?"

"What?" There was a loud noise on the other end of the phone as if he'd dropped his. A moment later, he was back online.

"Detective, did you ever have any leads about who was in the woods with Lena Halsey the night she OD'd?" Jake asked. "This is Detective Cashen."

"No," Delacourt said. "Where's this coming from? Did you talk to Lovell?"

"If I'm understanding what you told me," Jake said. He pulled over to the side of the road. "Halsey informed you that Larry Lovell took his money but never delivered an answer on who was in the woods with Lena that night?"

"That's correct. It was like ten grand. I think he paid him. For nothing."

"Halsey told you this. You're sure. He said Lovell never got him any solid answers?"

"Yeah. That's what he said. Why? Is Lovell telling you something different? I swear to God, that guy is a damned liar. If he's trying to lay the blame for that case at my feet ... well ... that's par for the course with him."

"Thank you," Jake said. "Again, sorry to bother you with this. I just wanted to make sure I had the facts straight for when I talk to Lovell." Jake wasn't sure why he lied. He just wasn't ready to let anyone else but Birdie in on his thought process.

After a few quick pleasantries, Birdie hung up the phone.

"Jake," she said.

"He lied," Jake said. "Halsey lied. He knew Joey DeSilva and Jax were implicated in his daughter's death. He never said a word. He's been at Ray DeSilva's side every time I talked to him until today."

"But how could he have ... Jake ... Joey was AWOL for years? She only recently got back in touch with Ray after Mariah Ortiz got in her ear and she ..."

The events of the past few weeks played back in Jake's mind like a movie on fast forward. Dale Halsey was there when Ray DeSilva identified his daughter's body. Dale Halsey was there the first two times Jake tried to interview DeSilva. He'd only interviewed DeSilva once by himself. Today. And when he did ...

"He knew," Jake whispered. "My God. He knew."

"Who knew?"

"Halsey," Jake said. "Jesus. Birdie. He lied. That first time at the morgue. He told me he had no idea Ray had been in contact with Joey. But today, Ray showed me their text exchanges. He let something slip. He said he told Halsey he was going to meet with her. Ray felt guilty. Because he was getting a chance to see his daughter again and Dale never could. He said Dale told him he shouldn't feel guilty about that. Dale knew Ray was in contact with Joey. He knew it. And when I asked him about that at the morgue he told me he didn't think Ray had talked to Joey in years. It was a lie. Jesus. If DeSilva told Halsey where he was meeting Joey. If he showed Dale the same texts he showed me. My God. It means Halsey knew exactly where Joey and Jax were staying, too."

Jake punched his fist against the steering wheel. The answer was there, right in front of him, pretending to shield Ray DeSilva the whole time.

Thirty-Three

"Jake, you don't have it."

Meg Landry stood in front of the large window in her office overlooking the courthouse.

"I have two major lies and a motive," Jake said.

"That's not probable cause."

"It's leverage."

"You have no physical evidence tying him to this. No eyewitnesses who could pick him out in a lineup. What if he won't come in? What if the interview goes badly? Or he brings a lawyer? Or asks for a lawyer?"

"Where's this coming from?" Jake said. "You've never questioned my interrogation skills before."

She put a hand on her forehead as she spun to face him. "I'm not questioning them now. It's just. We need this case cleared. Now more than ever."

"Why now more than ever?"

She went to her desk and sat down. "Because in about ten minutes, a story's going to break. Someone leaked the names from Willis Bondy's list. The *Beacon* is basically going to come out and say it came from me."

"Did it?"

"Of course not."

Jake planted his feet on the floor and got up out of his chair. "Then who cares. That story was going to come out anyway eventually. And it's not your mess. It's Willis Bondy's. And it's Rob Arden's if he doesn't get smart and distance himself from Bondy."

"If people think I'm leaking that kind of information? I'm already ten points down. In two months, Ed Zender's going to be your new boss unless ..."

"Stop," he said. "You're letting these people get inside your head. That's all this is about. Who cares about Willis Bondy? You didn't do anything wrong."

"People think a human trafficking ring came into Blackhand Hills under my watch. And they're going to think I leaked those names to try and save my own skin. It'll stick. Just watch."

"You're good at your job. So am I. That's the only thing either of us can control."

"Jake," she said. "You have to button this one up. Are you sure it wouldn't be better to wait to interview Halsey when you have something more solid?"

"Erica's working on getting the subpoena of Larry Lovell's case file. We'll get formal statements from every witness he talked to. If I wait to talk to Halsey until that happens, he's gonna catch wind of it."

"Jake?" Darcy stuck her head in. "Your man is here."

She didn't say appointment. She didn't say witness. She said man. It underscored the stakes for Jake in a way he knew Darcy didn't mean.

"He's in the interview room. I gave him coffee."

"What's his demeanor?" Jake asked.

"Friendly. Curious, maybe."

"Thanks. Let me go do this, Meg. Trust me."

Jake looked at her. Really looked at her. Landry looked like she'd aged ten years in the last few weeks. The run-up to her election would add even more stress.

"Good luck," she said. "I'll be watching."

"Good."

Jake grabbed his suit jacket off the chair. Darcy held the door for him. He stopped to grab his leather folio from his office desk, then walked into the interview room where Dale Halsey waited.

———

"Thanks for coming in," Jake said. He reached across the table and shook Halsey's hand. "Sure you don't want anything besides coffee?"

Halsey held a hand up. "I'm good. This is fine."

"I suppose I should get right to it. I really do appreciate you driving all the way out here."

"You said it wasn't something you wanted to handle over the phone. I told you when we first met I'm willing to do anything I can to help you on this case."

"How's Ray DeSilva holding up?"

"He's better," Halsey said. He dressed casually in a maroon golf shirt and tan cargo pants. Jake sensed no nervousness in him at all. Halsey sat with one arm draped over the chair beside him and his right leg crossed over his left thigh. His hands were rock steady as he sipped from his Styrofoam coffee cup.

"He's back at the hardware store," Halsey said. "That's a big improvement. He's a social guy. It's good for him to be there interacting with people. It fuels him."

"That is good news. Listen. I've got some uncomfortable questions I need to ask you about Ray. I wish there were some way I could sugarcoat it. But I've heard some things in the last few days that are making me rethink some stuff where he's concerned."

Halsey brought his cup to his lips and drank. Steady. Smooth. He set the cup down.

"In what way?" he asked.

"Well, it's more I've gotten a clearer picture of the kind of person Joey DeSilva was. How she lived her life in the last few years. I'm starting to believe she wasn't just collateral damage in this case."

"What do you mean?"

"Can I trust that this conversation won't leave this room?"

"Of course. I meant what I said. I want to help. I owe it to Ray."

"You're a good friend. I see how you are with him. I don't think he would have made it through the last month without you. You're a constant presence in his life. By his side when he came to the morgue. Probably the worst day of his life. And at the hospital. Reaching out to talk to me and keep tabs on this investigation for him. I hope Ray appreciates how good a friend you are."

"It's not just me. The Lean On Us membership has stepped up for him. We have a very special bond. I wish it weren't rooted in trauma."

"Well, anyway. I just wanted to let you know it hasn't gone unnoticed by me. Which is why this conversation isn't easy for me."

"Detective, why don't you just come out with it? What's got you worried about Ray?"

"Well, like I said. It's a lot to do with Joey. I think Ray has a ... how do I say it ... colored or distorted view of who his daughter was? Those awards of hers he keeps on the wall. Scholar-athlete. Her stellar grades. Her plans. I'm starting to believe that's all just a fantasy Ray's crafted to hide who Joey really was."

For the first time, Dale Halsey's face changed. It was subtle. Just the downturning of his mouth. A shadow in his eyes.

"You know what I'm talking about," Jake said.

"Joey was a troubled girl, I'll admit that."

"She was more than troubled. She was a bully. I'm hearing from a school resource officer that she was a holy terror since losing her mother. Incidents that were swept under the rug because of it. Because teachers and administrators felt sorry for her and liked her father. But she was ... well ... she was a bad kid, Dale. She hurt people. And she ran with a rough crowd."

Halsey let out a sigh. "Yeah. Those things are true, I'm afraid. But what does it matter now? She's gone."

"Well, it's not just her reign of terror with kids her age. Listen, I've got statements from at least three witnesses that it was Joey who did the recruiting for Jaxon Waters. Sure, he was rough with her. Abused her. Terrified her. But she wasn't blameless. She brought several young women into the business. She was right there with Jax, turning them out. And some of those women got hurt because of it. Their stories are consistent. Jax was his own kind of monster, but they were afraid of Joey."

Halsey stared at his coffee cup.

"Dale, you've known Ray for a lot of years. When your girls were still girls. Before his wife died. My concern is this. If you can confirm what I've been told. There are a lot of people in Westeridge who think Ray was better off after Joey took off. That she made his life a living hell."

Halsey rapped his knuckles on the table. "Again. What does any of that matter now? Do you think it means he loved her any less?"

"No. But ... it's just ... look. I would understand it. In his mind ... hell ... in reality ... Jaxon Waters took his daughter from him. She was involved in bad stuff before she met him. But Waters was on a whole new level. If he'd never come into Joey's life, things could have been different. So what I'm saying. I would understand it if Ray had a beef with Jax Waters. The kind that might make violence justifiable in his mind."

Halsey met Jake's eyes.

"He knew where she was," Jake said. "That's the thing that just sticks in my craw. Ray knew where Joey was that weekend. She texted him. Gave him directions. Ray didn't open the hardware store those two days. Nobody can vouch for where he was." A lie. But one Jake doubted Halsey could dispute.

"What are you saying, Jake?"

"I'm saying. Ray DeSilva had a motive to do Jaxon Waters some harm. And if he went out there. Maybe just to talk. Maybe to go get his daughter. Maybe that was his intention. You know? But things can get out of hand. We know Jaxon Waters was a violent man. Or maybe there was an argument. Joey wasn't gonna leave him. Or she said something hurtful. The kind of thing you can't take back."

"You think this was Ray? You think he took out Jaxon Waters and then killed his own daughter?"

"I'm asking you," Jake said. "Knowing that Ray himself might have felt he was better off without Joey in his life. Maybe he realized things were too far gone. I mean, I'm not a father. But maybe something like that could push a man to do something unspeakable. Something that to others might look cold-blooded. But in reality, it was merciful. Or justified."

"Are you going to arrest him if I tell you what I think?"

"I'm just asking what you think at this point."

"Do I think Ray DeSilva was capable of murder? Of murdering Joey?"

"Yes. That's what I'm asking you, Dale. Do you think Ray DeSilva could have done this?"

He ran a hand across his jaw. He picked up his now empty coffee cup and tapped it on the table.

"I don't know. Maybe. Maybe. But do you have anything to go on other than this hunch?"

Jake took a breath. The dominoes were set. He pushed the first one over.

"Did you know Ray had plans to meet with Joey that weekend?"

Halsey pursed his lips and shook his head. "No."

"He never mentioned it. Never told you he'd been in contact with her?"

"Nope."

"But you'd remember something like that, wouldn't you? He came to group therapy because of Joey. Because he was trying to process and grieve for what she'd put him through. He went to the cops and tried to file a missing person's report. Don't you think it's odd he never told you she'd made contact with him after what, three or four years of nothing?"

"I don't know. Maybe he thought it would hurt me. My daughter can never reach out to me again. He knows that."

"Right. Right. That makes sense. God. Dale. I don't know what to say. I'm sorry. I've spent all this time talking about Ray's trauma. Ray's grief. This has to be tough on you. All of this. Coming to the morgue like you did. Watching your friend fall apart. It has to bring back a lot of really tough memories for you about what happened to Lena. I can't imagine it. I know what a fentanyl death looks like. You want to think it's peaceful. That a person just gets drowsy and falls asleep. Never wakes up. Only they don't. It rips through them. Eats them."

Halsey crushed his empty cup. "Yeah."

"Senseless doesn't even begin to describe it. I don't think there's a word strong enough for it. And it's preventable. If they'd gotten her to the hospital ..."

"Why are we talking about this?" Dale said.

"I'm sorry. I really don't mean to make you uncomfortable. I'm just saying. I can try to understand the anger you'd have to feel. And if Ray was able to see his daughter again, no matter what she'd done. You aren't the same as Ray. I mean, he comes to group therapy all those years. But his pain isn't the same as yours, is it?"

"It's not a competition."

"No. No. I know that. Joey wasn't the only one with a dad. And we know not all dads are good dads. But ... listen ... I shouldn't be telling you any of this. This is an ongoing investigation. But two of these girls who Waters turned out? Samantha Blanco and Morgan Prater? Dale, they got hurt. Waters didn't protect them. Joey didn't protect them. They were sent out with men who did things to them. Hurt them. Beat them. In one case, Morgan was sent back with a message. A message written in bruises all over her body. And Jaxon Waters did nothing. Joey did nothing. They patched her up. Gave her some makeup and sent her back out to earn."

"They were monsters," Halsey said. Jake felt the second domino begin to fall.

"Dale, I'm sorry. I truly am. Lena wasn't like Joey. Or Morgan or Samantha. She was still innocent, in a way. From what I understand, she looked up to Joey. Idolized her. Didn't she?"

"When they were younger, yes."

"Joey was good at leveraging that. It's how she got all those girls to fall in line. Big promises. A chance to escape whatever was going wrong in their lives. And she told them she'd take care of them. She didn't though. She let them suffer. When she was the last person who could have saved them, she let them fall. She let them lie there. Hurting. Bleeding."

"I never had the heart to say it," Dale said. "To Ray, I mean. He's a father. He loves his daughter. Anyone can understand that."

"Of course they can."

"But Joey? She was always in trouble. And no matter what she did, she was never held accountable. Ray would never give her any consequences for her bad behavior. He was afraid to discipline her. She'd threaten to run away. Threaten to kill herself. She'd blame him for Louisa's illness. Can you believe that? Told him one time that he should have taken her to a different doctor or noticed sooner when Louisa wasn't eating. And if he had, they'd have caught her tumor sooner."

"That's awful," Jake said. He waited for a beat. Dale Halsey's face was a mask of rage. Curled lips. Contorted muscles.

"And he was going to take her back," Jake said. "Even after all of that. She had him wrapped around her finger. If Joey said jump, Ray would ask how high. Right?"

Dale nodded.

"It had to have been almost impossible for you not to say anything when he told you she wanted to meet with him."

Halsey squeezed his eyes shut and dropped his head.

"Because he did tell you, didn't he? Your best friend?"

"What do you want from me, Jake?"

"You knew Ray was going to meet with Joey again? You knew she asked him to jump."

He didn't answer. Didn't deny it.

"Ray told you he was meeting Joey in Blackhand Hills, didn't he? It's okay. You can be honest now. Ray told me he told you."

It was there. Right in front of Jake's eyes. The shift. The set of Dale's shoulders changed. He stiffened. Gone was the casual posture. He sat up and folded his hands on the table in front of him. Jake waited. These were the most crucial seconds of this man's life. Jake went still. Resisted the urge to ask him again. To have him recommit to the lie. To say another word. To breathe. Dale looked down. He rubbed one thumb against the knuckle of the other. He knew. Slowly, Dale lifted his eyes and focused on Jake.

Jake exhaled.

"Yeah. He told me," Dale said.

"Why didn't you tell me that in the beginning, Dale? Why did you tell me you didn't know Joey reached out to her dad?"

"I didn't think it mattered. What does it matter?"

"Dale, I spent some time in Westeridge yesterday. I met with Detective Delacourt. You know what he said?"

"No."

"He said of all the cases he's worked on in his over twenty years as a detective, Lena's case is the one that still keeps him up at night. He actually wanted me to tell you that if I talked to you about this again. That he wishes ... that he'd have given anything if he could have brought a conviction against whoever gave Lena those drugs. And who left her to die that night. When help was just a 9-1-1 call away."

Dale's eyes turned to glass. He stared at the center of Jake's chest.

"He could have brought a conviction though, isn't that right?"

No response.

"He told me you hired a PI. Larry Lovell. I met with him too. And you know what he told me. Don't you?"

Halsey shook his head. "Don't do this."

"Dale? Tell me what happened. Look at me. I understand it, okay? I know what kind of death Lena had to endure. I've seen it. I know. If she were my daughter or someone else I loved ... man ... I don't know."

Halsey kept shaking head.

"You said it yourself. That girl. Joey. She managed to get away with it all. Her whole life after her mother died. She was never held accountable. You and I both know a conviction would have been a long shot. Lovell's witnesses were sketchy at best. Drug users. Criminals in their own right. Who would have believed them?"

Halsey slammed his fist to the table.

"It was mercy, wasn't it? In its own way?"

"He killed her!" Dale shouted. "He gave her that cup full of poison and laughed when she started to fall."

"That's what the witnesses Lovell found said. They all got a kick out of it."

"She was her friend! She wouldn't have been out in those woods if Joey wasn't there! If I'd known who she was hanging out with, I never would have allowed it. I would have dragged her back home by her hair and locked her in her room if I had to. I wouldn't have minded if she hated me for it."

"Because at least she'd still be alive. There are so many what-ifs, Dale. I can only imagine what that does to a person. Trying to live with that. Those witnesses? They were told to leave, weren't they? Joey promised she'd take care of Lena."

"She let her die! She stood there and let her die! Like a dog foaming at the mouth. Seizing. In agony. Trying to breathe. Trusting her. And she did nothing. And for years, she knew. She lived her life knowing. She would do it again. She *has* done it again. Those girls you said. They're safe now, aren't they?"

"Yes," Jake said. "They're safe. You made them safe, didn't you?"

"Yes! Goddammit! Yes. I made it so Joey and Jax couldn't hurt another innocent girl. Couldn't ruin another father like me. Or a mother. I had to. You understand, don't you?"

"I do."

"I had to! I had to make him stop. He drugged those girls. That's how he made them do what he wanted at first. What he would have tried to do to Lena. So I stopped him."

"You shot him?"

"Yes," Dale cried out. "I shot him. But it was too quick. So quick. Not enough pain."

"And Joey wasn't innocent either, was she?"

Dale shook his head. "She let my Lena die. She stood by and let her die. Her friend. Lena trusted her. Looked up to her. Idolized her, like you said. And she just let her die. For what? Detective Delacourt said they probably never would have brought charges against anyone at that party. She wouldn't have gone to jail if she'd called the ambulance."

"You made her pay for it?"

"I made it so she couldn't hurt anyone else like my Lena. Or Ray. God. I know how that makes me sound. But Ray is better off."

"Everyone says that," Jake said, barely above a whisper.

"Yes. She was no good. Some people are just no good."

"So you shot her too?"

Dale nodded. "Yes. Goddammit. Yes. I shot her. I shot her. I shot her!"

Jake laid both his hands on the table, palms down. In his mind, he heard the last of the dominoes fall.

THIRTY-FOUR

"Sheriff, so you're refusing to comment on the fact that a vocal opponent of your campaign was harassed in a public place by your orders?"

Meg Landry stood in front of a bank of microphones. Two minutes into the Blackhand Creek murder press conference, everything went sideways.

"Harassed?" she said. "Nobody was harassed. My detective lawfully served a search warrant upon Mr. Bondy. There was no harassment."

"Would you like to comment on the allegations made in this morning's *Beacon* that two inside sources can verify a deliberate leak was made, disclosing the identities of witnesses to your investigation? And what motive could there have been for that other than political gain? You're ten points down in the polls?"

Meg picked up the piece of paper in front of her and read from it.

"The only announcement I'm here to make today involves the arrest that was made in the murders of Jaxon Waters and Josefina

DeSilva Waters out at Blackhand Creek. Dale Halsey of
Westeridge, Ohio was charged with two counts of first degree
murder this morning. Mr. Halsey has confessed to the crimes. My
office is cooperating fully with the Worthington County
Prosecutor's Office. I'll defer questions to them regarding the
charging document and when Mr. Halsey will be arraigned. I'd like
only to add that all suspects are innocent until proven guilty in a
court of law."

"Was Willis Bondy ever a suspect?" a reporter shouted out.

"What? What difference does that make? I just gave you the
identity of the suspect, the only suspect arrested in conjunction
with a double homicide at Blackhand Creek."

"Meg," Jake whispered to her. "Wrap it up. Don't take the bait.
This is coming from Zender's camp. They're trying to rattle you in
front of the cameras."

"Thank you," Landry said. "As I said. I'll defer all the other
questions regarding the Waters' murders to the prosecutor's office.
That's all for now, people."

She gathered her notes as reporters shouted more questions. Jake
put a hand on Meg's back and led her out of the press room.

"Goddammit!" she shouted as soon as the door shut behind them.
"They don't even care that you made an arrest. They just want to
crucify me for something I didn't do. Something that doesn't
matter. I'm not the one who solicited prostitutes out at that cabin.
Bondy did that. And somehow I'm getting more heat over it than
he is?"

"It'll blow over," Jake said as they walked back to her office. Birdie
was waiting outside the door.

Neil, Landry's media liaison, came out of the office holding a pad of paper. "Ansel's five minutes out. He's had a meeting with Halsey and his attorney."

"Good," Meg said. "Let Boyd Ansel take the heat for a while. This ball is officially in his court."

Birdie and Jake followed her inside. Meg said something privately to Neil, then came into her office. Jake and Birdie took seats in front of her desk. Landry slipped out of her jacket and sat down in her chair with force.

"You did good work. Both of you. That was a master class in interrogation, Jake. Erica, your legwork on this one was invaluable. I just wish I could officially promote you over it. You'll both get plaques, I'm sure." Her last sentence was laden with sarcasm. She knew how much Jake and Birdie cared about plaques.

"I appreciate everything you've tried to do," Birdie said.

Meg waved her off. "It's crap, Erica. A heaping pile of it they expect you to stomach. I'm sorry. If I had any leverage at all, I'd use it for you. To be honest, I'm a hindrance to you as long as I'm this far down in the polls. Hopefully even Ed Zender can recognize what an asset you'd be in his old job. Jake, how'd it go with your victim's father?"

Jake drove down to see Ray DeSilva late last night. His friend Flora was still staying with him. That was a blessing.

"He was stoic," Jake answered. "Honestly, at this point, I don't think he cares anymore who killed his daughter. I mean, he's grateful an arrest has been made. But he's mostly still numb. He said nothing surprises him anymore. That he's already taken the worst news he ever will."

"He and Dale Halsey were supposed to be best friends," Birdie said. "That's going to hit him later. Hard. He's probably still in shock."

"Likely," Jake agreed. "But he's got people around him now. And despite Halsey's conduct, the Lean On Us are still showing up for DeSilva."

"They're showing up for Dale Halsey too," Meg said. "Ansel texted me an hour ago. They've hired a defense attorney to represent Dale Halsey."

She looked up and motioned to someone behind Jake and Birdie. Jake turned. Boyd Ansel himself walked in.

"Your ears must have been burning," Meg said. "I was just telling my detectives what you told me about Halsey's defense team."

"I wouldn't call it a team," Boyd said. "It's one lawyer out of Dayton. Good guy. Easy to work with."

Jake braced himself. "If he changes his story ..."

"He's not," Boyd said. "Not so far. But what can you tell me about the fruits of your search warrants on his house, car, and phone?"

"Phone will take a while for the full report. ONIC did me another favor. Halsey was smart. The night of the murders, it looks like he left the thing at home. Car looks clean. I'm working on the murder weapon."

"He wants to deal," Boyd said. "This guy? Halsey? It's hard not to feel sorry for him. Of course it's unthinkable what he did. Killing that woman. His supposed best friend's daughter. No matter what she did in her past, Halsey knows the kind of pain that causes."

"In his twisted way," Jake said. "He thought he was protecting other girls from his daughter Lena's fate."

"The thing is," Boyd said. "If he ever took the stand, I think he might be able to sell that story to a jury. He's very convincing. And inexplicably sympathetic."

"Despite everything," Birdie said. "He's helped a lot of people. The members of Lean On Us will show up in force if this thing goes to trial."

"I know all of that," Boyd said. "I think he does, too. He's not looking to recant his confession. He's looking to cut a deal."

"Second degree?" Jake asked.

Boyd shook his head. "Can't do it. He made a plan. Got the information from DeSilva as to where that girl was staying. He used it. Drove out there. Lied in wait. It's premeditation from top to bottom. And he could have let her go. He admits he shot her once and she started to run. He ran after her and hunted her down. He never gets out, Jake."

Jake shook his head. He knew what a jury might see. It's what he saw. There was that small part of him that understood what drove Dale Halsey to do what he did. That believed, as horrible as it was, the world might be better off without Jaxon Waters and Joey DeSilva in it.

Not that that was ever the point.

"It's your case," Ansel said to Jake. "This is a capital crime. No question. I know I've got discretion on any deals I make with Halsey, but your input matters to me, Jake."

Jake looked at Boyd. He was a different man than his predecessor, Tim Brouchard, in every way.

"I appreciate that," Jake said. He considered what Boyd was saying. If Jake wanted it, he'd be willing to go to bat on the death penalty.

Jake thought about Lena Halsey. What he'd said to Dale was true. Her death wasn't painless. She suffered. She would have been terrified up until her heart's last beat. But even with all that, it wasn't up to Dale Halsey to mete out vengeance for her. That was never the answer. He also knew Dale was right. Arnie Delacourt could have tried to bring charges against Joey and Jax for their part in Lena's death. But there was more than a good chance they never would have seen the inside of a jail cell over it.

"No," Jake said. "If Halsey's willing to plead to first degree, no death penalty, it's a good outcome. Who knows? Like Erica said, he did a lot of good through Lean On Us. They're sticking by him to some degree. Maybe he can still do good behind bars. Whatever you can work out so Ray DeSilva doesn't have to sit through a murder trial. It's the right thing to do."

Boyd nodded. "Good. He's willing. His lawyer is too. I should have this wrapped up by the end of the day."

"Fantastic," Landry said. "I'll leave that for you to communicate to the media. I'm still scraping off the tire tracks from the bus they threw me under."

"For what it's worth, Sheriff, I don't think you deserve the heat you've taken over this investigation. If there's a cancer in Blackhand Hills, you didn't cause it. And also ... for what it's worth, you have my vote in November."

Meg smiled. "It's worth a lot, Boyd. But you might want to keep that to yourself. You'll be on the hot seat in the next election cycle after me."

"I'll take my chances." Boyd gave her a wave and left the office.

"He's a good guy," Meg said.

"He's turning into a decent prosecutor," Jake agreed.

"Which means he's gonna get eaten alive at the polls too," Birdie said. Her face fell. "I'm sorry, Sheriff. I didn't mean ..."

Meg put a hand up. "It's okay. I know what you meant. And none of that is your problem. It's mine. It's the job. I knew it when I took that oath. But I'm proud of you two. As condescending as that might sound. This one wasn't easy. While I'm here, I'll keep fighting for both of you. Until the bitter end. Until they pry the sword from my hands."

Jake lightly smacked the arms of his chair. "Don't lay your sword down just yet, Sheriff. The election's two months away. That's a lifetime. Anything could happen."

Anything. It was true. But he knew it would take a miracle for anyone other than Ed Zender to be sitting in her chair come January.

As Jake and Birdie left Meg alone and headed back to their own office, Jake started thinking about ways to make that miracle happen. Because he knew if Meg Landry left, he'd have to follow.

They walked into the detective's office. Birdie had a banker's box sitting on Gary Majewski's desk. He was due back at the end of the week and she'd be back in field ops. She started packing up the few personal items she'd brought down to brighten the place up. One of them was a picture of her and her brother Ben taken the day she finished basic training. Ben had his arm around her, beaming as the sun lit his eyes.

"We'll find a way to get you back here," Jake said. Birdie held on to the photograph, running her fingers around the frame.

"It's not in your control," she said. "It's not in Landry's either. But I'm okay. I like field ops too."

"You're wasted there."

"Jake," she said. "I'm used to following orders, remember?"

"What I remember is that I couldn't have cleared this case without you. And I meant what I said. You're wasted out in field ops."

"Thanks for saying it," she said. She had a sad smile as she put Ben's picture in the box with the rest of her things.

"I'm sorry," Jake blurted.

Birdie lifted the box and rested it on her hip as she turned to him. "This isn't your fault. You're not in command."

"I don't mean ... I'm not sorry about the detective spot. I mean, I *am*. But that's not what I'm talking about. I'm sorry about Keith and what happened at the bar. I shouldn't have stuck my nose in your business. I was out of line."

Birdie gave him a wry smile. "Do you really believe that? That you were out of line? Or did Gemma put you up to this?"

She wasn't going to make this easy on him. "Okay. I'm not sorry for caring. For wanting to step in for Ben."

Birdie put her free hand up. "Stop. I appreciate the sentiment, but you're not Ben. You're not my brother. I don't need a big brother in that way, Jake. What I need is a partner. A friend. As for the rest of it? I know how to take care of myself. And if I find I *do* need help, I'll ask for it, okay?"

Jake put his hands up in a gesture of surrender. "Okay. I get it. I really am sorry."

Birdie took a breath. Jake sensed she was about to lay into him again. Instead, she smiled in a way that lit up her whole face. "Apology accepted." She stepped forward and shoved her box into Jake's chest. He grunted as he caught it.

"What's that for?" Jake asked.

"This is me asking for help," she said. "Help me carry that back downstairs."

"What the hell do you have in here, anvils?" he asked. Jake adjusted his grip on the box just before he would have dropped it.

"Wimp," she said as he followed her out of the office. "Are those muscles of yours just for decoration or are they occasionally useful?"

Jake laughed, remembering she used to say the same thing to Ben when they were younger. As she pushed the button on the elevator, Jake looked down. Ben's smiling face looked up at him from the photograph she'd laid on the top of the box. Jake could almost hear him laughing.

THIRTY-FIVE

Three Weeks Later

"Socks," Gemma said. "Ryan, you didn't pack enough socks. You go through three pairs a day. You're used to me washing everything for you all the time. You won't ..."

"Mom!" Ryan said. "I've got it." The boy's face went beet red. He stared at Jake, wide-eyed, trying to convey an unspoken message for him to deal with his mother.

"Hangers!" Gemma said. She stood in front of the closet right inside Ryan's new dorm room. It was suite-style, with two lofts on either side of the room and a sitting area in between. He'd share a bathroom with two other guys but only had one roommate. That roommate, a shy kid from Toledo, had just left the room to scare up another rolling bin to bring the rest of his things from his car. He'd come up alone. No parents. Jake knew Gemma would never have let that fly.

"I can go get hangers if I need them," Ryan said. "There's a supermarket right across the street from campus."

"On the other side," Gemma said. "That's too far to walk."

"He's got his bike, Gemma," Jake said. He busied himself with setting up Ryan's computer and printer. Before that, he'd put Ryan's loft together and that of his roommate.

"His bike? Then how's he supposed to ride home with a bag of hangers? We'll go get some and bring them back."

"No!" Ryan shouted. "I mean. It's okay. Hangers aren't an emergency, Mom."

"I can always send a care package," she said. "Oh ... but I need the mailing address. Where's that paper they gave you that has all of that stuff on it?"

"I don't know," Ryan said. "I'll find it when I unpack the rest of my stuff."

"Let me help you do that at least," Gemma said.

"Uncle Jake," Ryan muttered to him. "Will you please ..."

"I can only try," Jake said. He finished running Ryan's printer cord behind the desk and into the hidden outlet tucked behind one leg of the loft. His next task was mounting Ryan's flat screen to the wall whenever the boys decided where they wanted it.

"This couch is too big maybe," Gemma said. "We measured. I don't understand why it's so cramped under these lofts."

"It's fine!" Ryan protested.

"Maybe two bean bags would have been better. I saw one of the other boys down the hall had those set up. It looked really nice. Then you can move them wherever you want. It might be better for conversation."

"Mom!"

Gemma quickly turned. It gave Jake a quick glimpse of her face. His sister was on the verge of tears. She was gonna blow. There was only one thing to do.

"Ryan," Jake said. "I think you and Cody can figure out how to mount the TV. It might be a good idea to live with the space for a day anyway. See what makes sense. You've got your toolbox Grandpa put together for you. Everything you need's in it."

"I can handle it," Ryan assured him.

"That's it then," Jake said. "Gemma, we better hit the road if we want to avoid rush hour traffic."

"I wanted to walk down to the cafeteria," she said. "Ryan, we should make sure your ID works. That's how you access your meal plan. Are you sure the Silver Plan is enough? We could have done Platinum."

"I'll figure it out," Ryan said through gritted teeth. Cody, his new roommate, had just shown up with his last bin of stuff.

"Those were such a good idea," Gemma said, picking up a large blue plastic tote from Cody's bin. It had a black handle that doubled as backpack straps if he needed it.

"Where did you say your mother got these, honey?"

Ryan groaned behind Jake.

"IKEA, I think," Cody said. He was a wrestler from Whitmer High School. He and Ryan had connected on a school sponsored roommate matching app. Things were a hell of a lot different from when Jake went to college. Then he'd just shown up and took his chances. Cody was a skinny, gawky kid with sandy-blond hair that covered his eyes. So far, he'd barely gotten a word in edgewise. Gemma's nervous chatter filled the room.

"All right then," Jake said. "Cody, we're heading back down. I can take your empty bin so you don't have to make another trip."

"That'd be great, Mr. Cashen," he said. The kid stuck his hand out to shake Jake's, solidifying his good impression.

"Nice to meet you, Mrs. Cashen ... er ... Mrs. Stark," Cody said.

"Gerald," Ryan said, his tone heavily laced with snark. "Though she says she's working on changing it. Again."

Jake shot a look at Ryan then mouthed the words, "Give her a break."

"I just want to make sure you've got ..."

"I've got it," Ryan said, but his voice was softer this time. He went to his mother. "Mom. I've got everything I need. And if I don't have something, I'll figure it out. I'm fifteen minutes from Akron. Not in some third world country."

Gemma bobbed her head up and down rapidly. That was it. She was starting to fall apart. Jake stepped in. He gave Ryan a hug and a slap on the back.

"Proud of you. Shoot me a text if you need anything."

"I will," Ryan said. Then he went to Gemma. She went rigid as he gave her a quick hug. Jake took over, putting an arm around his sister's shoulders. He led her out into the hallway and shut Ryan and Cody's door before she could think of another reason to stay.

She broke down before he got her back in the car.

"He's my baby," she said as Jake buckled her in.

"I know."

"It's so far away."

"It's two and a half hours."

"Did I? Jake ... did I do everything?"

Jake turned to his sister. He handed her a tissue from a pack he kept in the center console.

"You did everything right, Gemma."

"Will he be okay?"

It hit him then. Not for the first time. Ryan was almost the same age as Lena Halsey had been the night she went to that party with Jax and Joey Waters. Almost the same age as Joey DeSilva the last night she spent under her father's roof before she ran off with Jax.

Dale Halsey thought he'd done everything right. So had Ray DeSilva. The strength it took to be a parent, he thought. The fear. He realized then, also not for the first time, that his sister might just be the strongest person he'd ever known.

He reached for her, smoothing a hair away from her tear-filled eyes.

"He's going to make mistakes," Jake said. "He's gonna drive you crazy, I think. But yeah, sis. You did everything right. And he's going to be okay."

Gemma reached for him then. She pulled Jake into a bone-crushing hug. She clung to him as if she were drowning. Maybe she was a little bit. So he hung on to her until she finally came up for air.

Then, he put the truck in gear and drove past the giant Putnam University crest at the edge of campus. Beneath it was the university motto written in Latin.

In Itinere Finis Est

In the journey lies the end.

A cryptic letter from a prison inmate pulls Detective Jake Cashen back into one of the darkest chapters in the history of Blackhand Hills. He's poised to reopen a chilling murder case once thought closed. But some stones are meant to be left unturned. What crawls out this time could upend the entire Worthington County criminal justice system.

One-Click So You Don't Miss Out!

Turn the page and keep reading for a special preview...

Interested in getting a free exclusive extended prologue to the Jake Cashen Series?

Join Declan James's Roll Call Newsletter for a free download.

SNEAK PREVIEW OF LETHAL HARVEST

Lethal Harvest
by Declan James

Sam Ingall made himself as small as he could against the inside car door as his father took a breath, preparing to yell.

"Don't tell me you know!" his father said. "You don't know. You're two weeks late cutting your grandma's grass. She depends on you. She's too old to do this herself and too stubborn to hire it out. She's paying you good money to do something that should only take you an hour. And make sure you do the trim the right way this time. I saw what you did last month. It looked like crap. You ask me, she shouldn't have paid you at all that time. When you don't do what you're supposed to do and you take money from her anyway, that might as well be stealing. You're almost fifteen, Sam. Time to get your head out of your ass."

Sam gritted his teeth, stopping himself from saying "I know" one more time. It would only make things worse. Mercifully, his father had just approached the winding gravel driveway leading up to his grandmother's farm. She had four hundred acres of corn fields.

Early October, and the ears came up to Sam's forehead. You could get lost in them. He fantasized about doing just that.

The gravel crunched under his dad's tires and Sam put his hand on the door latch, waiting to jump out as soon as he could.

"She said she'll leave the spare key to the shed on the front hall table for you," his father said. "Make sure you lock everything up and put it right back where you found it. I don't want her to have to hunt for it. And that goes for the tractor and trimmer. You gotta park that thing in the back and out of the way. She gets in there still. Hang the trimmer on the hook. She doesn't need to be tripping over stuff and breaking a hip because you're too lazy to do things the right way."

"I know," Sam said, before he could stop himself. He watched his father's eyes bug out.

"Quit telling me you know. You don't know. I had to come out here and do *your* job for you last week. You spend too much time on that damn Xbox your mother bought you even though I told her not to. I'll pick you up in two hours. Everything better be done right. And you ask Grandma if there's anything else she needs while you're here. She shouldn't have to ask you."

"Got it," Sam said. The car had come to a stop. Sam vaulted out of his seat and tried not to slam the door behind him. His father was still yelling as he walked away. Sam didn't look back. He felt the tension go out of his shoulders as soon as his father drove off. At least he'd have the next two hours in peace.

His grandmother's utility shed was tucked behind the giant house. Grandma's house was one of the oldest in the county. Some people in town were trying to have it put on the historical register. Sam thought it was just spooky and drafty. He hated when she asked him to go down into the root cellar to get whatever canning supplies she needed. With its dirt floors, lack of lighting, and cobwebs everywhere, the place seemed like something out of a horror movie. When they were little, Sam's older cousin used to tell him she kept bodies buried down there. Even then, Sam knew his cousin was lying. But it still made his skin crawl.

Sam walked around the house. Grandma had geraniums hanging from pots under the roof of her covered porch. There were twenty of them. He knew she'd ask him to water them even though this late in the year, they quickly wilted. He made a note to hook up the hose on his way back from the shed.

He got to the shed and reached for the door handle. At the last second, he remembered his father said Grandma had left the keys in the front hallway.

"Dammit," Sam whispered to himself. He was hoping to avoid seeing his grandmother today. She liked to talk his ear off about the "old days" when his grandfather was still alive. Sam didn't remember the man. He died a few years before Sam was born. He didn't know why the old woman didn't just sell the place. She leased the corn fields out to another farmer. She couldn't make her way to the second floor of her own house anymore because of arthritis pain in her feet. Sam knew his parents had been trying to convince her to move into one of the assisted living places in town. She wanted to keep the farm so she could leave it to her sons and grandsons. But none of them really wanted to deal with it.

No, Sam thought. They just want to send me out here to deal with it, sweat my balls off, and sneeze to death from the pollen and ragweed.

Sam made his way up the porch steps of the old white farmhouse. Grandma's wind chimes rang out as the breeze picked up. There was a storm coming. It'd be here by late afternoon. More reason for Sam's dad to bitch at him not to dawdle.

Sam tried the front door. It was locked.

"Great," he muttered. He knocked. No answer. Sam peered through the window next to the door. He could see Grandma's ancient orange cat, Pumpkin, sitting on the back of her front room couch, swishing his tail.

"Grandma!" Sam called out. "It's Sam. I need the key to the shed."

No answer. "Son of a bitch," Sam muttered under his breath. He hoped she hadn't fallen again. The last time, his father threw out his back trying to lift her. She spent six weeks at a rehab nursing home only to fall again when they sent her back home.

Sam decided to go around back. She had a family room back there she called a Davenport. It got more sunlight so she liked to sit there and work on her embroidery. She'd probably fallen asleep in her chair. He stepped off the porch and made his way around to the back of the house. If he found her there, there'd be no avoiding a lengthy conversation. It would put Sam at least a half an hour behind. If his dad showed up and Sam wasn't finished mowing the lawn, he'd start yelling again, even though it wouldn't be Sam's fault.

Sam got to the back door. He could see through the windows into Grandma's back room. Her basket of embroidering things sat next to her floral recliner, but his grandmother wasn't sitting in it.

"Grandma!" he called out again. No response.

"Great," he said. "Just great." He had no way of getting into the shed now unless he figured out how to break into it or the house. He'd have to climb through her kitchen window.

The wind picked up in earnest. Behind him, the stalks of corn swayed. Sam stepped away from the back window right into a giant pile of cat shit. Swearing, he tried to wipe it off on the tall grass.

That's when he saw a couple of broken corn stalks right at the edge of the yard. Every once in a while, kids would come out there and have parties in the stalks. For a moment, Sam wished he could be one of them. He walked over to the broken stalks. His anger rose. He never got to hang out with his friends like that. There was always some chore he had to do. Or homework.

God, he thought. It would be so easy to just get lost in that corn. Hide when his father came looking for him. Just disappear. He took a step into the field. The wind shifted again, picking up some foul stench. Something dead. A raccoon maybe. Or another one of the feral cats Grandma insisted on feeding.

Sam wiped his shoe again, knowing the cat poop was probably still embedded in the treads of his tennis shoes. He picked his foot up to check. His eye caught something lying in the dirt at the base of the corn stalks.

It took a moment for his brain to catch up with what his eyes were seeing. A large, wet lump. Matted fur. No. Not a lump. It was too round. Not fur. That was hair. Long strands of gray. Every instinct in Sam's body told him to run. Told him not to reach down and turn the thing over. But it was as if he existed outside himself. He extended his leg, placing his foot on the top of the lump. He rolled it over.

A pair of sightless eyes looked back at him. Her mouth was frozen open in a forever scream. As Sam took his foot off the head, his grandmother's dentures rolled out and landed at Sam's feet.

Don't miss Lethal Harvest, Book #7 in the Jake Cashen Crime Thriller Series.

➡ https://declanjamesbooks.com/lethal

About the Author

Before putting pen to paper, Declan James's career in law enforcement spanned twenty-six years. Declan's work as a digital forensics detective has earned him the highest honors from the U.S. Secret Service and F.B.I. For the last sixteen years of his career, Declan served on a nationally recognized task force aimed at protecting children from online predators. Prior to that, Declan spent six years undercover working Vice-Narcotics.

An avid outdoorsman and conservationist, Declan enjoys hunting, fishing, grilling, smoking meats, and his quest for the perfect bottle of bourbon. He lives on a lake in Southern Michigan along with his wife and kids. Declan James is a pseudonym.

For more information follow Declan at one of the links below. If you'd like to receive new release alerts, author news, and a FREE digital bonus prologue to Murder in the Hollows, sign up for Declan's Roll Call Newsletter here: https://declanjamesbooks.com/rollcall/

ALSO BY DECLAN JAMES

Murder in the Hollows

Kill Season

Bones of Echo Lake

Red Sky Hill

Her Last Moment

Secrets of Blackhand Creek

Lethal Harvest

With more to come...

STAY IN TOUCH WITH DECLAN JAMES

For more information, visit

https://declanjamesbooks.com

If you'd like to receive a free digital copy of the extended prologue to the Jake Cashen series plus access to the exclusive character image gallery where you can see what Jake Cashen and others look like in the author's mind, sign up for Declan James's Roll Call Newsletter here: https://declanjamesbooks.com/rollcall/